EROSION

LG Thomson

LG Thomson

Happy reading!

ISBN-13: 978-1500798550
ISBN-10: 150079855X

ISLAND

1
FRIDAY

Jonathan's stomach lurched as the silver boat bounced over the waves. He tore his gaze from the hypnotic, churning water and sneaked a look at Fran. She was relaxed, chin tilted into the wind. Sea-spray spattering against her smiling face. She'd tied back her hair, tucked it into her hat. Pity. Jonathan considered Fran's long, auburn hair to be her best feature. She should have let it flow free in the wind. Then the picture would have been complete. Her, radiant in the wild outdoors. Hair billowing in glossy tendrils behind her. Him, green-faced, slumped in a nauseous heap beside her.

He'd visited her on the island before. There hadn't been any choice. Not if he wanted to see her at all through the summer. But he'd never made the crossing so early in the year. Not when the tides were big, the tiny boat pushing against them. He'd been able to pick his moments before. Delaying his visit for a day or so, if it looked as though the wind would be up. This time, there had been no choice. The date was fixed.

It was bad enough when the sea was calm and the water clear. The short crossing made him nervous even then. Today it was thick and green. Ripe with swollen, rolling waves. He took a deep breath. Tried to swallow his queasiness. It was no use. Even with his eyes closed he could feel the endless up and down, up and down. His stomach heaving in time to the undulating rhythm of the swell. Threatening to evacuate its contents. Forcing him to think of the breakfast he'd had and wished he hadn't. Thick smears of glossy butter melting and slithering from toast. Creating fatty slicks in the sticky, orange sauce of baked beans.

He groaned, turning his clammy face away from Fran. Straightaway feeling her hand on his arm. Her fingers squeezing him through his waterproof jacket.

"Are you okay?" she asked. Voice raised to be heard above the drone of the engine.

He gulped down a lungful of sea air before looking back at her. Ignoring the acid reflux flowing into his mouth, he stretched his lips over his teeth until they were within nodding distance of a smile.

"Fine," he croaked, tasting salt on his lips. "Loving it," he added for good measure.

"I know," she replied. "It's great."

"Great," he echoed, swallowing down a tiny morsel of vomit.

His lifejacket gave no comfort as it chafed against his chin. All it did was reinforce the idea that there was a chance he could end up in the water. And if that happened, lifejacket or no lifejacket, he'd be sucked under in a second. The roiling, briny soup filling his lungs. He stared at their destination. Time was elastic. The journey taking forever. The island still seemed too far away. Too long until they were pulling into the jetty and he could set foot on dry land again. He glanced back at the mainland. It was a memory. A gulf of water between it and them.

Standing at the wheel, Zander caught the glance. Grinned at him. Jonathan forced himself to grin back. He gave Zander a quick thumbs-up and immediately felt like a fool.

He sent a prayer to Poseidon, and every god that ever existed, not to let him throw up in front of the grizzled boatman. Exposing his abject fear of the sea to Fran would be bad enough, but the humiliation of puking in front of Zander would be too much to bear.

Almost as disturbing as the thought of throwing up in front of Zander and Fran was the constant clanging that came from the bow of the boat.

Clang.

Clang.

Clang.

A constant, unnerving, metallic beat threatening to split the boat in two.

He'd once asked Zander what the sound was.

"Shackles," came Zander's brief response.

Jonathan stared at the island and tried to block the sound from his mind.

Clang, clang, clang went the death knell of the shackles against the aluminium hull.

2
SATURDAY

Harry whistled softly as he clambered through the dunes. Hazel trudged behind him, her feet slipping in the sand. She'd been listening to Harry whistling to himself for thirty years. It was starting to get on her nerves.

He glanced back. "Come on love, keep up."

Hazel slowed her pace.

Something had changed. She didn't know if Harry had noticed and was pretending not to, or if the shift in the dynamic between them had passed him by. They certainly hadn't talked about it. They hadn't talked about anything meaningful for a long time.

Harry's short, stout frame disappeared behind a sand dune. Hazel stopped and stared at the view ahead. A view devoid of Harry. She dropped her walking pole and shrugged off her backpack. It landed on the sand with a soft thud. The sound of rebellion. She giggled, feeling naughty, like she'd bunked off school for the day.

She stretched out her arms and turned slowly around. Not another person in sight. Not even Harry. Especially not Harry. No doubt he was marching on, oblivious of her absence.

A ray of sunshine broke through a chink in the clouds and, for a few glorious minutes, turned a sliver of beach from muted shades of grey to golden yellow. Hazel unzipped her jacket and pulled off her hat in celebration of the moment. She had a mad desire to strip off her layers of clothing and run naked through the dunes.

Harry's head appeared over a forest of marram grass, spoiling the view and the moment. His hand scythed through the air as he gesticulated for her to come on.

The gap in the clouds closed as suddenly as it had opened, and the world turned grey again. Hazel picked up her pack and pulled it on. She rammed her hat back on her head and picked up her pole, but left her jacket flapping open.

Harry waited for her at the crest of the dune. Impatience oozing from his pores. Hazel took her time getting to the top.

"What's the big rush?" she asked.

Harry stared at her open jacket. "You'll catch your death," he said. He turned and walked on, leaving Hazel staring at his back.

She allowed a gap to open between them. When it was wide enough that the scrape of the marram swaying in the breeze masked the sound of his whistling, she started after him.

The gap closed again when Harry stopped to survey the seashore. They'd been visiting the island for several years. The annual trip one of their rituals. This time, they had come on a special volunteering weekend early in the year. The breeding season had not yet started and there were no terns nesting on the beach. It was a chance for them to explore a part of the island usually off-limits.

Harry turned to face Hazel, a smile on his face. There was something about the way he looked at her. Harry, but not Harry. She noticed how thin his lips had become over the years and wondered if he still had his talent for lies and deceit.

He looked back at the beach, greedily sucking in the vista.

"It's magnificent," he said, "just magnificent. You could travel the world over and not see a sight like it."

Hazel gazed across the shoreline. It was true - the scenery was magnificent, but Harry's words sounded boastful and self-satisfied, as if he was somehow responsible for its existence.

She looked back at Harry. It was as though she was a stranger seeing him for the first time. His eyes were watery. His jowly cheeks stung pink - a combination of cold air and exertion. He'd never been a handsome man. Too short with stubby legs and always a touch overweight. Now, examining him like this, she realised that she found him downright unattractive.

He glanced at her.

"Everything alright, dear?" he asked.

"Fine."

He looked at her curiously for a moment.

"Good. Let's push on then."

He said it as though they were on a major expedition. She scowled at his back as he stomped on. She doubted he would have the energy for anything more taxing than what was really a rather gentle walk. How then did he find the energy for having an affair?

Hazel stopped. Her feet glued to the ground. Eyes wide. Yes, of course. He was at it again. Now that she'd articulated the thought, she realised how obvious it had been. Harry was having an affair.

"I thought we might take a walk round to the jetty. See if there's any sign of the boat coming over with the rest of the party."

He spoke over his shoulder at her. Not turning to see what she thought of his idea. He was already whistling again. Assuming she'd be right there behind him, the way she always had been.

Hazel watched him bumbling on ahead of her, his whistling needling her brain. She realised something else in that moment. Their marriage was worthless. All those years. Her youth. Her energy. All wasted. Above all, Hazel realised that she hated Harry.

Something snapped inside her. She threw her pole aside. Ripped off her hat. Dark fuzziness enveloped her. She sent forth a silent scream. It was followed by the frothing and flowing of righteous anger through her veins.

When her mind cleared, Hazel felt curiously powerful. As if her anger had given her strength. She picked up her hat and stick and gazed thoughtfully after Harry's diminishing figure. He wasn't going to get off lightly. Not again. There would be no tearful hugs, no forgiving and forgetting.

This time, she would show no mercy.

3

Rob came up behind Eleanor and pulled her close.

"Isn't this great?" he said, nuzzling into her neck.

Eleanor shrugged him off. She dropped the rucksack she'd borrowed for the trip and looked over the room they were to share for the weekend. It didn't take long. A set of bunk beds took up most of the available space. An ominous smell seeped from the stained mattresses. The rest of the furniture comprised a set of drawers under the window and a spindly wooden chair. A gas mantle on the wall and a brass hook on the back of the door completed the fixtures and fittings.

"Great? I think Early Gulag might be a more apt description," she said, "but I guess I can cope for a couple of days."

She peered out of the small window. It looked onto the slope of the hill rising steeply at the back of the bothy. Even on a bright summer's day the room wouldn't get much light.

"Not much of a view, but at least we can let some fresh air in."

She struggled with the latch for a moment before realising the window opened inwards. The rusty hinges creaked uneasily as she opened it.

Cold air wafted in. It smelt of damp earth. Not much of an improvement on the mattresses.

Rob sidled up behind her again and put his arms around her.

"We won't be missed for a while. What do you say?" He kissed her neck.

Eleanor screwed up her face and pulled free.

"I don't think so," she said.

A wounded look passed over Rob's face. Eleanor felt a pang

of guilt. She hadn't meant to be so harsh. Problem was, he could be so annoyingly clingy. No matter. He'd bounce back. He always did.

"I don't want to spend any more time in here than I have to," she offered, by way of softening her rejection of him. "The only good thing I can say about it is at least we don't have to share with Marcus. Sharing a boat ride with him was enough. That guy gives me the creeps."

Rob put a finger to his lips. He glanced around as if Marcus might suddenly emerge from the wall. "Keep your voice down. He's probably okay when you get to know him."

He sat on the edge of the lower bunk and opened up his rucksack.

"He told me the island is cursed," Eleanor said.

Rob glanced up at her. "You're joking. When did he say that?"

"On the way up from the boat. when you were talking to that Barry and -"

"Harry," Rob corrected her. "Harry and Hazel. Nice couple."

"Whatever," Eleanor said.

She wiped the seat of the chair with a glove and sat down. "They looked like a pair of Toby Jugs. Probably been ending each other's sentences for years."

Rob laughed. "Yeah, I suppose they are a bit like that. So, what did Marcus say exactly?"

Eleanor extracted a make-up bag from a compartment on the side of her rucksack.

"Oh, he was banging on about the people who lived here years ago."

She frowned as she studied herself in a compact mirror. "Bad hair day," she muttered. "He said they ate gull eggs and seaweed, and who knows what."

She teased her short, dark hair with her fingers.

"Yeah," Rob said, "there was a village here years ago, and I guess they did eat gull eggs. Don't fancy them myself, but it's hardly curse-worthy."

"Well according to Marcus, one of the women took a craze. She bludgeoned the rest of the islanders with a rock while they slept. Killed them all. Even the babies. She dragged the bodies to the cliffs and threw them into the sea. Then she threw herself after them. And ever since then the island has been cursed."

Rob stared at Eleanor as she tightened her lips and applied a sheen of lip-gloss.

"Utter bollocks," he said. "I've been coming here for years and I've never heard anything like that."

"You think he was making it up?"

"Absolutely. There's nothing cursed about this place, Eleanor. Nothing at all."

4

Fran's face ached with the effort of keeping a smile fixed on it.

"It's great to be back on the island," Marcus said. "I've missed it." He took a step towards her.

"It has that effect on people," Fran said, still battling with the smile.

She tried to speak casually but her chest felt tight. As if Marcus had sucked up all the air in the room.

His hair had receded further since the last time she'd seen him but otherwise he looked just as he always did. Intense, pale and creepy. The light from the open door reflected on his glasses masking his eyes with white rectangles.

"It's not just about the island, Fran," he said.

"No?" her smile faltering.

"I've thought about you a lot since last year. I sent you a couple of emails, but you didn't reply."

Her face flushed. "I meant to-"

"Doesn't matter." Marcus interrupted. "The point is, it's good to see you again."

She hadn't noticed him moving, but he seemed closer. As though he was taking a step towards her every time she blinked. Any nearer and she'd be able to feel his body heat.

She stepped back, bumping her hip against the corner of the big wooden table.

"Careful," Marcus said. His tongue darted out and moistened his lips. "I bet you bruise like a peach."

"Tough as old boots, me." Fran gave a nervous laugh. She glanced at the door, willing someone else to appear. Anyone. "It's always good to catch up with people."

"You shouldn't be so modest, Fran. You're not just people. I-"

Marcus's words were cut off by the arrival of a red-faced man lugging a box of firewood.

"This should keep us going for a while," the newcomer said.

"Let me give you a hand with that, Archie." Fran said.

The smile on her face was genuine now. She could have hugged Archie.

Fran grabbed one end of the box. Marcus stepped back as she and Archie carried it to the fireside. Archie poked the fire, fed a couple of logs into the flames and gave a satisfied nod.

"Do you want the top or bottom bunk?" Marcus asked him.

"I'll take the bottom - if you don't mind?" Archie replied.

Marcus shrugged. "Fine by me."

"I love an open fire," Archie said. He nudged Fran in the arm with his elbow. "You're looking a bit skinny. You're no still a veggie are you?"

"'Fraid so," Fran laughed.

She sneaked a look at Marcus. He had retreated to the bunks in the corner of the room and was delving into his rucksack.

"You need to get a decent steak down you before you fade away," Archie said, "or at least a plate of mince and tatties."

"I think you said that last year," Fran replied, "and I'm still here."

She watched Marcus out of the corner of her eye as he unpacked. He had all the right gear. All the top brands. None of it looked as though it was straight out of the wrapper, but he wore it like a costume.

"Yup, still here and still gorgeous. Eh, Marcus?" Archie asked.

Marcus looked up from his unpacking.

"What's that?" he asked, as if he hadn't been listening to every word.

"I was just saying that Fran's looking as gorgeous as ever."

Another flush flooded Fran's face as Marcus swept an appraising glance over her. She resolved that whatever else happened this weekend, she was not going to end up on her own with Marcus again. She gave Archie a playful push to cover her embarrassment.

"Stop it," she said.

Archie chortled. "Tell, you what, I'll stop winding you up if you tell me what's on the menu tonight."

"Always thinking about your stomach," Fran teased. "Hazel's offered to cook. You met her already, didn't you?"

"Aye, lovely woman," Archie said. "What's she cooking?"

"Veggie curry, I think. You like curry don't you?"

"As long as there's no any lentils in it. I hate fucking lentils." He paused to think for a moment. "Unless it's lentil soup made with a sheet of ham ribs."

Archie gleefully rubbed his hands together at the thought.

"About this curry?" he asked.

"What about it, Archie?"

"I don't suppose there's any chance of her slipping a wee sausage in it, just for me?"

5

Jonathan walked into the bothy and immediately felt like walking straight back out. The room was crowded. Too many people, all giving it the big yadda-yadda. It was like getting smacked around the ears with a wet towel.

Fran spotted him before he could slink out. She rushed over to him.

"There you are," she gushed. He hated it when she gushed. She was pink-in-the-cheek. A little bit high from the mingling. Jonathan hated mingling. Had wondered how much of the weekend he could get through without being forced into it.

"Everyone, everyone," Fran called. "This is Jonathan."

He cringed as the babble died down and seven strangers turned to face him. Fran grabbed the nearest by the arm and huckled him towards Jonathan. She made a brief introduction before being sucked back into the throng.

The stranger's name was Rob.

Rob beamed Jonathan a big, friendly smile and thrust out his hand. He had the look of a guy who'd eaten a good, hearty breakfast every single day of his charmed life. Not that he was fat. Not yet anyway. Just very, very solid. Good looking too, in a wholesome, square-jawed kind of way. The type of guy any mother would be proud to call son. Jonathan made nice and shook hands.

Rob's grip was three seconds too long and on the granite side of firm. Jonathan filed him under *macho fuckhead*.

Rob made getting-to-know-you noises. Jonathan nodded. Still playing along, but he couldn't be bitched with it. He watched Rob's mouth work, catching flashes of his big, white teeth.

Catching the odd word, despite himself.

The island, blah, blah, blah. Eleanor, blah, blah, blah. Rugby, blah, blah, blah. He noted the sincerity in the guy's big brown eyes. He came out with this shit like he believed it. Jonathan waited for a pause in the verbal torrent and threw himself into it.

"Nice meeting you, Rob, but I have to cut out of here. Fran asked me to meet the boat."

He was out of the door before Rob could draw the breath to make an offer of help.

Rob would definitely have offered. He was that kind of guy. The kind who carried his dad's tool-bag around for him when he was a kid. Probably still did.

Jonathan shut the door firmly behind him. He took in few deep breaths of fresh air. Muffled though it was by the closed door, he could still hear the babble. Man, he was glad to get out of there.

He set off for the jetty. Being outside energised him. He enjoyed the sensation of striding out. Feeling like he could walk for hours on end. Energy high. Happy to be alone for a while. He had to laugh - here he was, in one of the most remote areas of the British Isles yet having to snatch a few minutes of solitude.

He walked down the hill, watching the boat as it ploughed through the waves towards the island. Bringing over the last of the volunteers. Another voice to add to the clamour.

The sea was wilder than when he'd come over with Fran the day before. The previous night had been brilliant. Just the two of them on the island. Cut off from everything and everyone. Fran calm. Focusing her attention on him. No babbling. No mingling.

He wished it could always be like that.

6

Fran stared at the closed door for a beat.

"Where did Jonathan go?" she asked Rob.

"Down to the jetty," he replied. "Said you asked him to meet the boat. Oh, hi Eleanor. You've met Fran, haven't you?"

"Yes. Can we talk?" she said to Rob. She looked at Fran and flashed a smile that barely reached the end of her lips . "You don't mind, do you?"

"No, of course not."

They retreated to the other side of the room. Fran glanced out of the window, watching as Jonathan walked down the hill. She didn't remember asking him to meet the boat.

She had that funny sensation again. The feeling of never really getting to know him. One minute feeling closer to him than she'd ever felt to anyone. Like soul-mates. Bound together. Each incomplete without the other. The next feeling as though he'd slipped through her fingers like mist. Leaving her nothing to hold onto. Wondering if there really was anything between them. If any of it was real.

"Seems like a nice guy."

Marcus had crept up behind her. Was standing too close. Talking in her ear as if he was whispering sweet nothings. She drew away from him, her fingers rubbing at her ear and neck where she'd felt his breath against her skin.

"Yes," she said. "He is."

"I hope he realises how lucky he is." Looking into her eyes. Pinning her down with his stare.

"I'm the lucky one." She forced a smile and broke away from his gaze.

She looked around the room and managed to catch Cal's eye. He wandered over to her.

"How's it going?" he asked. An easy smile on his lips.

"Great," Fran smiled back. "Have you met Marcus?"

She felt only a little guilty about dumping Marcus on Cal. Cal wouldn't mind. He got on with everyone.

She excused herself, avoiding looking at Marcus as she did so. She couldn't bear the thought of being caught in the tracker beam of his stare again.

7

By the time Jonathan arrived at the jetty the last volunteer was already clambering out of the boat. They were clad in luminous yellow oilskins. It wasn't until she cast the oversized garments off that Jonathan realised they'd been shrouding a petite woman.

She tossed the heavy jacket, followed by the trousers, to a grinning Zander, and yelled her thanks. Jonathan had never seen a smile like it on Zander's face.

The woman turned as he approached and gazed at him with big blue eyes. Curls of blonde hair escaped from beneath her hat. She was laughing at something Zander said. The sound flowing over rosebud lips. She looked so small and delicate that Jonathan had a sudden desire to protect her. He felt as though he could pick her up, put her in his pocket, and keep her safe and warm.

"That was one wild ride," she said to him. She looked back at Zander and waved him off. "See you in a couple of days," she called.

"Maybe," Zander called back, his grin wider than ever. Jonathan could have sworn he saw the man wink.

"Zander said I was the last over," she said.

"Yes," Jonathan replied. "The others are at the bothy."

They watched for a few moments as the boat churned through the thickening swell back to the mainland.

"Well I guess that's us marooned," she said. "for the next couple of days at any rate. Great isn't it? I'm Gemma, by the way."

She took off her glove and held out her hand. Jonathan took it in his, holding it gently, the way he might hold an injured bird.

"Jonathan."

"Pleased to meet you," she said.

Warm fingers encircled his hand. Her skin felt soft pressing against his. Jonathan returned her generous smile with ease.

"And you," he replied.

Conversation flowed easily between them as they walked up to the bothy. He didn't have to struggle to think of something to say to her. Nor did he get the urge to escape at the first chance, the way he normally did when he met new people.

Halfway up the hill he stopped and looked back out to sea. It took him a few gut-wrenching moments before he managed to pick the boat out in the rising waves. He finally caught sight of it just as it steamed into the safety of the bay on the other side.

"I wouldn't worry about Zander." Gemma looked at Jonathan like she had him all figured out. "I swear he's got saltwater in his veins."

She gazed back out at the sound. "I think he's more comfortable at sea than we are on dry land. Especially when it's wild like now. He loves it. He's one crazy guy."

"He'd have to be," Jonathan said. "I don't know how he can stand it. On any day, let alone today."

"You don't like the ocean?"

"Not much." Jonathan surprised himself with his admission.

"But you've come to an island for the weekend?"

"To quote Chief Brody - it's only an island when you look at it from the sea."

"I guess so." Gemma laughed. Jonathan joined in.

"Chief Brody - Jaws, right?"

Jonathan nodded.

"So, is it sharks you're afraid of?"

"Not really. They don't help... maybe it's the depth. The thought of not knowing what's down there. To tell the truth, I've never really thought about it. I generally avoid it."

"Thinking about it or going near it?"

She gazed at him with eyes as blue as forget-me-nots, coaxing his answers out with a smile.

He shrugged. "A bit of both, I guess."

"Yet here you are."

A tendril of guilt unfurled inside him, causing him to hesitate before answering.

"Well, that's because of Fran."

"Oh - I see. She and you..?"

"She's my girlfriend," Jonathan replied.

A beat of silence passed. Maybe two. Her still looking at him. Him still falling into her eyes.

"Lucky Fran," Gemma said.

"I'm the lucky one... just one thing?"

Gemma tilted her head at him. "What's that?"

"Don't say anything to her..."

"What's to say?"

"I mean about me being... not liking the sea."

Gemma raised her eyebrows. "You mean you've overcome your deepest fears to be with her and she doesn't even know?"

"Please." Wishing now he hadn't opened his mouth.

"Don't worry." She patted him on the arm. "Your secret is safe with me. I won't say a word."

8

Funny how one tiny piece of knowledge could change how a person viewed a situation. Example: before she clicked that her husband was having another affair, Hazel wouldn't have thought anything of the way he was behaving with Gemma. She would have assumed that the babble of conversation and laughter coming from the table was just typical Harry behaviour.

Harry being friendly. Harry being chatty. Harry telling jokes.

She might even have been proud of the fact that he was making such an effort to get on with one of their fellow volunteers. That it was lovely how he was going out of his way to make the young, attractive, woman feel at ease. Hazel glanced over her shoulder, observing Harry as he attempted to cross the generation divide.

They were sitting beside each other at the table. Gemma said something Hazel didn't catch. Harry laughed as he leaned into the young woman and patted her on the back of her hand. Hazel bit her lip and turned back to the vegetable curry.

"Do you think that will be enough?"

Cal standing at the sink beside her. Hazel looked at the basin of potatoes he'd peeled.

"Yes, I think that's plenty," she said.

He was tall, lean and sinewy. Practically radiating vigour.

Behind her, Gemma giggled at one of Harry's oft-repeated jokes. Hazel gritted her teeth.

"Excuse me," Cal leaned past her, reaching for the kitchen roll.

For the briefest of moments, one of his hands rested on her hip. A thrill rippled through Hazel. She suddenly wondered what

They all started sniffing the air like a pack of daft dogs. Everyone making comments about how great it smelt. Archie included.

Despite his aversion to vegetarian food, his mouth was watering. Seemed a waste of a good curry not to have some meat in it, but if there was one thing he hated more than veggie food it was cooking. Thing was, if he was going to cook meat for himself then he'd have to do his own dishes as well. And if there was one thing Archie hated more than cooking, it was doing the dishes. It was a big fucking no-no all round. So he'd do what he always did when he came here - go with the veggie flow. Back on the mainland, first chance he got he'd stop for a slab of dead animal slapped on a buttered roll.

Pity it was a ninety-minute drive to the burger van in Garve, but the wait wouldn't kill him. Not that he'd have to wait that long. He'd brought himself a wee sneaky something for sustenance. It wasn't much, but it would help get him through the long meat-free days ahead.

Fran handed out plates of food. She must've won the *I'll help Hazel* contest.

Archie hadn't been paying attention. He watched her now though. Good looking girl. He usually preferred women with a bit more meat on their bones - he truly was a dedicated carnivore - and he liked them stacked on top. He was most definitely a tit man. Fran didn't fit the bill at all. She was a right Skinny Minnie and had tiny wee tits. But there was something about the way she held herself that kind of got to him. As well as fancying her a bit, he genuinely liked her.

Not that he'd stand a chance. She was way too into that queer boyfriend of hers. Archie would have to content himself with being pals. Fair enough. He wasn't exactly short of female company. What could he say? He knew he wasn't God's gift, but women liked him. He made them laugh. Made them feel good about themselves. And they were always going on about the twinkle in his eye. He didn't know what the fuck that was about, but as long as he was twinkling them right into bed, who was he to complain?

He wasn't the only one in the room who fancied Fran. He'd seen the way that twerp Marcus looked at her. Practically salivating. Archie felt like telling him to put his tongue back in his mouth. What Marcus didn't get was that, boyfriend or no boyfriend, a girl like Fran wasn't going to look at a dink like him in a million years.

Fran sat Archie's dinner on the table in front of him. He smiled at her, told her thanks very much, and contemplated the plate.

A mound of brown rice (brown!) sat in a stodge beside a ladleful of lumps coated in curry sauce. If he didn't know better he could pretend the lumps were chicken. Best not to think that way though. He'd only be disappointed when he bit into a piece of potato or, God forbid, a lump of bloody cauliflower. What the actual fuck was the point of cauliflower?

Hazel was telling Fran to sit down. She'd finish up serving. Around him, everyone was gabbing away. All playing nice. No-one eating until everyone was seated. Man alive, he was hungry enough to eat a scabby vegetarian.

Fran finally sat down. Hazel put a plate of curry in front of her then Harry got his.

Archie eyed Harry's plate, comparing it to his own. Harry had a right old heap of curry steaming away in front of him. Archie nudged him.

"A wee bit of favouritism going on there?" he asked.

Harry laughed. "Your need is greater than mine."

Before Archie could utter a word about speaking in jest, Harry had already swapped their plates over.

"To tell the truth," Harry leaned into Archie and spoke in a low voice, "I'm not that keen on Hazel's vegetable curry. But don't tell her I said so."

He winked at Archie and tapped his nose.

"It's alright," Archie replied. "Your secret's safe with me."

Finally, Hazel sat down with her own meal, and the eating commenced.

The chatter ceased for the next few moments while everyone chowed down.

"Lovely curry," Cal finally said.

"Well done, Chef." Rob raised a tin of lager.

The rest of them followed suit, raising their drinks in a toast to Hazel.

"Thank you." She gave a modest smile. "But I think I may have been too heavy-handed with the fenugreek."

Denials and reassurances arose over the table.

Archie muttered along with everyone else, but the curry didn't taste right to him. It wasn't just because it was veggie. He'd been coming to the island for years and been subjected to veggie food every time. None of it had tasted like this.

He glanced around the table. Everybody else was getting tucked in. No-one seemed to have a problem with it, Harry included. Bloody noisy eater he was too. A right old chomper.

Maybe it was the bloody fenugreek Hazel had been on about. Gave it a bitter kind of taste. Archie added fenugreek to his list of pointless foods. He swigged down a few mouthfuls of lager and wished that he'd clung onto his own smaller portion.

At least there was plenty of booze on the go. He didn't have them all sussed out yet, but one thing he could say about this lot was that at least they enjoyed a drink. That Eleanor one was fair quaffing the red.

He'd been stuck here with some right po-faced bastards before. You'd think it would kill them to enjoy themselves. At least Fran had been here for the past few years. He'd been able to go and have a fly drink with her when there were too many stiff-necks around.

He chewed another forkful of curry, wondering how much he could get away with leaving without it being an insult to Hazel. Just as well he'd brought his wee treat for later, or he'd be starving.

The curry definitely hadn't hit the spot.

10

"Can I have your attention please?"

The dishes had been cleared and the alcohol was flowing. Nine relaxed faces turned to Fran. With the exception of Eleanor, they were regular volunteers. Coming at least once a year, helping out on the island for a week at a time through the season. Greeting the visitors who came to view the seabird colonies. Helping with maintenance tasks. They'd come here now to help with a special out-of-season volunteer weekend.

"I know most of you are familiar with the bothy and the island, but there are a few housekeeping duties I have to get out of the way."

Fran ran through the first aid and fire safety procedures and explained how to use the hand-held radios.

"As you know, there is no mobile signal on the island, so we rely on the radios in case of emergencies."

"I quite like the idea of being cut off from the rest of the world," Archie said.

"Oh me too," Gemma said. "It's fantastic."

Fran smiled brightly at her.

Gemma had given Fran no reason to dislike her, but dislike her she did. She suspected that deep down she might be jealous of the petite, pretty blonde. Fran carried no excess weight. If anything, she was skinny, but, beside Gemma, her long body seemed unwieldy. She felt gargantuan and clumsy. And somehow very unfeminine.

Jealousy was not a trait she admired in others, and she wasn't proud to be harbouring such feelings herself. Particularly against someone who had done her no harm. Guilt compelled her to compensate by being over-friendly.

She wondered if her smile looked as fake as it felt.

"Are we likely to have an emergency?" Eleanor asked.

Fran was glad of the distraction. The ache on her face eased as her bright smile faded to a more natural hue.

Eleanor, a city woman if ever there was one, had seemed tense earlier. She'd since relaxed. The process no doubt helped by lashings of red wine.

"It would be unusual," Fran said. "I've spent the past three seasons working on the island, and in that time I've had to call out the coastguard once - for someone who had slipped on the cliff path and twisted her ankle. Obviously not very pleasant for the woman involved, but not much of a drama. Okay?"

Eleanor nodded, reassured by Fran's response.

Fran continued. "I used the radios to check in with the coastguard yesterday when Jonathan and I arrived. They are both working fine. One will be kept here at the bothy - hung up there beside the instructions and grid reference. The other one will be with me."

So far so good.

"Now that the housekeeping is out of the way, we can get on to the fun stuff. I know we've all been chatting, but I think it would be useful if we introduced ourselves to the group. I'll start. Okay, I'm Fran and I've been the ranger here on the island for the past three years." She looked at Rob, who was sitting nearest to her.

"Hi everyone, I'm Rob."

Fran sat down, breathing a sigh of relief as Rob gave a little spiel about himself and the introductions moved round the room.

It was always tricky pulling a new group together, but it seemed to be going okay. Better than she'd hoped, if she was honest. She caught Jonathan's eye. He gave her a short nod.

Letting her know she was doing just fine. She knew he didn't like mixing with groups of strangers and was surprised and delighted when he'd agreed to come. Albeit on the condition that they got to spend some time together, alone. They'd had that last night, and it had been wonderful.

Marcus's voice brought her attention back to the room.

"I'm Marcus and my favourite past-time is hating my ex-wife."

Fran glanced around as people stiffened. The only ones in the room who didn't seem adversely affected by the sudden shift in mood were Archie and Cal.

A smile was twitching on Cal's lips while Archie looked as though he was fit to burst with laughter.

"Nice hobby," Eleanor muttered.

Marcus raised an eyebrow. "Only joking," he said with a thin smile. "Even I'm not that bitter."

"You're a funny guy, Marcus," Archie said. "Is it my turn now? Okay, I'm Archie. I like getting away from it all every now and again, getting some peace and quiet. Being a contrary sort, I also like a bit of life around me. I like to eat and drink and have a laugh. Sorry to say I've never been married, but I love the ladies - especially Marcus's ex-wife. Lovely woman."

Everyone laughed. Even Marcus couldn't stop himself from smirking.

Fran laughed too hard and too long for what had been a feeble kind of joke. But it had been a welcome tension breaker. Her laugh faltered as she noticed how close Gemma was sitting to Jonathan. She'd managed to squeeze herself beside him on the bench. Any closer and he'd be wearing her as a tattoo.

She said something to him. He smiled and said something in return.

Fran told herself that Gemma was only being friendly, and that Jonathan was only being friendly in return. She told herself that it was unreasonable of her to expect, to want, him to be his usual reticent self. She'd put him in this situation. She could hardly blame him for behaving in a polite and friendly manner.

She told herself all of that, but she didn't believe a word.

Gemma was last to introduce herself.

"Hi everyone." She smiled. Small, even, white teeth against soft, pink lips. "I'm Gemma, and I love meeting new people."

I'll bet, Fran thought. She felt sour inside.

"Okay everyone," Fran stood up again. She wasn't entirely sure that Gemma had finished but, frankly, she didn't care. "We've got a lot to get through tomorrow."

Her tone sounded a little strident in her own ears, but it grabbed everyone's attention.

"First on the list is baiting the rat stations. There are eighteen boxes located around the periphery of the island." She indicated a map pinned to the board. "The rat population has been kept under control for the past few years and we want to keep it that way. The idea is to put the bait out when there are few other food sources available, so this time of year is perfect. It's simply a matter of locating the boxes and putting fresh bait in them. I need two teams of two people for that."

"I'm up for that," Jonathan volunteered.

"Me too," Gemma chirruped. Before Fran could steer her in another direction, Harry jumped in.

"We'll be the other rat team," he said, indicating himself and Hazel.

Jonathan alone all day with Gemma. The whole deal stitched up before Fran said another word. She stared at Hazel who was laughing long and hard at Harry calling them a rat team. Fran wondered if it was just tea Hazel had in her mug. Thinking to herself at the same time that she absolutely trusted Jonathan. Didn't she?

"What's next, Fran?" Cal asked.

Fran pulled her attention back to the task list.

"I need a couple of people to walk round the boardwalk

sections of the path and mark the parts where repairs are needed."

"Eleanor and I will do that," Rob said.

"Great," Fran said, marking them down. Still thinking about Jonathan and Gemma, out there together. Alone. If she trusted him, it didn't matter.

"Next is clearing the cross-drains on the path."

"I'm up for that," Cal said. "What about you Archie - think you can handle it? Maybe you can work off some of that gut."

"What gut?" Archie sucked in his belly. "Don't be fooled by this," he said, slapping it, "I can work the socks off a big softie like you any day of the week."

"You're on, mate," Cal said.

There was laughter in the room, but Fran wasn't laughing. And she wasn't thinking about Jonathan spending the entire day alone with Gemma. She was staring at the list. There was only one task left. And only two people left to do it.

"Fran?"

She looked up at Marcus. He was looking at her like a snake eyeing up its next meal.

"What will we be doing?" he asked.

11

Eleanor watched surreptitiously as Cal stretched out his long, lean legs. His foot brushed against hers. He smiled at her, mouthed *sorry*. Too polite to interrupt the rambling tale Rob was regaling them with. Eleanor coyly returned the smile, wondering if the touch had been accidental.

He held her gaze for a second longer than necessary and she knew it had been no accident. She let her eyes slide from his face down to his chest and along the length of his body. By the time she got to his feet, which he'd placed scant inches from her own, she was in the mood for more than a game of footsies.

She eyed Rob. He was in full flow, telling one of his shaggy dog stories. She'd heard it all before. His t-shirt was straining over his belly. It wasn't a good look. She could hardly talk. Rob wasn't the only one who'd gained weight over the past month or so. If it wasn't for all the time she'd put in at the gym, she'd be looking like Mrs Blobby. Too many takeaways in front of the telly was one of the problems. Too much red wine was another. Talking of which - Eleanor took another sip from her glass, making sure to avoid the chip on the rim.

Hazel laughed, shaking her head as Rob came to the end of his tale.

Hazel was an incredibly ordinary looking woman. Nothing about her stood out. She wasn't fat, wasn't thin. Wasn't beautiful, wasn't ugly. She wasn't tall, but not so short you'd comment on it. She was strictly background material. The kind of woman you passed in the supermarket without really seeing. Almost invisible. But she laughed like she meant it. In fact, she looked so happy in the moment that Eleanor felt a teeny pang of jealousy.

She couldn't remember the last time she'd laughed like that. Was wondering now if she'd ever completely given herself up to any moment. She always seemed to be worrying about what she looked like or what other people were thinking about her.

She took another sip of wine. Ironic, considering that it was drinking too much red wine that got her into this in the first place. She would never have agreed to come if she hadn't been drunk. In the end, she'd agreed to it to keep Rob happy.

See, she did care about him.

He was so bloody keen to get her up here. Despite all the evidence to the contrary, he had convinced himself that she'd love it. That she would end up sharing his passion for clambering up muddy hills and traipsing through insect-ridden countryside.

She snuck another look at Cal. Rob had been right about one thing. The scenery was pretty good.

Cal caught her looking. She blushed and looked away.

Blushed for goodness sake. Like a schoolgirl.

She put it down to the wine. She was feeling kind of giddy.

As the flush subsided, her gaze slid back to Cal. He was laughing at something Archie had said. There was still a wide smile on his face when his eyes suddenly locked onto hers.

A wave of sexual arousal surged through Eleanor's body.

Cal's eyes narrowed. For the briefest of moments, he looked at Eleanor as if he knew exactly what was going on in her head.

Well, come right on in, she thought. The water's fine.

12

Fran lay in bed, all tensed up in the dark. All alone. From beyond the door she could hear the flurry of hushed activity. People going to and from the toilets and shower room. Preparing for bed. She hoped Jonathan was one of them.

She heard Harry ask Hazel in a too-loud voice where his toothbrush was. Hazel shushed him. Snapping at him in an irate whisper that it was in his toiletry bag. Where else would it be?

Fran empathised with Hazel's irritation. She was feeling pretty bloody irritated herself. Marcus had managed things beautifully. All he'd had to do was sit back and say nothing. It was almost as though he and Gemma had planned it together.

Fran punched her pillow but misjudged the swipe. Her knuckles scraped against the wall. She swore and reached for the torch.

Her skin was broken, droplets of blood already oozing out. It was just a graze, but it hurt like hell. She sucked on her grazed knuckles and thought about where it had gone wrong.

What she *should* have done was pre-assign the tasks.

She switched off the torch and lay back in the dark. Staring at nothing. Squeezing her damaged fist tight. Taking comfort from the pain. Wishing she could inflict some of it on Gemma.

She tried to stop her thoughts from straying to what tomorrow would hold, but they persisted in wandering. She'd be working with Marcus all day. Gathering the debris that had been washed onto the beach during the winter.

Her stomach churned at the thought of being alone with him. But what could she do? He hadn't done anything wrong. Hadn't broken any rules. None of the written ones anyway. He hadn't touched her. Hadn't said anything inappropriate. Not really. Nothing she could pin down. There wasn't anything she could actually accuse him of.

Life would be wonderful if she could simply swap Marcus and Jonathan over. The danger was that it would look self-serving and churlish. She wasn't here to spend a weekend with her boyfriend. She was here to work.

It had been hinted to her that this weekend was a test of her management skills. That how she did would count for, or against, her promotion higher up in the organisation. Making changes to work teams for personal reasons would most definitely be regarded as unprofessional.

It was nobody's fault but her own that she was in this situation. Hindsight being a wonderful thing, she realised that she shouldn't have persuaded Jonathan to come with her. But it was done now and she would have to deal with it. So, while she was on the beach with Marcus, Jonathan would be tramping the far reaches of the island with pert little Gemma.

Pert little Gemma. Laughing at every comment Jonathan made. Leaning over him. Touching his arm. Hanging on to his every word like he was the Delphi Oracle.

As for I-don't-like-people-strangers-making-small-talk-Jonathan, he had lapped it up.

It hadn't helped that every time Fran accidentally turned her head in his direction, Marcus caught her eye and gave her a surreptitious wink.

The entire evening had been hideous.

As soon as it was late enough not to be rudely early, she announced that she was turning in for the night. Long day ahead tomorrow. Early start, etc, etc. Heavy hint central.

Harry and Hazel started making moves straight away. She'd looked at Jonathan, hoping he would go with her, but he was too busy shaking his head in amusement at something Gemma had said.

Fran closed her eyes tight but all she could see was Gemma making eyes at Jonathan.

Footsteps in the hall. She wanted it to be him. Hoped it would be. But it probably wasn't.

The door opened. She peeked from beneath her eyelashes. Jonathan's frame silhouetted against the low gaslight in the hall. He hadn't stayed so long after all.

He closed the door and felt his way through the dark room, swearing under his breath when he banged into the chair. Fran suppressed a giggle.

Sounds of him undressing. His hands patting the bed, trying to find his way into the zipped-together sleeping bags. She shifted, giving him space.

"You awake?" he whispered.

"Mmmm." she answered dozily. Pretending she'd been asleep. That she hadn't been at all worried about him spending time with Gemma. Not a problem. No insecurities here.

He ran his fingers lightly down her back. She turned around to face him. He traced a finger around her face and down her throat. Gently tugged at the neckline of her t-shirt.

She sat up, pulled it off, cast it aside, lay down beside him. With a feather touch, he trailed his hand around her breasts and down over her belly until he reached the soft mound of her pubic hair.

She let out a small moan, but he teased her a while longer, tracing circles on her thighs. Just when she thought she couldn't take it any longer, in one smooth move he parted her thighs and nimbly manoeuvred himself between her legs.

She gasped as he went down on her then gave herself up to the pleasure of his flickering tongue.

13

Hazel opened the bunk-room door a crack and peeked into the hall. All was quiet. She was about to open the door wider when she heard the flush of a toilet. She stayed perfectly still, watching as Jonathan emerged a few moments later. He walked to the other end of the hall and disappeared around the corner. Presumably to Fran's room.

She waited a moment longer before creeping into the hall. Fran and Jonathan had gone to bed. Harry was in the shower. The rest of them were still through in the bothy. This was her best chance.

Harry would be in there for an age yet. Farting. Splashing. Clearing his sinuses. She didn't want to think about what else he might be up to. She wondered if he curtailed the sound of his ablutions when he was with his mistress.

The gas mantles gave off a dim light, but Hazel suspected it was nerves rather than not being able to see properly that caused her to fumble the latch. Her heart thudded heavily. She hoped it wouldn't give out on her.

She glanced around. Double-checking she was on her own. Took a deep breath. Lifted the latch. Opened the door. The hinges screeched. The sound bouncing off the walls, echoing along the hall. Hazel froze. Eyes wide. Feet stuck to the floor.

The door hadn't sounded like that earlier on. Like something out of a Hammer Horror film. But earlier on it had been light. Legitimate business went on when it was light. Now she was skulking around in the shadows. Acting guilty. Looking guilty. The dark made all the difference.

She waited for someone to appear. To challenge her. Ask her

what on earth she was up to. But no doors were flung open. No feet pounded towards her. She could hear Harry gargling. There was no sound from the other end of the hall. She was alone in the shadows. Unlit torch in her hand. Film canisters in her fleece pocket.

They said it was good to make your heart work a bit harder every once in a while. Hers was certainly getting a good workout now. She had to admit though, she was getting quite a kick out this subterfuge. It was the most excitement she'd had in years.

When it was clear that no-one was coming, she entered the store. She closed the door behind her, switched on the torch and sat it on a shelf. The tub of rat poison was exactly where she'd left it. She prised the lid off the container and took the film canisters from her pocket.

Harry had nagged her about getting a digital camera, but she'd stuck doggedly to her 35mm. It was what she was used to. And she liked the film canisters. Harry thought she was being silly, but they were handy for all sorts of things. For example, they were just the right size for saving two-pound coins. Or for storing poison.

She had used three canisters. It seemed a bit excessive now, but she'd wanted to do the job properly. It hadn't seemed prudent to ask if anyone knew how much rat poison it would take to kill- No not kill. How much poison it would take to *distress* a rat of human proportions.

A rat of human proportions. The thought struck her as funny. Almost as funny as when Harry had named them the Rat Team.

This time, Hazel held her mirth in. She had the peculiar feeling that if she started laughing now she might never stop.

She opened the first two canisters. They were full. She carefully emptied the contents back into the tub of poison. The third canister was almost empty. She tapped it on the neck of the tub to dislodge the remaining granules.

By the time Harry had finished his ablutions, Hazel was tucked up in bed. The gas light was still on, but as she was in the bottom bunk with her head shrouded in the hood of her sleeping bag, it didn't bother her in the slightest. She didn't answer when Harry asked if she was awake.

The whole bed frame shook as he hauled himself into the top bunk. She wondered for a moment if he was going to come crashing through the frame. Mattress, sleeping bag, Harry and all. He'd most likely crush her to death if he did. Such a clumsy man.

Within seconds he was snoring. He had a thick, heavy snore. Sounded like it was trying to grab the back of his throat and choke him. If only.

Hazel felt sorry for Gemma and Cal. They would be sleeping in the other bunks. That is, if they could get any sleep. But neither of them seemed particularly shy. She rather thought they wouldn't be averse to poking Harry in the ribs if need be.

She pulled her sleeping bag tight around her ears. As she snuggled down to sleep, she wondered how long it would take for Harry's special curry to take effect.

14

Eleanor's gaze flickered from Rob to Cal and back again. Rob's problem was that he tried too hard. He was like an over-grown boy scout. The world full of new experiences waiting for him to launch himself at. Everyone he met was a potential new friend. As for sex, full marks for enthusiasm and energy, but at times he went at it like he was working towards a new merit badge. In-out, in-out. Repeated thrusting with little variation.

Cal, on the other hand, had this really relaxed vibe about him. The corners of his eyes crinkled deliciously when he laughed, which was often. He was laughing now at some daft thing Archie had said. Even that creep Marcus seemed to amuse him.

Cal had one of those quiet laughs, didn't make much noise. Not like Rob. He had to let the world know when he thought something was funny. He was letting rip with a monstrous guffaw right now. A prime example of him trying too hard.

Eleanor cringed and rolled her eyes. Marcus caught her in the act and treated her to a sardonic grin. She tossed him a look of disdain. The grin on his face broadened, growing fat on her reaction. Eleanor decided to ignore him completely for the rest of the weekend. Shouldn't be too hard to do, tomorrow at least. He'd be with Fran all day, clearing the beach.

As Rob told a story she'd heard a dozen times before, Eleanor idly wondered if there was something going on between Fran and Marcus. She was sure she'd seen him wink at Fran a couple of times through the evening. She could see why Marcus would go for her. Fran was one of those outdoorsy types, all fresh air and no make-up. A walking, talking advert for healthy living. She even managed to look good in a fleece.

On the other hand, she did not get what a woman like Fran would ever see in a worm like Marcus. Yet, she could sense some kind of tension between them. There was definitely something going on. Seemed a bit risky inviting your lover on a weekend along with your boyfriend. Maybe they had a threesome thing going. No accounting for taste. Eleanor grimaced at the thought. If this was the territory her mind was roaming, it was time to turn in for the night.

She waited for Rob to draw breath and made her excuses. Rob immediately said that he'd be right through. Good grief, couldn't she get fifteen minutes to herself? She wanted to swat him like a fly. The sooner this weekend was over the better.

A T-shaped extension had been built onto the gable end of the original bothy. It housed two bedrooms, one of which was the ranger's accommodation, the bunk-room, toilets, shower room and store. It seemed a bit mental having to go outside before she could get to her bed, but not much about this place made sense.

Eleanor shivered as she hurried along the path to the door at the other end of the building. Wishing she had something better to look forward to sleeping on than that stinky mildewed mattress. She glanced around. Dark. Lots and lots of dark. Anything could be out there. Lurking. It gave her the creeps. It now seemed entirely possible to Eleanor that the place was cursed.

Darkness pressing in. Surrounded by sea. Miles from the nearest help. From civilisation. No wonder the woman had gone demented. Murdering her friends, neighbours, family, before committing suicide. If Eleanor had to spend much longer here, she'd be throwing herself off the nearest cliff.

She tried to resist doing it. Tried not to give into her fear. If she looked, she'd make it real. She looked. Over her shoulder. Of course there was nothing there. No monsters. No madwoman clutching a rock. Nothing, but an empty bloody island. The whole story Marcus's idea of a joke. Ha, bloody ha. She rolled her eyes.

Stopped.

And stared.

She gazed up at the sky, almost gasping at the beauty of it. There was no light pollution. For the first time in her life, the splendour of the night sky was revealed to Eleanor in all its glory.

"Amazing, isn't it?"

A voice behind her, speaking softly.

Eleanor jumped. She'd been so caught up in her star gazing that she hadn't heard the door opening or the soft tread of footsteps on the path.

She turned her head. Cal. Standing close to her. Smiling. His eyes glittering in the starlight. Eleanor's stomach quivered.

She looked back at the sky. "I've never seen anything like it," she said. "Look - there's a shooting star. I've never seen one before. There's another one."

"I think that one's a satellite," Cal said. "See, you can follow its path."

"A satellite - really?"

She turned her face towards his. He was standing so close, there was barely space for a sigh between them. He was as aware of her body as she was of his. She was sure of it. They were having a moment.

Their lips so close, it would take barely a move for them to be kissing.

She caught her breath.

"Look at that!" Rob's voice boomed out.

Eleanor jerked away from Cal. A guilty flush prickling her skin.

Rob strode towards them, Gemma at his shoulder.

Eleanor eyed him nervously, but Rob was gazing obliviously at the sky.

"Did you see that shooting star, Eleanor? Did you make a wish?"

"I saw it," she said. She had moved away from Cal. Was barely within hand-shaking distance. Nothing to see here.

"I saw it too," Gemma said. But she wasn't looking at the sky. She was staring at Eleanor, her lips curled in a smile.

Eleanor looked away from her. "It's freezing out here," she said. Fronting it out. "Let's go inside," she said to Rob.

"Okay, babe. Whatever you say."

He put his arm around her and gave a tight squeeze.

"Steady on, tiger," Eleanor said.

Rob released her. As he did so, she thought she saw his gaze flicker towards Cal. A hard glint in his eye. Then it was gone. Probably just a trick of the light. Rob hadn't seen anything. There hadn't been anything to see.

As they wished the others goodnight, Eleanor was aware of Gemma's knowing eyes watching her. Eleanor decided there and then that she couldn't stand the woman.

All the same, what had she been thinking? There was no denying that she and Cal had a moment. The thrill had been palpable. She couldn't believe how attracted she'd been to him. He was barely more than a stranger. It was crazy.

She felt thrilled and terrified at the same time. But no matter how she felt, no matter how strong the connection between them, nothing was going to happen. There was no way she could betray Rob like that.

If things really were over between them she had to face up to it and end their relationship. She couldn't just go and humiliate him, by having sex with someone behind his back. Especially not here, on this bloody special island of his. She'd ruin it for him forever.

No, she'd get through the weekend, and when they were home, she would tell him it was over.

15

At last, Archie was alone. Marcus had gone to the toilet before settling down for the night. Everyone else had already gone off to bed.

As soon as the door closed behind his room-mate, Archie was out of his chair like a greyhound out of the trap, and into his rucksack like a rat down a drain pipe. He'd been looking forward to this moment all night.

He prodded and poked with no luck. Where was it? He pushed layers of clothing aside and peered into the rucksack. It was a mess of shadows. He couldn't see anything in this bloody light. He needed a torch. No, there was no time to waste. He'd have another feel about first.

He burrowed his hand right down to the bottom. He was groaning with frustration when his fingers scraped against a paper bag.

He grabbed hold of it and pulled it to the top of the rucksack. It didn't matter if it got a little mangled on the way. It was going to get one hell of a lot more mangled where it was going.

He held the rumpled bag in his hand for a moment, enjoying its illicit, meaty weight. His mouth was salivating like one of Pavlov's poodles. The anticipation was bloody marvellous. He didn't think he'd ever looked forward to eating something so much in his entire life.

Archie eagerly tore the bag open. The pie was squashed. Its insides oozing through cracked pastry. Lovely, golden, flaky pastry. Congealed gravy. Big lumps of tender beef. All the glorious meatiness contained within the greaseproof bag.

Archie scooped one of the larger pieces into his mouth.

Crumbling pastry. Thick, salty gravy. Mushy-melt-in-the-mouth meat. He closed his eyes, savouring the flavour. Very fucking delicious, thank you. All the more so for being his wee secret treat.

Just as he swallowed the mouthful, his eyes sprang open.

There had been a tang. A possible sour note. A hint of something not quite right. His pie couldn't have turned, could it?

He sniffed at the bag. Seemed okay. He'd bought the pie fresh that day. Had made a special stop for it in Ullapool. He scooped up another mouthful. Thoughtfully chewed it. It tasted fine. Perfect, in fact. He quickly ate the rest of the larger pieces then lapped up the remaining crumby mush straight from the paper.

His face was still in the bag when the door opened.

Archie looked up as Marcus walked in. Talk about caught in the act. Marcus stared at him, his eyebrows going through the roof.

Archie licked a smear of gravy from his lips.

"What on earth are you doing?" Marcus said.

"What the fuck does it look like?"

Archie's voice was thick. The final morsels of pie clagging his throat. He swallowed, savouring the last of the meaty-gravy-pastry flavour.

Marcus eyed the crumpled bag in Archie's hand.

"Billy fucking Bunter."

Archie crushed the bag into a tight ball and threw it on the fire. It flared up, sizzling briefly before burning out.

"Fuck off, dweeb," he said.

"You greedy bastard."

"It was only a fucking pie."

Archie wiped his mouth on the back of his hand. The final notes of his treat had gone sour on him.

"No need to ask then."

"Ask what?"

"Who ate all the pies?"

Marcus laughed. It was a thin, unpleasant sound.

"Tell me something, Marcus," Archie said. "Do you work at being a cunt or does it come naturally?"

Marcus shrugged and went to the bunks.

Archie clenched his fist. He felt like smacking the smarmy prick. The only thing stopping him was how upset Fran would be. Fisticuffs between the inmates was a big fucking no-no. Still, it was tempting. Could probably take the cunt down with one quick bop on the nose.

Resisting temptation, he went next door to use the facilities. Despite brushing his teeth, he returned with a sour taste still in his mouth.

Marcus was all tucked up in bed. Either asleep or pretending to be. Bastard seemed to think he was un-fucking touchable.

Never mind, one way or another, before the weekend was over, Marcus would get what was coming to him.

16

SUNDAY

Fran watched as white horses cantered and spumed on the rollers. The fresh air was invigorating, but the breeze was stiffening and there was quite a swell. She wondered if Zander would go to sea on a day like this. She watched as wave after wave crashed relentlessly over the rocks at the end of the beach. Foaming and spraying. Probably not, though you never could tell with Zander. She reckoned that under his wild-man-of-the-sea act there was a touch of genuine madness.

She loved being on the beach in winter. Wild and empty, it felt like a secret. Strictly speaking, she supposed March counted as spring, but it sure felt like winter. It looked like winter too. Apart from the white of the surf, everything appeared in muted shades of grey. Even the sand on the beach, so warm and golden in the summer, had a grey sheen.

Standing far enough up the beach so that the surf missed her feet when the waves surged in, she looked out to the horizon. Compared to the vastness of the sea and sky, she felt insignificant. She also felt very much alive. She smiled as a spray of saltwater tingled her face.

The receding waves sucked at the sand. Churning it into the water. No, not even Zander was mad enough to set to sea on a day like this. They were on their own. Cut off from the rest of the world. No mobile phones, no internet, no television. For all they knew, some big calamity could have befallen the rest of the world without them knowing a thing about it. They could be the only people left alive anywhere.

"Look at this!"

Marcus's voice cut through her thoughts. She turned her back on the sea and walked up the beach towards him. The downside of being cut off from the rest of the world was that Marcus was here too.

She ticked herself off. He'd worked hard all morning and there had been no hint of untoward behaviour. No sly looks or smirking. No winking. No invasion of her personal space. She was thinking that maybe - just maybe - she'd got him all wrong.

"What is it?" she asked.

"Look, almost a matching pair."

He held up two rubber boots. One yellow. One orange. Each cracked and scarred.

"Amazing what you find," she said.

Marcus turned the boots upside down and gave them a shake. Seaweed, sand and an empty crab shell tumbled out.

"There's a couple of fish boxes half buried in the sand up there."

"Let's go get 'em," Fran said.

Marcus tossed the boots onto the heap of debris they'd accumulated. When they were finished, the pile would be covered in tarpaulin and secured against the wind until it could be collected by boat and taken to a skip on the mainland.

The fish boxes were lodged in wet sand. By the time they'd dug them out, Fran's arms were aching. She dropped her shovel, fell back on a sand dune and let out a groan.

"I thought we'd never get them out," she said.

Marcus removed his glasses and wiped the sweat from his brow.

"We've earned our supper today," he said.

"That's for sure."

The sun broke through a gap in the clouds.

"Oh, lovely," Fran said.

She closed her eyes for a moment, luxuriating in the unexpected warmth. Sun on her face. The pounding roar and hiss of the surf. Marram grass rattling in the breeze. The ache ebbing from her arms. Heavenly bliss...

Something - someone - touched her.

Fran yelped. Opened her eyes.

"Sorry," Marcus, standing over her. "Didn't mean to startle you."

Fran sat up. Disorientated.

"I must have dozed off."

She'd been asleep and he'd been touching her. Just his hand on her arm - or something more?

"Just for a moment," he said.

She glanced up at him. His eyes were hidden by the reflection on his glasses. She couldn't see his eyes, but she could feel them, watching her. Studying her.

He wasn't tall, maybe five nine, but in his current position he towered over her. She clambered to her feet, wishing he'd step back, give her space.

Getthefuckaway.

He held out his hand to help her up. She ignored it.

"I can manage."

She stood up and brushed the sand from her clothes.   Not looking at him. Feeling exposed. Embarrassed. Her mind racing. Berating herself for letting her guard down.

"Let's get back to work," she said. Her face turned away from him.

"There's something over there," he said. "In the strandline."

They walked along the beach. Fran a step behind. She fought the urge to break free and stride ahead of him. Couldn't stand the thought of him watching her back. Checking her out. Him looking at her when she couldn't see him. Like a predator.

She dropped her pace a little. Letting him get further ahead. Wishing it was Jonathan here with her. He was never far from her thoughts. She tried not to think about him and Gemma together. Just the two of them. Laughing, chatting. Getting to know each other.

She was being stupid. Jonathan loved her. He would never let her down.

Marcus stopped. He was staring at a mound of mangled seaweed, toeing something with his boot.

"It's a sheep," he said when she arrived.

Fran looked down at the beast. Its eye sockets were empty. The flesh had been stripped from its head, exposing its teeth in a permanent skeletal grin. Its body, bound in a heavy fleece, looked remarkably intact.

"Where do you think it came from?" Marcus asked.

"Dunno," Fran said, reluctant to engage in conversation. "Maybe it went over a cliff on the mainland."

"Poor thing," he said. "What a way to go. It must have been terrified when it fell. Do you think it screamed? Can sheep scream?"

She stared at him. The sun had once again been masked by thick clouds and she could see his eyes perfectly clearly. Could read nothing in them.

"I don't know," she said.

"Just as well it's still too cold for flies," he said. "A little bit more sunshine, a few more degrees of heat, and it will be heaving with maggots."

Fran screwed up her face. "Don't be so gruesome."

"It's all part of the natural process, Fran. I thought you of all people would have appreciated that."

She turned her back on him, started walking back down the beach.

"We've got work to do," she said.

"You're the boss." He sounded amused.

Fran scowled.

She heard his footsteps, crunching through dried seaweed as he followed her. His eyes on her. Watching the sway of her hips.

She stiffened at the thought. Wished Jonathan was here with her now.

Behind her, the dead sheep lay grinning in the mangled seaweed.

17

Jonathan checked the map.

"The next one should be just about here," he said.

Gemma scoured around the uneven ground for the bait box. "Here it is."

She smiled at him. She smiled a lot. Talked a lot too.

He shrugged off his day pack.

Fran had been in a funny mood again when she woke up. Yeah, she was under pressure. Wanted the weekend to go well. Yeah, yeah, yeah. Blah, blah, blah. Like it really mattered. She had already worked for them for three seasons. They already knew how good she was. Jonathan reckoned all the pressure Fran was under was coming from herself.

Between her moods, the sickening boat trips and the clowns he was stuck here with, he was really, really wishing he hadn't let her talk him into coming.

A shag had sorted her mood out the night before and it had done the trick again this morning. Hearing the volunteers moving about in the hall outside Fran's room had added a certain frisson. They'd muffled their giggles under the sleeping bag.

It had just been a quick fuck and fumble, but at least it had straightened her face out.

Afterwards, he made a point of telling her he loved her.

"Really?" she'd asked.

"Really," he'd replied.

She needed a lot of reassurance these days.

It could be wearing.

She'd trailed a finger over his chest, looked at him coyly.

"What do you think about Gemma?"

"Gemma?" he'd snorted. "She's a daft wee blonde. Not in your league at all."

"Penny for them?" Gemma was peering at him. Eyes wide, a knowing smile tugging at her lips.

"Sorry?"

"Penny for them?" she repeated. "Your thoughts. You were miles away."

"Sorry, I was just thinking about something."

"No kidding. I hope Fran realises how lucky she is."

"Was it that obvious?"

He wasn't any too keen on the knack Gemma had for getting inside his head.

"Just a bit," she said. "I hope some guy feels like that about me someday."

A small bubble popped in Jonathan's head. He recognised dangerous territory when he saw it.

"Are you going to check the box?" he asked.

It wasn't what he'd call a smooth change of subject, but it had been a quick manoeuvre away from having to reassure Gemma that she was indeed wonderful and that someday her prince would come.

He might not have the insight into her mind that she apparently had into his, but he was pretty damn sure that she already knew how attractive she was. Him ladling out compliments for her to lap up was a mess of flirting he did not intend on getting suckered into.

"Anything you say," she said.

He pretended not to notice the sidelong glance she gave him.

Gemma opened the bait box. "Empty," she called.

Stepping carefully over the hummocky ground, she picked her way back to him. Jonathan opened his bag and reached in for a tub of poison.

Gemma screamed. Jonathan looked up as she stumbled into him.

The sudden lurch of her weight knocked him off balance. He instinctively grabbed hold of her as he fell. She landed on top of him, knocking the air out of his lungs.

"Oh God," her voice, breathless. "I'm so sorry. I tripped on the heather."

Her face above his, their noses almost touching. He noticed tiny flecks of green in her blue eyes.

"It's okay," he said.

"I'm a complete klutz."

"It was an accident. Don't worry about it."

Jonathan felt warm. Very warm. He didn't know if she was radiating heat or if he was generating it all himself.

"You're so sweet."

Her lips were soft and pink. Her breath smelled of peppermint. He grabbed her by the arms. Rolled her off him. Turning quickly, before she could feel him hardening against her.

He was on his feet again in an instant.

She grinned up at him, like she knew exactly what was going on.

He held out a hand to help her up, wishing she'd get the hell out of his head.

She wrapped her fingers around his and nimbly leapt to her feet, ending up almost as close to him as when they'd been lying on the ground.

She released her grip, but her fingers lingered in his hand. She tilted her face up at him. It looked very much like an invitation. His cock was rock solid.

She parted her lips. Spoke softly, almost whispering. Another bubble popped in his head.

"Thanks," she said.

"What for?" He asked, his voice as hushed as hers.

"For not getting angry."

He wondered why they were whispering when they were away out in the middle of nowhere.

"It was an accident, why would I lose my temper?"

Then he wondered why he was feeling so guilty when he hadn't done anything. Except get a hard on.

His cock throbbed.

He couldn't help it.

She moved in closer. Her lips brushed against his. A gossamer touch. Barely there at all, but it sent a shock through him like a bolt of electricity. Dozens of bubbles exploded in his head.

He pulled away from her. Stumbled, almost falling again. Gemma reached out to him. He put his hands up. Blocking her.

"I'm fine," he said.

He turned away from her. She'd tripped into him deliberately. He was sure of it. He'd been tempted. He couldn't deny it. Sorely tempted.

A pang of guilt seared through him.

His cock shrivelled.

He didn't know why he felt guilty.

He shouldn't feel guilty.

He hadn't done anything wrong.

18

Archie groaned.

"What's up?" Cal asked.

"My guts," Archie said. "They've been playing up all morning." He pursed his lips and sucked in a stream of air. "Must have been that veggie curry last night. I keep saying that vegetarian food isn't natural. Oh Jesus!"

He bent over, clutching his stomach. When the spasm passed he looked up at Cal with a pained expression.

"I don't think it was the curry," Cal said, "or else we'd all be suffering."

"Are you sure you're okay?" Archie asked. "No pains or suspect grumblings?"

"I'm perfect, mate."

"Oh hell. In that case, it must have been the pie."

"What pie?"

"A wee bit of meaty sustenance I brought with me. Ate it last night. I thought it tasted a bit funny but I ate it anyway."

Cal laughed. "Serves you right."

"It's no funny. Ah Christ, no!"

"What is it - are you alright?" Cal asked.

"I think I've just shit myself."

"Really?"

"Oh hell, yes."

"You'd better get back to the bothy and get yourself cleaned up."

"I think I'll have to."

Archie hobbled away, the sound of Cal's quiet laughter nipping at his heels as he went.

He tottered towards the bothy as quickly as he could manage but running with shit dribbling down his legs was more difficult than he would ever have imagined. It swilled in his underwear. Made his trousers stick to his legs. He was a desperate man in a desperate situation.

Trouble was, his guts weren't done yet. All he could think about was getting to the toilet and voiding himself.

The stench was diabolical. It was going to take more than a few sheets of recycled bog paper to sort him out. He'd have to have a shower. A thorough one. Give himself a right good clean. Scour himself with a Brillo Pad and a tub of Vim, if that's what it took. And he thought it probably would.

Then he'd have to dispose of his shitty pants. Maybe his trousers too. They were beyond saving. He'd have to bag them and bin them.

A wave of nausea swept through him. Sweat popped on his brow. He let out a mournful cry. As much in embarrassment at his predicament than anything else, but oh how his guts ached.

He shouldn't have tried to blame the veggie curry. That wasn't fair. Veggie curry be damned. He'd known it was the pie as soon as the first gut cramp had hit him. He'd farted, thinking the expulsion of gas would relieve the pain. Except the fart hadn't been a fart.

He couldn't believe he'd shit himself. Couldn't believe he was in this mess. Jesus, his guts hurt. If he hadn't been such a greedy wee bastard, none of this would have happened. Oh the pie, the pie. The fucking pie. A few mouthfuls of guilty pleasure then nothing but misery.

That bastard Marcus was going to love this.

19

Harry squatted beside the bait box, tub of rat poison in his hand. He wasn't showing any symptoms of being anything other than his usual self. Hazel snorted. He looked at her.

The man had the constitution of an ox. Even so - surely the poison should have had some effect by now.

He stood up.

"What's wrong?" he asked.

She should have used more. She hadn't wanted to kill him, though. She wasn't a murderer, for goodness sake. She'd only wanted to inflict some discomfort on him. Get some payback for the pain he'd inflicted on her. Retribution for the years she'd wasted by staying with him.

She couldn't have used any more though. Not without the blue dye from the poison becoming obvious in the curry. Still, she had put in a fair dollop. It should have had some effect. Not no effect.

It was very frustrating.

Look at him now. Staring at her with that gormless look on his face.

"Hazel, love - what's wrong?"

"Don't you dare *Hazel love* me!" She spat out the words.

A perplexed look passed across Harry's face. As if he could not possibly comprehend why she would throw his endearment back at him.

It was that look as much as anything else that caused her to crack.

She couldn't hold it in any longer.

"I know Harry," she blurted, "I know what you've been up to."

The colour drained from his face as she glowered at him. His mouth opened, closed, opened again, but no words were forthcoming.

"The affair, Harry. I know about the affair."

"But, what… how - I don't know-"

He mumbled and stumbled, but when the words wouldn't come he gave up and hung his head.

He stood before her, deflated, pathetic. Poor Harry. Poor, poor Harry.

Harry the liar. Harry the deceiver. Harry the adulterer. Hazel couldn't stand his pitiful display for a second longer.

He was standing within slapping distance, but he wasn't worth the effort.

Slowly, he raised his head. There were tears in his eyes.

"I'm sorry," he said.

"Who is she Harry? I want to know. I want to know everything."

20

"Amazing," Eleanor said.

She was standing as close to the cliff edge as she dared. Two hundred feet below, the sea pounded into the rock face, sending up huge shocks of white spray.

Though the cliffs were stained with guano, there were few birds around. A lone black back gull swooped and soared above them. A pair of herring gulls shrieked at each other.

"It's incredible when the seabirds are nesting," Rob said. "You see all those ledges on the cliffs?" Eleanor nodded. "That's where they nest. Guillemots. Razorbills. Fulmars. Puffins. The puffins dig little burrows. People are crazy for puffins. They come from all over to see them. The noise is tremendous when all the birds are here."

"I'd like to see that," Eleanor said.

"See," Rob said, "all this outdoors stuff isn't so bad after all, is it?"

The broad smile on his face reminded her of when she'd first agreed to go on a date with him.

"No, it's not so bad," she agreed, looking away.

Even without the bird life, the view was stunning. The churn of the water and pounding of the waves at the base of the cliffs was mesmerising. She watched as breaker after breaker surged in. Lashing against the rocks in a continual cycle of ebb and flow. Slowly, relentlessly, wearing them away.

"Whoa, steady on."

Rob's hand on her arm, gently pulling her back from the edge.

"The ground can be unstable - you don't want to get too close."

He was still smiling. Taking pleasure from her enjoyment. From the fact that this was something he had introduced her to.

Eleanor suddenly felt terribly sad. Here he was, all happy and blissfully unaware of what she already knew - it was over between them. And not because of Cal and the moment she had shared with him. Cal had nothing to do with it. Her attraction to him was a symptom, not the cause.

She didn't want to hurt Rob, but she wasn't the person he wanted her to be.

Try though he might, he could not mould her into that person. That was the nub of it. He kept trying to make her something she wasn't. This weekend was a prime example. No matter what he read into it, her enjoying a view did not make her a convert to the great outdoors. Rob needed to find someone who genuinely shared his passions. Someone like Fran.

She should have ended it ages ago, before they became a habit.

Better late than never. She'd let him have his weekend first. She wouldn't spoil it for him. But as soon as they were back in civilisation, that was it. Sayonara, my friend. It was a bit of a bugger though. Now that she'd made up her mind, she'd have preferred to get it over and done with.

She watched as he fumbled at one of his pockets. Maybe he'd brought some chocolate with him. Her mood brightened at the thought. A couple of squares of dark Lindt would go down a treat right now.

Nope, too small for chocolate. Way too small.

Rob held up a small green box and smiled at her.

Eleanor's eyes widened. Her mouth gaping like a fish out of water as the realisation of what he was about to do sledge-hammered into her.

Taking her reaction for joyful astonishment, Rob opened the box. For one horrible moment, Eleanor thought he was going to go down on one knee. Instead, he stepped towards her, turning the box in his hand so that she could see the ring.

It was a diamond solitaire, very simple and very beautiful.

"Eleanor..."

Shaking her head, she stepped back. This was the last thing she'd expected. The last thing she wanted. She didn't want to be tied to Rob for the next five minutes, never mind agree to spending the rest of her life with him.

"... Eleanor, will you marry me?"

She stared at him, stunned. Feeling like a small animal caught in the glare of oncoming headlights.

His eyes shone at her. His face beamed joy as he waited for her to say yes.

He stepped towards her, closing the gap between them.

She shook her head.

"Eleanor?"

"No, Rob." Her voice as shrill as the gulls. "I don't want to marry you!"

21

Archie tugged at his boot laces. He felt weak. The knots too complicated for his fumbling fingers. The boots too heavy to pull off. He leaned against the bothy wall as he struggled with them. Finally, he pulled them free.

He took a moment to recover from the effort before peeling off his soiled trousers and underpants. He dropped them in a heap. They were too filthy to take inside. He'd have to bag them later. Didn't want anyone to see them. Too ashamed.

Cold air stung his bare legs.

He looked down at himself and let out a strangled sob. His legs and feet were covered in black shit and he stank. He'd eaten some dodgy takeaways in his time, and he'd had more than his share of the shits after a night on the lash, but he'd never experienced anything like this. This was extreme.

He felt a trickle of snot run from his nose. He wiped it on the back of his hand. It left a dark streak. He peered at it. Not snot. Blood. *What the fuck?*

He took a closer look at the black mess streaking his legs. Blood and shit. Blood in his shit. There was *blood in his shit*. That's why it was black.

This hadn't happened because he'd eaten a dodgy pie. This was something altogether different. This was a whole other world of pain. He had some fucking disease. E coli or that flesh eating bug. That was it. He didn't have the shits. He had a disease.

He staggered into the bothy. He felt frail. His insides were bleeding. He was ill. Properly ill. Panicky thoughts tumbled around his head. He didn't get ill. He never got ill. But he was ill now. Felt dizzy. But he had to get to the shower. Had to get cleaned up. He was dirty. Covered in blood and shit.

He lurched to the shower room. He didn't have his towel with him. No energy to go get it. He'd have to borrow the one that was in there. He was sick. No-one would mind.

He turned the water on. Stripped off the rest of his clothes. Stepped into the shower. He gasped when the cold water hit him, then relaxed as warm water came through. He leaned against the wall and looked down at himself. He used his thumbnail to scrape away thick smears of matter pasted to his skin. Watched in satisfaction as the filth washed away.

Still damp from his shower, and naked and weak as a newborn mole-rat, Archie somehow managed to stumble and crawl his way into his sleeping bag.

He hadn't dried himself properly. Had barely dragged the towel over himself. He certainly didn't have enough energy to get dressed. Didn't have the energy for doing anything other than lying down.

Lying down was good. Standing made him woozy.

He wished the fire was lit. A nice big fire so that he could feel the warmth and listen to the crackle of the burning logs. He was too feeble to light a fire. No energy for anything. Couldn't even think straight. Sort of light-headed. And sore. He had pains in his muscles. Like flu.

It wasn't a crying-out-in-agony pain. Just as well. He didn't have the energy for crying. It was more of an all-over ache.

He wondered what was wrong with him and if anyone else had it. He wondered what they would say when they saw him lying in bed. Was he infectious? Fran would be mad. He was supposed to be somewhere doing something. With Cal.

His mind flitted from one thing to the next, without grasping on to anything. He thought about cold meat pies and curries that didn't taste right. It was a funny thought, but it didn't last long.

22

"But think about it, Hazel," Harry pleaded. "Zander will never be able to get over on a day like this."

"We'll see about that," Hazel said.

To hell with the weather. She had made up her mind that she was leaving. Leaving the island. Leaving Harry.

"What about the bait boxes?"

"Bait boxes! You think I care about bait boxes? After what you've done?"

"But Hazel-"

"They're a waste of time anyway. The poison doesn't even work."

The words out before she knew they were coming.

"What do you mean?" Harry stared at her, a puzzled look on his face.

"Oh, never mind!" Using her anger to front it out. It wasn't difficult. She had plenty of it.

She spun away from him. Couldn't stand to look at him for a minute longer.

She began the hike back to the bothy. Legs pumping. Thoughts racing. The rational part of her mind realised that what Harry had said was true. Even if they could raise him on the radio, Zander would never be able to get over today. Not unless it was a life or death situation. The sea was too rough.

Maybe she couldn't get off the island today, but that sure as hell didn't mean she had to spend any more time with Harry. If he was so concerned about the bait boxes, he could carry on doing them by himself. She was going back to the bothy and that was that.

Harry yelled for her to wait on him.

Already walking hard, Hazel picked up her pace. He could bobble along behind her for a change.

At least he'd stopped crying. His crocodile tears made her feel sick to her stomach. He was lucky she hadn't brought her walking pole with her, otherwise she might have been tempted to stab him in the eye with it.

For the meantime at least, he'd stopped telling her that he was sorry. His apologies were nothing but meaningless babble. If he meant it at all - if there was any sincerity in the man's soul - he would never have deceived her in the first place. Let alone for all this time.

No doubt he had also told his mistress a pack of lies. Swore blind that he would leave his wife to be with her. That his marriage was a sham. That they never slept together anymore. In other words, all the usual lies wife-deceivers were so glib at delivering.

Perhaps it was written in the code of conduct for adulterers - thou shalt lie continuously to wife and mistress both.

If only it was true that they hadn't been sleeping together. It was not a regular occurrence, but it did happen. Now, on top of everything else, Hazel would have to make herself an appointment at what used to be called the clap clinic. Oh, the humiliation. She could only hope that the other woman had not passed anything on to Harry.

The other woman had a name. Hazel had prised it out of Harry. It had been a beauty. A real stinger. No wonder he had been so reluctant to give it up.

Teresa. It was a name Hazel knew well. Teresa.... the very same Teresa Harry had been having an affair with all those years ago.

She'd been a neighbour then, and, Hazel had mistakenly thought, a friend. The type to pop in for a coffee and a blether. And pick up your husband on the way out.

71

Teresa had moved shortly after the affair had been exposed. Harry swore blind that he hadn't seen her since - not until last year. They'd bumped into each other in town and gone for a coffee together.

Talked and talked they did. All very cosy and so very, very innocent. He told her about his grandchildren. She told him about her divorce. It was her second. Wouldn't you know it, they enjoyed chatting so much, they arranged to meet up again. Funny how Harry hadn't mentioned it, what with it being so innocent and all.

He said that he didn't mean for it to happen. *It was just one of those things.* He didn't love Teresa. He loved Hazel. That's right. He loved her so much, he'd had two - two, count 'em - affairs with the seemingly irresistible Teresa.

He'd said it was over. In a pig's eye it was over. It would be like last time - only over because Hazel had found out about it. The thought - the very thought - of them pawing over each other was repulsive.

Before she knew who he'd taken up with, Hazel had been mad enough with Harry to poison him. Now something more direct appealed. She would have quite happily smashed him in the face with a shovel. Or stabbed him. Repeatedly.

No longer Harry's faithful, stupid, drudge, she felt it was quite within her to actually carry out one of these acts. So much so that she didn't trust herself to look at him in case she lost control there and then.

Until that point, she had never realised she was capable of such anger. Or that anger could generate so much energy. It was quite exhilarating.

23

Rob stared at Eleanor, looking as though he wouldn't be any more shocked if she sprouted wings and flew off with the herring gulls.

He'd bought her the ring, expecting her to say yes. Well, they'd both had a bit of a jaw-dropper then, hadn't they? She hoped he wouldn't cry. She didn't think she could stand that. She'd never seen him do it, but he'd seemed close on a couple of occasions.

Rob could be very emotional, but he didn't cry. Instead, a peculiar expression came over his face. One she hadn't seen before. He looked down at the ring for a second then snapped the box shut with one finger.

The box disappeared into a pocket. Rob squared his shoulders, pulled himself straight. His face had hardened, his big brown eyes narrowing to slits. He didn't look much like a puppy dog now. More like a hound from hell about to take a chunk out of her.

Eleanor didn't recognise this Rob. Didn't much like the look of him either. Her instinct was to get away, fast, but her feet felt as though they were embedded in the clifftop.

"It's Marcus isn't it?" he said.

"What?" As surprised now as when he'd produced the ring.

"I saw the pair of you making goo-goo eyes at each other last night. I didn't want to believe it, but here we are." He glowered at her.

She gave an uneasy laugh and shook her head.

"You couldn't be more wrong. Seriously, not even if he was the last man on... I mean, Marcus? My God."

It was ludicrous. Her and Marcus? The man was repulsive. How could Rob have gotten it so wrong? Nervous laughter welled up in response to the weird situation.

"Don't laugh at me," he said.

A giggle escaped from her lips.

"I said don't laugh at me."

Eleanor took a deep breath.

"I wasn't laughing at you Rob. It's just-"

"I ask you to marry me, and you laugh in my face?"

"Rob, it's not like that."

"You know, you really are a bitch. You think it's okay to hurt people - that you can take the piss, do whatever the fuck you want?"

She cringed at his tone.

"Rob, this is getting out of control. Rob?"

He was breathing heavily and had a look in his eye Eleanor didn't care for. She backed away from him, her feet all set for moving now.

"Rob?"

"Bitch!" He snarled and made a grab for her.

Eleanor flinched from his grasp and ran.

Rob went after her. His fingers jolted into the small of her back. She pitched forward. Her feet slipping on the grass. She landed on her stomach, scant inches from the cliff edge. Terrified, Eleanor rolled onto her back, away from the precipice. Rob loomed over her, face twisted in fury.

He dropped down, one knee on either side of her body, and pinned her wrists with his hands. She struggled against his weight. He stared down at her, the flesh of his face hanging, making deep sockets around his eyes.

He was too strong. Too heavy. Struggling was a waste of energy. Her survival instinct kicked in. She lay still. Looking up at him. There would be a chance. There had to be a chance.

All she had to do was wait.

Gradually, the hard edge fell away from him. He released one of her wrists and cupped her face with his hand. He gazed at her tenderly for a moment. Eleanor held her breath. It was going to be okay.

Rob stroked her gently along her jaw line.

"Why did you have to do it?" he whispered.

The pressure from his fingers increased. His face hardened again. It wasn't going to be okay.

"No." Eleanor's voice sounded small and far away.

The pressure from Rob's fingers increased. Digging under her jaw. Felt as though he was going to rip it off. She squirmed, but she was trapped under his weight.

His fingers dug in deeper. The pain became intolerable.

She would have to do something.

"Eleanor, all I ever wanted was you."

Tears filled his eyes.

Eleanor smashed the heel of her free hand into his face. Blood spurted from Rob's nose. He squealed and rocked back on his heels.

Eleanor wriggled free. She scrambled away from him. He swiped at her legs but his aim was off. She kicked out at his face. Her foot landed lucky. Caught him on the brow bone. Sent him tumbling back. Towards the cliff.

He landed heavily, his momentum tobogganing him to the deadly precipice.

Eleanor screamed.

Rob's hands scrabbled for a hold. His fingers gouging into the sparse vegetation. He managed to snatch onto a snarled root.

He came to a halt with his body hanging precariously on the edge.

Beneath him, pieces of rock crumbled and fell towards the thrashing waves.

He caught sight of Eleanor running towards him.

"Stop," he croaked

She stopped. She could see the ground giving way beneath him. He was going to fall. She got down flat on her belly and stretched out a hand towards him.

He stared at her, jaws clenched, the veins in his neck bulging. "I'm sorry," he gasped.

"It's okay, just take my hand. It'll be okay."

He reached towards her. Their fingers brushed. A small chunk of the rock face gave way. Not much. Just enough.

Eleanor's fingers were still snatching at cold air as her scream echoed around the cliffs.

24

Jonathan led the way to the next bait box. The light swish of Gemma's clothes as she walked behind him made his scalp tingle. After the kiss that had hardly been a kiss at all, she had tried to engage him in small talk. He barely responded.

The conversation died before it could draw its first proper breath. Now they walked in silence, with a tension between them that hadn't been there before. And all he could hear was the ever-present swish, swish, swish of her clothing.

This constant reminder of her presence unnerved him. Made him think about her weight on top of him. Her body pressing into his. Her pink lips. Her sweet breath. He felt himself becoming aroused again.

He spotted the bait box. He wanted to walk by it, pretend it wasn't there. He could hardly bear the thought of stopping, of having to look at her. But neither could he stand the thought of not stopping. Not looking at her.

"Shouldn't we be there by now?"

Her warm honey voice trickling into him.

"It's just here," he said.

He stopped. Let the backpack drop from his shoulders. He looked at the ground. Looked at the bait station. Looked anywhere except at her.

She touched the back of his hand. Tiny electric shocks rippled through his skin.

"Jonathan?"

He raised his eyes, looked into hers. Green flecks dancing in sparkling blue.

He didn't know how it happened. Only that it did. Her lips

on his, soft, yielding. Her mouth tasting of peppermint. He kissed her back. Gently at first, then more urgently. She responded, pressing against him.

She worked her hands under his jacket, pulling at his clothing until she found bare skin.

Jonathan groaned as she kissed his neck, nibbled at his ears, explored his mouth with her pink, darting tongue. She was hungry for him and he wanted her, wanted her now. He fumbled at the front of her jacket. She eased the zipper down for him. He had one hand on her lower back. Pulling her into him. The other pushing under her clothing. She massaged him through his trousers. He moaned and pulled down the cup of her bra, releasing her left breast.

She groaned, saying his name, over and over. The vibration of her lips against his ear driving him as crazy as the sensation of her erect nipple against the palm of his hand. She had soft, round, full breasts.

Not like Fran's.

He froze.

"Jonathan?"

He pulled back from her.

She stared at him, lips parted. Her chin red. Her skin grazed by his rough kisses and unshaven face.

"What's going on?" she asked.

He looked away from her. "I'm sorry. I can't do this."

She touched his face, turned it towards hers.

"It's okay," she said. "Really, it's okay. Whatever happens here is between us."

She closed the gap between them. Pressed herself against him once more.

He stepped back, hands raised, refusing to touch her. Scared that if he did, he'd be lured in again.

"I said no."

She gazed at him coolly then lifted her top up, revealing a

tantalising glance of her naked breast. In one smooth action she slipped it back inside the silky material of her bra, but not before he'd gotten an eyeful of her smooth, creamy flesh and the luscious pink nipple. He fought the urge to grab her and fuck her to within an inch of her life.

"Like what you see, Johnny Boy?"

Her voice taunting him.

He flushed. Angry at being caught looking. Angry at wanting her so much. Hating her for making him want her.

"Or is that your problem? Too much female flesh for you to handle?"

No honey coating on her words now. It was razor blades all the way.

"What?"

His ire simmering. Close to the surface.

She gazed at him defiantly.

"Well, you won't be used to it, will you? Fucking Fran must be like screwing a skeleton."

Slashing and slicing.

"Leave Fran out of it."

"Does she rattle when she comes?"

"Shut up!"

"No tits, no hips - she's just straight up and down. It must be like shagging a boy."

"Shut the fuck up, Gemma!"

"O-M-G! That's it - isn't it?" Gemma opened her eyes and mouth wide in three mocking Os. "You're stuck in the closet, Johnny Boy. I bet that's why you're with Little Miss Wholemeal Fran. It must be easy pretending you're with a guy when you're shagging her. Does she take it up the ass for you?"

Jonathan scowled at her. "You are disgusting, you know that? Totally vile."

Gemma laughed. "Is that the best you've got? What a phoney you are."

She poked him in the chest.

"I bet you fancy Zander, don't you? You'd love the feel of his big calloused hands all over your skinny arse. Tell me one thing - I swear I won't tell a soul - does Fran know her boyfriend is gay?"

He batted her hand away.

"Why don't you just shut up. You don't know anything."

Eyes bright, cheeks flushed, Gemma was in full vitriolic flow and would not be shut up.

"You know, there's not a chance of you copping off with Zander. He likes women. I should know. I spent a weekend with him last summer and we fucked like alley cats."

"Shut up - I'm warning you."

"You?" She said mockingly. "Big bad Jon-a-than? What. Are. You. Going. To. Do. To. Me?"

Punctuating every word with a prod in his chest. Each prod wracking up the tension in Jonathan's body.

"You're sure as hell not going to screw me - so what are you going to do?"

He gave her a sharp push.

She stumbled backwards, jeering at him.

"You want to play now? A little rough and tumble?"

He pushed her again. Harder this time. She stumbled back again. Still laughing at him. He yelled at her to shut up and gave her another shove. Hard enough this time for her to fall backwards.

"Oh!" she exclaimed.

She went down heavy. Landed with a wet crunch. At least it shut her up.

Thing was, she wasn't making any sound at all now.

As he stared at Gemma, Jonathan suddenly felt very heavy. She was lying where she'd fallen. Not moving.

His anger drained away, leaving nothing behind but cold fear.

25

A fresh scar in the cliff, lighter than the surrounding sandstone, marked the spot where the ground had given way beneath Rob. Eleanor crawled on her stomach to the edge and forced herself to peer over.

Rob had landed on a large, flat stone. His right leg twisted cruelly at the knee. He looked like a discarded doll. Wave after wave lashed against the rock, sending fountains of spray across his body.

A powerful roller swept in. Rob tumbled like flotsam in the foam as it broke over the rock. Eleanor gasped. He'd surely be swept into the sea. Dashed against the base of the cliffs. But when the water receded, he was still there, though more mangled than before. His limbs jutting unnaturally from his body.

He was utterly broken. Undoubtedly dead.

She stared down at him, feeling helpless and wretched. Her eyes blurry with wind and tears. Blaming herself. Blaming Rob.

She was on the point of turning away, crawling to safety, when he opened his eyes.

She swept away her tears, not daring to believe. But yes, his eyes were open, staring up at her. He was alive. Rob was still alive.

She looked around, desperately seeking some way of helping him. But there was nothing she could do. Not here, on her own.

She cupped her hands around her mouth and hollered down at him.

"I'm going for help!"

She doubted he could hear her. The sea was pounding beside him and her words had probably been carried away on the wind, but he would have seen her. He would know that she knew he was alive. For now, it was the best she could do.

She clambered away from the precipice, got to her feet, and ran. Leaving him there alone was distressing, but there was nothing else for it. She needed to raise the alarm.

She ran until her lungs were ablaze, until the stitch in her side was like the stab of a blade. She ran until she didn't think she could run any further, but still she kept on. Boots pounding over the rough path. Heart thumping. She ran until her foot snagged. Her ankle turned. She tripped, flying forwards, arms stretched out as the ground rushed up to meet her. Yelping as skin sheared from her hands and wrists like cheese on a grater. She skidded to a halt, banging her knee against a rock. She groaned and lay still for a moment, breathing in the smell of the earth until she could taste it. She felt as though she'd been put through a mangle.

Last year's grass scratched against her forehead, but she could smell the promise of new life. Life. Death. The associations sent a shudder through her body.

She sat up and inspected the damage. The heels of her hands and wrists were grazed. Grit embedded in the tiny cuts. One of her acrylic nails had been torn off revealing her own stumpy nail bitten raw underneath. Her knee throbbed. Her ankle ached. But she wasn't lying broken at the base of a cliff. She was alive and Rob was relying on her.

She got to her feet too quickly. The ground tilted. She staggered like a drunk and threw up. One short, sharp retch emptied her stomach. She coughed, spluttering over the small pool of vomit. Disgusted, she stepped away from it.

Her ankle held. Another step. Another. Increasing her pace. Not daring to run in case her knee gave out or her ankle turned.

Hobbling as fast as she could, Eleanor followed the path as it angled towards the island's interior. She would find somebody soon. She had to.

The path gave way to a narrow boardwalk running over rough ground. The rims of her boot soles caught in the uneven spaces between the slats, forcing her to slow down. She tried walking on the ground at the side of the boardwalk, but she snagged on wiry heather roots and the boggy ground sucked at her feet.

Frustrated, she returned to the boardwalk, involuntarily tensing her legs until she reached the gravel path at the other end. Ignoring the twinge in her ankle, she picked up her pace. Half trotting, half limping, until, finally, she caught sight of someone ahead. It was Cal.

She called out. Her voice emerged as a croak. She tried to swallow, but her throat was dry. She'd abandoned her pack on the cliff-top, and in it, her bottled water. She glanced around as if expecting a sparkling stream to appear, but there was nothing but scraggy heather and mossy rocks. Nothing for it but to push on. The path twisted and dipped over the rough terrain. She lost sight of Cal until she was almost upon him.

He was by himself, clearing a drain at the side of the path. She croaked his name. He looked up. The greeting on his lips fading away as he took in the state of her. He leapt onto the path and ran towards her.

"What's wrong, what's happened?"

She stared at him, working her mouth. Nothing coming out.

He gripped her upper arms.

"Eleanor!"

Black dots dancing in her peripheral vision. Cal's voice coming from far away.

"Eleanor, talk to me!"

His voice louder.

Her eyes focused on his. She'd felt herself sinking, but she was coming back now. Like a diver coming up from the depths, moving from dark to light. Finally breaking through the surface of the water. She took a deep breath.

"There's been an accident."

26

Hazel's determined march came to a faltering halt at the bothy. A pair of boots had been discarded by the door. Beside them lay a heap of dirty clothing. Trousers and underpants. Hazel recoiled from the foul stench arising from them.

Wondering what on earth was going on, she pulled a handkerchief from her pocket and used it as a mask to shield her mouth and nose.

"What on earth…?" Harry, slightly out of breath, caught up with her.

His presence was bad enough. He irked her even more by echoing her thoughts. "My God, what a stench. Whose clothes are they?"

"I don't-" Hazel began to reply automatically, her words muffled by the handkerchief, before catching onto herself. No matter what was going on, she was not going to be tricked into engaging with the enemy.

She made to open the door.

"Do you think that's wise?" Harry, havering behind her.

She lowered her mask and turned on him.

"What do you suggest? Do you think we should stand out here like a pair of ninnies? Someone is obviously in distress and, distasteful though it is to you, they may need our help."

It gave her great satisfaction to see him flinch from her. Her actions were no longer up for discussion. Nothing she said or did required his approval. It was an incredible release.

She turned to the door, boldly swung it open and stepped into the hall. Only then did she hesitate. She stood for a moment, taking stock while Harry hovered behind her.

Dark streaks smeared the floor. The iron tang of blood thickened the sickly odour of human waste. Taking care to avoid stepping on the dubious marks, Hazel picked her way along the corridor.

"Hello," she called, "is anyone there?"

There was no answer.

"Hello - it's Harry here," Harry called from behind her. Muscling in on the act.

Hazel tutted and tossed him a scowl. Harry gave her a what's-wrong-with-you shrug. She felt like giving him a slap. Instead she tentatively followed the sickening trail. It lead around the corner to the shower room. The door was ajar. Hazel knocked on it before sticking her head around and looking in.

There was a residue of grime in the shower base. The walls and curtain were streaked with diluted smears. A towel had been discarded in a soggy, filthy heap. Hazel recognised it as Harry's and couldn't resist a smirk. Served him right for leaving it in there. Closing the door on the mess, she turned to him.

"It's been used but there's no one there now. You check the bedrooms, I'll check the bunk room."

To Hazel's great satisfaction, Harry immediately obeyed, disappearing back along the hall.

She went into the bunk room and checked all four beds. There was nothing untoward. Nobody lying in bed. Nobody lying anywhere. Everything seemed as it should be. All except for a smear on the wall beside the external door. She went over for a closer inspection. It looked like a smudged handprint. As though the person had leaned on the wall as they were opening the door.

Harry entered the room behind her. "Nobody in the bedrooms," he said. "Anything here?"

"Just this." Hazel indicated the smear. "They must have gone through to the bothy."

She opened the door and walked along to the bothy, Harry at her back.

Immediately she opened the door, Hazel detected the metallic tang of blood layering through the usual bothy aromas of cooking smells, smoke and mildew.

She glanced around. Unless someone was hiding under the table, the only place anyone could be lurking was the bunks in the corner. She took a quick glance under the table. Nobody there. The bunks looked empty. She was right up beside them before realising that someone was buried in the sleeping bag on the bottom mattress.

She took a guess as to where their shoulder was and gave them a gentle shake. A low moan emerged.

"Who is it?" Harry asked.

Ignoring him, she gently peeled down the top of the sleeping bag.

She let out a gasp and stepped back.

"Oh my good God!" Harry exclaimed.

Even in the shadows of the lower bunk it was obvious that Archie was in bad shape. Dark rings circled his eyes. Blood had smeared and dried on his pale face. He moaned again. It was a pitiful sound, particularly pathetic as it emerged from one normally so ebullient.

Over her initial shock, Hazel crouched down beside him.

"Archie, can you tell me what happened?"

Archie's eyes fluttered open. "I'm sore, Hazel." he said. "Hurts all over... sore guts... made a mess... sorry... bad mess... greedy bastard... greedy Archie... ate a pie... dodgy curry..."

He moaned and closed his eyes again.

Curry. He'd said *curry*.

Hazel experienced a sudden draining sensation. Felt as though her legs were going to give way. She grabbed onto the side of the bunk, steadied herself.

She looked at Harry. Nothing wrong with Harry. Looked back at Archie. No, it couldn't be. She'd been so careful…

"Hazel?"

Harry staring at her.

27

"Gemma?"

Jonathan's voice was barely a whisper. He'd been standing still for what felt like a very long time. His resistant gaze drawn towards her immobile body.

All the time he'd been standing there, she hadn't moved. Not so much as a twitch. All the same, when he finally took a step towards her, he did so with caution. A tiny part of him was afraid that when he was close enough she'd attack him. Screaming, clawing, biting. Retaliation.

The bigger part of him was afraid that she was not going to move at all.

He was right beside her now. His feet at her shoulder. She was very pale, very still. The colour gone even from her pink lips.

He crouched down beside her. Her unblinking eyes were freaking him out. He was loathe to touch her, but forced himself to reach out and feel for her carotid artery. Her skin was warm but there was no pulse. Maybe he'd missed it. He tried again, but there was no pulse to find.

He slipped his fingers behind her head, and lifted it, hoping the movement would elicit a response. A moan, a scream, even a volley of spite. Anything but this deathly hush.

Beneath her head he found the reason for her pallid silence. There was a triangular rock under her head. It cut through the ground like a shark's fin through water. The tip had penetrated her skull.

Jonathan's stomach curdled. He pulled his hand away. Gemma's head thudded against the shark's fin rock again. And once again there came that sound. The wet crunch of splintering bone as her skull was penetrated, her brain pierced.

He rocked back on his heels, staring in growing horror at his blood-smeared fingers. There was no denying it. She was dead and he had killed her.

Murder. He had committed murder.

A wave of fear rolled through him followed by a shot of adrenalin. His first instinct was to run. He got to his feet and took a few stumbling steps before catching onto himself. Where did he think he was running to? He was on the island. Trapped here until Zander came over the next day. He couldn't go anywhere. Couldn't get away.

But he couldn't just leave her lying there. He had to stop and think. He looked at the blood congealing on his hand. There were specks of matter mixed in with it. Splinters of bone. Splatters of brain. He had to clean it off and he had to think.

He took a few deep breaths. Inhaling through his nose. Exhaling through his mouth. Sucking the air in. Blowing it out. Injecting oxygen into his system.

When his heart rate had settled and his breathing was steady, he scoured his hands on a clump of scrubby heather. It had been an accident. He hadn't meant to kill her. He looked at his palm. He could still see traces of blood. He scrubbed at it again, reddening the skin. He hadn't meant it, therefore it was not murder.

Worst case scenario - culpable homicide. He rubbed harder at his hand. Culpable or not, he didn't fancy the sound of it. Homicide even less so. Ugly words. They sent you to jail for homicide. But he hadn't meant to kill her. He wasn't culpable. Not in the true sense of the word. It had been an accident, pure and simple. Tragic - but most definitely an accident.

All he'd wanted was for her to shut up. He couldn't say that, though. If he did, they'd blame him. That was how their minds worked. They twisted things. They'd make it into a big thing. Say that he really had wanted to kill her.

That he'd wanted to shut her up permanently.

Maybe there was a tiny bit of truth in that. But not enough to make it murder. Or even culpable homicide. He'd just wanted her to shut her filthy mouth.

He glanced down at her dead body. Hating her all over again for putting him in this predicament. Why hadn't she just shut up? Even now her mouth was open. And her eyes. Their relentless stare made him nervous. He should close them.

He crouched down to do so. His trembling fingers hovering over her face. Until finally his hand recoiled. He couldn't bring himself to touch her eyelids. What if he pulled them down and they sprang open again? He would freak. He was barely hanging together as it was. He hastily grabbed on to the brim of her hat and pulled it down over her eyes. That was better. Much better. He could concentrate now.

Think about what he had to do.

28

Eleanor, burning inside, aching all over. Her breath hot and raw. Ankle screaming. She couldn't go on. Couldn't keep running. Had thought that when she reached Cal, that would be it. He would take over, relieve her of this terrible burden. Systems would fall into place. Things would happen. Help would come. Rob would be rescued, and they could all leave the island. But no - Cal had gone to the cliffs and sent her to find Fran. She would call for help.

So Eleanor had started running again. Feeling like she was on a treadmill. A never-ending nightmare of twisted ligaments, burning breath and help that would not come. And all the while, Rob was lying on the rock, limbs broken, back cracked, suffering, dying. Maybe dead already. No. She couldn't think like that.

She half-ran, half-slithered down through the sand dunes, then she was on the beach. Feet sinking into the soft sand above the strandline. She could see Fran and Marcus along the beach, working with their backs to her. She called out, her voice lost beneath the rumble of surf.

Crossing the strandline, she headed for the firm sand below it but tripped on a tangle of seaweed and twine. Stumbled and tumbled, rolling on damp sand. Sea, sky, sand, merging one into the other, until she came to a stop.

She lay on the sand. Eyes closed. The roar of the sea blending with the rasp of her breathing. She was all out. Nothing left. She was letting go. Drifting. Didn't care if she never woke up. A sound. Her eyes fluttered. A voice. Perhaps a seagull. Her eyes remained closed. Then it came again.

"Eleanor!"

And with it, the hollow pounding of feet reverberating through the sand.

"Eleanor - are you okay - what's wrong? Are you hurt?"

Hands on her. She opened her eyes. Boots in the sand. Legs. Hands helping her up. She tried to shrug them off. Didn't they understand? She wanted to be left alone. She wanted to sleep. But they wouldn't let her.

They made her sit up. One of them crouched down in front of her.

"Eleanor, what happened? Is anyone hurt?" Fran, her face anxious.

As well it might be. Recent events swirling through Eleanor's mind. The row. Rob falling. His body rolling in the surf. The realisation that she would never be able to close her eyes and pretend that none of it was happening. That whatever the outcome, she would have to deal with it. She started speaking. The words tumbling out. "Rob fell off the cliff... Cal's gone up there... you need to call for help."

Then it was all happening. Marcus helping her up. Fran taking the radio from her belt. Bombarding her with questions as she did so. Where had it happened? How badly hurt was Rob? Was he conscious? A click as Fran switched on the radio. A frown as she switched it off again. Then on. Then off and on again.

"What's wrong?" Eleanor asked. "Why aren't you calling?"

Fran looked at her. A frown etched deep in her brow.

"I don't understand it. The battery must be dead." Shaking her head.

"I thought you checked them?" Marcus said.

"I did. Both radios were fine."

"What about Rob?" Eleanor's voice rising. The nightmare going on.

Fran looking at her. Face serious, voice calm. "We'll go to the bothy and use the other one."

"I'll go up to the cliffs and see if I help there," Marcus said.

"Good idea," Eleanor said. "Cal and Archie are up there, right?" Looking at Eleanor.

"Cal's there," she replied. "I don't know where Archie is."

29

"What did you do with the curry I gave you last night?"

Hazel tried to ask the question lightly, as if the answer was really of no consequence at all. As if there was not a tightness in her chest. A flutter of panic in her stomach.

Harry gave her a quizzical look. "I ate it of course," he said.

"Are you sure?"

"Of course I'm sure. What else would I have done with... No, actually. I didn't eat it. My portion was bigger than Archie's and he was hungry and so... we swapped."

As he spoke, the quizzical look on his face was replaced by dawning realisation. He stared at Hazel, his mouth hanging slack.

Hazel looked from Harry, standing in front of her in perfect, if slack-jawed, health, to Archie in a state of extreme distress. She felt a prickling sensation under her skin as the colour drained from her face, leaving it tallow. Tension lines furrowed around her eyes and mouth, aging her five years in as many seconds.

"My God," she whispered.

"Hazel, what have you done?"

"I didn't mean for this…"

"Hazel?"

She raised her gaze to meet Harry's.

"Did you do something to the curry?"

She nodded, slowly. "Rat poison," she whispered.

"Rat poison... it was meant for me, wasn't it?" Harry's voice hoarse. Hardly there at all.

"I wanted to punish you for-"

"- the affair... Oh my good God."

Harry sat down heavily and covered his face with his hands. The white of his scalp was visible through the thinning hair on top of his head. When he raised his face, it was grey, drained of life, his eyes sorrowful. His skin hung loose, as if he had shrunk inside it. He looked like an old man.

"Oh Hazel, what have I done to you? This is my fault, isn't it? I've been a bad husband and now..."

Hazel stared at him. After what she had tried to do to him, an acceptance of blame, was the last thing she had expected. She blinked, trying to take in this new turn of events. This new Harry. Archie groaned, his sleeping bag rustling as he shifted in the bunk. The sound bringing her back to the reality of the here and now.

"Harry, we have to get help for Archie. We can use the radio."

"Yes. You're right. We must help Archie."

Hazel crossed the room to the radio. "What channel did Fran say for emergencies - sixteen - was it sixteen?"

"Yes, sixteen," Harry said. "But check the instructions on the wall - we've got to do this right, for Archie's sake."

Hazel picked up the radio.

"Hazel?"

She glanced at Archie. "What?"

"No matter what happens, I'll stick by you. I won't let you down again. I promise."

She nodded. Those things, the promises, the blaming, they could wait. The important thing now was Archie. Hazel switched on the radio. Nothing happened. She switched it off and on again. Still nothing. She looked up at Harry.

"Try it again," he said.

"I did. There's nothing happening."

"Let me try." She passed it to him.

The instructions were quite clear. All she was supposed to do was switch it on, and that's what she'd done. Several times. And nothing had happened.

"Well?" she asked Harry. He looked at her.

"It's not working," he said.

"That's what I've been trying to tell you. We need to get the other radio - the one Fran has."

"What beach is she on?"

Hazel studied the map on the wall. "I'm not sure," she said.

"We'll have to go out and look for her."

"That could take hours," Hazel said.

Harry sneaked a look at Archie's bunk, lowered his voice, "I don't think we've got hours."

30

As the bothy came into sight, Fran and Eleanor unconsciously stepped up their pace. A last sprint to the finish.

"Almost there," Fran said, breaking the silence that had grown between them. Getting to the radio in the bothy was their goal. Small talk hadn't figured.

Eleanor gave a brief nod in acknowledgment. Fran stole a sideways glance at her.

When they'd first met, Fran had Eleanor down as strictly high maintenance. All make-up and hair products. The type who would have a meltdown if she broke a nail. Seemed she'd got Eleanor all wrong, and she was glad to admit it.

Eleanor must have realised that Rob's chances were slim, but here she was, hair plastered to her head, make-up smudged and streaked, clothes torn, her body battered and bruised, yet still she was battling on, trying to help him. The woman had grit.

They were almost at the bothy now. She'd soon be on the radio. The coastguard would be there in fifteen minutes. You never knew. Maybe Rob would be okay after all. People had gone through worse and survived.

Two figures emerged from the bothy, saw them, started pointing and waving.

"That's Harry and Hazel," Fran said. "I wonder what they're doing back at this time?"

"I don't know," Eleanor replied. "But I don't like the look of it."

"Me neither."

"Thank God you're here," Hazel said as they drew close, "We were on our way to look for you."

"Why - what's wrong?" Fran asked.

"It's Archie," Harry said. "He's ill, really ill. We need to call for help - right away."

"Why didn't you use the radio in the bothy?" Fran asked.

"We've tried," Harry said. "It doesn't work."

Fran stopped dead and looked at them. "What do you mean, it doesn't work?"

"We've tried it over and over," Hazel said. "That's why we were coming for you - to get yours."

Fran's hand moved to the impotent radio on her belt. A rash of sweat broke over her body.

"My radio isn't working. We came back to use the one here. Rob's had an accident," she said, answering the unasked questions on their faces.

They trailed in behind her as she entered the bothy and went for the other radio.

It had to be working. They didn't know what they were doing, that's all. They'd panicked. Not switched it on properly.

She tried switching it on and off several times, but the digital display remained resolutely blank. She slammed the radio on the table. Hazel, Harry and Eleanor watched as she unclipped the other radio from her belt and tried it again.

It wasn't going to work. She already knew that. But she had to try. She tried, tried and tried again, but it was useless. She put it on the table beside the other. Pushing back her hat, she rubbed at her forehead.

"I don't believe this," she said.

Behind her, Archie let out a weak groan. She spun around and went over to him.

"Archie, how are you?"

She spoke gently, crouching by the bunk, and took a look at him. When she turned back to the others her face was pale.

"Isn't there usually another radio?" Harry asked. "A big one - where's that?"

Fran shook her head. "It gets taken back to the mainland at the end of every season for maintenance. It hasn't been brought back over yet. That's why we've got these." She stared at the radios lying uselessly on the table.

"I don't understand. They both worked fine on Friday."

She picked the nearest one up and turned it over. She flipped open the battery compartment. She looked up at the others then checked the second radio.

The batteries weren't dead. They were gone.

31

Jonathan grunted. He was discovering what the expression dead weight really meant. Gemma had seemed so petite when she'd been alive. He'd felt as though he could pick her up and put her in his pocket. Now that she was dead, it was like dragging a sack of coal over the rough ground.

Judging by the trail he was leaving behind, it looked as though he was dragging a sack of coal through the scrub. The plant life here was hardy - it had to be - and would soon bounce back, but he wasn't going to take any chances. He'd cover his traces after he'd got her to the bog-hole.

Once he'd weighed up his options, it hadn't taken him long to decide what to do. He could either tell the truth about what had happened and throw himself on the mercy of the legal system, or deny all knowledge of Gemma's fate.

Telling the truth was the more noble of the two, but it was risky. Innocent as he was, he could easily end up in jail and no doubt he'd lose Fran along with his freedom.

Even if he didn't end up in prison, there would still be a big investigation. It would be all over the news. No doubt a handful of ex-girlfriends would turn up, looking for their five minutes of fame to go with the pound of flesh they'd be seeking to extract from him. It would not be a pretty state of affairs, and he'd still lose Fran.

It didn't seem right that he was at risk of losing his freedom along with the woman he loved because of that little blonde whore. He hadn't done anything wrong. She'd come on to him. All he'd done was push her away. It wasn't his fault that she'd stumbled. He hadn't put the rock there.

Looking at it logically, no matter what, Gemma's life was over. It was boo-hoo sad, and no doubt there would be people who mourned for her, but was that any reason to ruin another two lives?

Jonathan wasn't prepared to take his chances with the justice system. That left him with only one option. He'd deny knowing anything.

First of all, he had to get rid of the body. He couldn't very well deny all knowledge of her whereabouts when she was lying right beside one of the bait stations.

He'd been scouting around, looking for somewhere to hide her, when he'd come across the bog-hole. It was perfect. The island was pock-marked with them. They came in various sizes, some barely a foot across, but all of them were deep and permanently filled with black, peaty water.

His arms and shoulders were burning with the strain of dragging her. He needed a break. He let go and stood up for a moment, stretching out. Her upper body slumped against his legs. He grimaced and stepped back, letting her head loll onto the ground. At least her eyes weren't spooking him now.

Before moving her, he'd happed her up like a mummy, pulling up the hood on her jacket, tying it tight so that it covered the wound on the back of her head. There was no use in leaving a trail of blood and brain behind him. Satisfyingly, the hood was tied so tight that it also covered most of her face. He didn't even have to look at her mouth now.

By the looks of the heavy clouds rolling in from the west it was going to start raining soon. That would help. A couple of good old west coast downpours would play havoc with forensics. Not that he was taking any chances. He'd already washed the mess from the shark's fin rock using water from the bottle she'd had in her pack. Then, in what he thought was a particularly smart move, he'd rubbed over the rock with a clump of moss and a handful of peat. There weren't going to be any traces of Gemma left behind.

Funnily enough, there hadn't been all that much blood. Especially not for a head wound. On the couple of occasions he'd cut his scalp, he'd looked like an extra from a war movie. She must have died quickly. That was a blessing. No suffering.

Maybe it was just as well she was dead. Otherwise, who knew what she might have said to Fran?

When he'd finished cleaning the shark's fin rock, he wiped his prints from the bottle and put it back in her pack. He weighted the bag down with stones and dropped it into the bog-hole. It went straight down, leaving no other trace than a few bubbles on the surface, and they didn't last long.

He'd thought about leaving her bag for them to find, but then thought, nah, let's make it a vanishing. Disappearing without trace. A complete mystery for all to ponder.

The ache in his shoulders had eased off. There wasn't far to go now. He bent down and grabbed Gemma's body under the arms and recommenced dragging.

32

Fran felt as though her arms were going to be wrenched out at the sockets. Eleanor was helping her to lug the sack of wood up the hill, but with every step the burden grew heavier.

The spare batteries had also gone walkabout. Harry, Hazel and Eleanor had all denied knowledge of their whereabouts. She'd asked Archie if he knew anything about them, he'd managed a groan of denial in response. Maybe one of the other five had hidden them as a joke. If so, it wasn't one she found the least bit amusing.

Whoever was responsible had a lot to answer for, but in the meantime the first priority was getting help for Archie and Rob.

In the faint hope that somehow they could pick up an errant signal, they each checked their phones. It wasn't happening for them. The entire island was a network-free zone. Ironically, this was one of the features many people enjoyed about going there. The ability to break free from the frenetic activity of everyday life. Of never being more than a text away. It didn't seem like such a benefit now.

The only thing Fran could think to do was build a fire up on the hill. It wasn't a usual occurrence and would perhaps be enough to snag someone's attention either at sea or on the mainland.

Not that she held out much hope for a passing boat in this weather. On top of that, it was Sunday, and the local fishermen tended to observe the Sabbath. At least in the sense that they didn't go to sea. A handful of houses clustered around the pier on the mainland, but none of them had a clear view of the island.

Keeping her doubts to herself, Fran mustered the small group into action. You never knew - if they managed to defy the wind and send a column of black smoke into the sky, someone might sit up and take notice. If the smoke didn't attract any attention, they could build up the flames once it was dark. Surely someone would notice a blaze on the island.

It wasn't much, but it was all they had, and it beat sitting around doing nothing.

They could have done with a few more hands helping out, but she decided to take the non-return of Cal and Marcus as a good sign. Perhaps they'd devised a way of getting to Rob. Jonathan and Gemma were still out at the bait stations and weren't expected back for another couple of hours. They were in for a shock when they returned.

"One last heave," Fran said.

They swung the sack so that it landed beside the small pile of wood already accumulated.

"My back," Eleanor said.

She rubbed the small of her back and groaned.

"My arms," Fran replied.

Harry was crouched in a hollow trying to get the fire going. He'd managed to raise a small flame, but even in the shelter of the hollow, it was struggling in the wind.

Fran eyed the sky. Looked like rain was coming in from the west. If they didn't get a decent blaze going soon, they'd have no chance. She watched as Hazel and Eleanor tried to shield the flame as Harry fed it small pieces of wood. They squatted around the hollow, all hunched up like the three witches from Macbeth.

By the pricking of my thumbs,
Something wicked this way comes

Fran shuddered as the unbidden words came into her mind. She pushed them aside. The space they'd filled was occupied by the realisation that she had precious little chance now of the promotion she'd been after. The weekend was a disaster.

She immediately berated herself for being so selfish. Rob had gone over a cliff, Archie was seriously ill, and all she could think about was her job. It was beyond selfish.

Selfish or not, a small voice continued to nark at the back of her mind. The plight of the two men was not of her making. Archie had some kind of horrible illness. He was suffering and she felt for him, she really did but she hadn't contributed in any way to his condition. Chances were, whatever it was, he'd brought it with him. If he hadn't come to the island, he'd still be ill. Her responsibility was to get help for him - and that was something she was desperately trying to do. As for Rob - he was an experienced hill walker and rock climber. He'd been to the island on numerous occasions. He was well aware of the conditions - so how the hell had he managed to fall off the cliff? Whatever had happened, it wasn't her fault. But no doubt she'd be held responsible.

Ditto the batteries. Someone in their midst had a very warped sense of humour, but it would be Fran's head on the block. It wasn't fair.

Fair is foul, and foul is fair.

Bloody Macbeth again.

She shook her head, clearing the unwanted words.

"It's caught!" Harry grinned.

A thin plume of smoke arose from the fire. The huddled trio gave a small cheer as the flames began to lick and crackle. The faint smile on Fran's lips faded as the first fat drops of rain spattered onto her jacket.

33

Jonathan gave one last heave and let go of the dead weight. He straightened up and exhaled, his breath whistling through pursed lips. The scuffed body lay beside the bog-hole. Just as well he hadn't had to drag it any further. He didn't have it in him.

Flexing his shoulders, he turned his face towards the sky and took a moment to enjoy the sensation of rain on his face. It was refreshing after all that heavy work. Almost as good as a cold beer.

The big, splatty raindrops had plenty of space between them. They were merely the overture of the torrent to come. Suited him just fine. The downpour would wash away any scraps of DNA he'd trailed behind him. He would leave no trace - just as the Scottish Outdoor Access Code requested. The idea pleased him.

He looked down at the body. He was already detaching himself from the idea of it being Gemma. Now he had to get the idea of it being a body out of his mind. He wasn't disposing of a body. Only guilty people disposed of bodies. He wasn't guilty. He was an innocent man in a tough spot. He had a problem to deal with and he was going to take care of it.

He would stay detached. Not think of it as flesh and blood. He had to disconnect himself from the visceral. The jacket had plenty of pockets. He scouted around for some decent sized stones to fill them. There would be a lot of air trapped in the layers of material, so he'd need plenty. He had to do the job right. Sink not float.

Once he had gathered a decent pile of stones and begun stuffing them into the pockets it was harder to cut himself off from the fact that he was dealing with a body. The hood had loosened. He could see part of her face. Not her eyes, thankfully. Having to look at her nose was bad enough. He averted his gaze. It landed on one of her hands.

It was splayed out, palm down. The smooth white skin had been scraped and scratched from being dragged over rough ground. He'd left a right old trail of DNA behind. The downpour had better be a good one.

Peaty soil had been clawed under her nails. Her index finger was jutting out in a way it had no right to. Must have broken it when he was dragging her. He hadn't been gentle. Hadn't treated her with any care. He had hauled and dragged. Swearing and cursing when something snagged, jerking him back, threatening to throw him off balance.

Now her finger sat at a cruel and unusual angle. Pointing at him. Accusing.

He snatched up a rock. She had no right to accuse him. He hadn't done anything wrong. It wasn't a crime to get a hard on. Pushing someone didn't make you a murderer. He stuffed the rock into one her pockets. It didn't matter. She - it - would be gone soon.

He'd managed to cram a fair number of stones into its pockets. There wasn't space enough for many more. Would it be enough though? All that air trapped in its clothing, not to mention the body itself gassing up. He had an idea. A flash of inspiration.

He undid the hood and pulled down the zip of the jacket as far as her chest. She would definitely sink if he stuffed the jacket with rocks. He pushed the first stone in. A hand-sized lump of silvery Lewisian gneiss. He poked it down as far as her waist. As he withdrew his hand, his palm rubbed against her breast. An image of exposed creamy flesh and erect pink nipple flashed into his mind.

Without thinking he squeezed.

107

34

Hazel watched as Harry fed the fire with kindlers. His lips puckered in a whistle just loud enough to be heard. He stoked the fledgling fire. Building it up so that it would be strong enough to defy the rain. He frowned as he worked, determined not to give in even although they already knew it was a lost cause. Rather like herself.

The energy which had been fizzing inside her, keeping her going, had dissipated. She'd humped wood up the hill, helped Harry with the fire, even given Eleanor a spontaneous hug when it had started burning and they'd let out a cheer. Now, standing still, she felt as though all her strength had seeped out of her into the ground beneath her feet.

She felt tired and heavy. The rain was coming on strong. The fire would not survive. Archie was lying in his bunk, desperately in need of medical care because of her actions. She wondered if she would feel less bad if it was her husband lying there instead. Would there be less guilt? Just as much? More? Did it even matter? She'd tried to hurt Harry, but it was Archie who was ill. She hoped and prayed he would recover and recover well, but no matter the outcome, she was finished.

If Archie died, she would be a killer. It was an impossible thought. Her, little old Hazel, the smiley woman who stopped to speak to people on the street, a murderer. The thought was beyond bizarre.

She would go to jail, and rightly so. And if Archie survived - what then? What would it be called - attempted murder? Assault with a deadly curry? No, that was flippant. It was the stress of the situation. Bending her thoughts every which way.

The truth was, whatever way she looked at it, Hazel could not get away from the fact that she had done a Bad Thing. She would be punished. She deserved to be punished. But in her heart she knew that she would not survive a prison sentence. She was not strong enough. She would not be able to bear being locked up, being institutionalised, treated like a number. Denied life's small pleasures. A walk in the hills. Tea and cake in a cafe. Time spent with her grandchildren.

She would die, incarcerated. Her name forever besmirched. Her story would end up in a Channel Five shockumentary alongside the likes of Rosemary West. Her children and grandchildren would be tainted by association. People would no longer name their daughters Hazel, the name, like Myra, sullied for generations to come.

Fueled by Harry's infidelity she had allowed herself to become shrouded in a dense fug of anger. She had lost sight of all the principles she held dear. She had failed to identify the repercussions of her anger. In short, she had made a cock-up of monumental proportions.

The rain no longer consisted of a few warning drops. The light splatter had given way to a downpour. The wind was picking up. Whistling around the hill. Slithering through the hollow where the fire had been lit. Splattering the flames. Laying them horizontal. Threatening to knock them out before they were quenched by the rain.

There was a dull buzzing in Hazel's head. She could not get her thoughts to align. The wind whooped, driving the rain. Sending it stinging into her face. She huddled into her jacket. If the fire was giving out any heat, it wasn't reaching her.

Harry tutted and fussed over it, trying to nurture the failing flames. He'd said that he would stick by her, no matter what. She wasn't sure that she wanted him to. The buzz of anger had gone, leaving her flat and depressed. Her head was a mess. Her thoughts in disarray. There was not much she knew any more.

Not much she could be sure of. All she was left with was one cold fact.

She still hated Harry.

35

Jonathan's hand pressed against Gemma's breast. Even through her clothing, he could feel her nipple stiff and enticing against his palm. His fingers squeezed into her soft, dead flesh. It was an unthinking action. Over in a split second. Before he even had time to think about what he was doing, he had recoiled. Jerking away from her as though he'd been electrocuted.

He stared at her, repulsed by his own actions. Repulsed by her. It. The corpse. The rotten, stinking corpse. It would already be decomposing. The tissues breaking down. Gasses building. He felt sick inside. This was a new low. He was no necrophiliac.

It was her. It all came from her. He'd started losing himself the minute she arrived on the island. She'd gotten into him. Inside his head. Rooting around like a worm in his brain. Pulling things out of him. Things she had no right knowing. Coming on to him. Toying with his mind, his emotions, his basic animal instincts.

In a moment of stark clarity, he recognised her for what she was. An enchantress. She was a witch and she'd cast a spell on him. To break the spell, he had to destroy her. Get rid of the body. He'd have burnt her if he could, but drowning would have to do. Everything would be sorted then. The curse would be broken, and he would be himself again.

No more time to waste. He'd loaded the witch with stones. Her feet were encased in heavy boots. That would be enough weight to get the job done.

He grabbed her. Rolled her. Tipped her awkwardly over the edge of the bog-hole, angling her in feet first. Plop, as they hit the surface. Her boots filled with water. Good enough for a witch. The black mire wasn't long in sucking her down.

Just like that, she was gone.

Jonathan watched with satisfaction as a myriad of bubbles broke the surface. He wondered how deep the hole was. If she had reached the bottom yet. Her flesh wouldn't be long in rotting. She would dissolve away as if she'd never existed. Her bones sinking into the murky sludge at the bottom. Lost in the dark, forever. If only all of life's little problems were so easily resolved.

He was on the verge of turning away, of going about his legitimate business, when something caught his eye. At first he thought it was an illusion caused by raindrops rippling the water. But no - there was something. Just below the surface. Something pale.

He crouched down for a closer look and gaped, fascinated, at her hand. Its pale skin glowing luminous white against the peaty backdrop. It seemed as though she was reaching up to him. As if she wasn't willing to succumb to her black, watery grave just yet. Or perhaps, he thought, she desired to take him with her into the depths. Who knew what went on in the mind of a witch.

Moments passed. Seconds, perhaps minutes, and still her fingers stretched out, snatching at the surface of the water. Reaching towards the boundary between their worlds.

Just as he was thinking he would have to do something about the situation, several large bubbles arose from the depths. They floated for a short time before bursting.

By the time they had popped and gone, so had the witch's pale hand.

36

Fran turned her back on the drenched fire. The shower had developed into a downpour. The flames barely had a chance to get going before they were extinguished. There was little they could do but admit defeat and return to the bothy. Lighting the beacon hadn't been much of a plan, but it had been something and had at least kept them occupied, given them hope. But what now? The only chance they had of getting help for Archie and Rob was if whoever had taken the batteries owned up.

She couldn't imagine why anyone would do something so stupid. Surely though they would return them when they saw-

Fran yelped as her foot went out from under her. She jarred her wrist as she landed. Eleanor turned, watching as Fran slithered down the sodden hillside before coming to a stop. She moved towards her, offered a hand to help her up.

"Thanks," Fran said.

Eleanor flashed her eyebrows in response. Her rain-splattered face looked utterly wretched.

They trudged the remaining distance together.

Inside, the bothy was cold and dark. A perfect match for their mood. Fran's hand trembled as she held out the match to light the fire. Her wrist didn't feel right yet.

Harry busied himself lighting the gas mantles before slouching in one of the ratty chairs. He looked like a beaten man.

Hazel cleaned up Archie's face with a damp cloth then sat by his bedside watching him. Eleanor was sitting on the sofa, staring into space.

Neither Cal and Marcus nor Jonathan and Gemma had returned. Jonathan and Gemma didn't know about Rob or

Archie. Cal had no doubt told Marcus about Archie, but neither knew how seriously ill he was. They would all be in for a shock when they got back.

They should be back by now. No doubt their progress had been hampered by the storm. She wondered if Jonathan and Gemma had taken shelter. She couldn't imagine where on that part of the island, but truth be damned, it was all too easy to picture the two of them snuggled up together in an imaginary cave, laughing and joking. Kissing.

She told herself not to be stupid. She hated this seam of insecurity she was mining. Besides, Jonathan had made it perfectly clear that he wasn't interested in Gemma. She knew that other people didn't always find him easy to get on with, but whatever anyone else thought, he was loyal. They would be on their way back right now. Heads bent in the wind, looking forward to getting back to food and warmth and the party atmosphere of last night. Some hope. Ignorance really was bliss.

Cal and Marcus would also be on their way back. They both knew better than to be stumbling about on the island in the dark, especially in this weather. Unless they'd found a way to get to Rob-

"Oh God!" Fran slapped herself on the forehead.

"What is it?" Harry asked.

"I forgot - Cal and Marcus don't know about the radios - they'll be waiting for-"

The bothy door flew open, cutting off her words. A gust of cold, wet, air swept into the room along with Cal and Marcus. Marcus slammed the door as Cal turned on them.

"Where the hell's the coastguard?"

37

Eleanor wanted to ask about Rob but the thickening atmosphere in the bothy acted like a gag. She shrank into the corner of the sofa as expressions of incredulity and anger fought it out on Cal's face.

Fran explained about the radios. Cal snatched them up, checking for himself before turning to the group.

"Who the hell's got the batteries?"

His wrath bulged, filling the room as he was answered by wide eyes, shaking heads, sealed lips.

"There's something else you should know," Fran said. "It's Archie - he's really ill."

She explained about them trying to light the beacon.

Her small voice was answered with a snap from Cal.

"Archie? I thought he had the runs from eating that dodgy pie."

"What pie?" Fran asked.

"I caught him stuffing his face with it last night," Marcus said.

"A pie did that to him?" Fran shook her head, "Poor Archie."

Cal stripped off his dripping jacket and threw it over a chair. Hazel scuttled aside as he went to the bunk to check Archie. The woman looked like a wizened apple. As if the events of the day had sucked all the juice out of her. She should consider herself lucky, Eleanor thought. At least she wasn't responsible for the mess they were in. At least she had nothing to feel guilty about. She hadn't kicked her boyfriend off a cliff. She hadn't sent the man who loved her plummeting to his death.

Eleanor's fingers dug into the sofa as hysteria quietly fountained within her.

Cal stepped back from the bunk and turned to face them.

"He doesn't look so good."

Understatement of the year. With his waxy pallor, Archie looked like a corpse-in-waiting.

"Do you think eating a bad pie could do that?" Fran asked. "It seems extreme."

"I don't know." Cal's anger had been replaced with concern.

"I don't think he's got any worse," Fran said. "Maybe he'll start to improve."

Cal looked at Fran for a moment then gave a nod. "Yeah, maybe."

Talk. It was all talk. Nobody was doing anything. Eleanor's fingers clawed the material. Crumbs and grit wedging under her nails.

"I know who took the batteries," Marcus said.

Eleanor's fingers stopped moving.

Marcus weighed one of the radios in his hand. He had centre stage and he knew it. He stared at them, one eyebrow raised.

"Well for goodness sake, tell us," Fran said.

Marcus drew the silence out for a moment longer before answering, "It was Archie."

"Archie?" Cal asked. "Why on earth would Archie-?"

Marcus cut him off. "Last night - don't you remember - he was jabbering on about liking the idea of being cut off from the rest of the world?"

"That's right," Harry sat up, "He did say something like that."

"Easy enough to achieve," Marcus replied, "The radios are our only means of contact. All he had to do was -"

"Take out the batteries," Fran finished in a whisper. She looked at Cal. "Do you think?"

"Somebody did it," he replied. "Why not Archie?"

"Find out what he's done with them." Eleanor's voice came out shrill. Faces turned towards her. "What are you waiting for?" she demanded.

Cal went to the bunk and shook Archie's shoulder.

"Archie? We need to know where the batteries are so that we can get help for you. Do you understand?"

Archie groaned. Cal shook him a little harder.

"Archie, where are the batteries?"

A sound, smaller than a groan emerged from Archie. Cal let him go.

"It's no use. Even if he did take them he's not even in a fit enough state to tell us where he put them."

He ran his hand over his head.

"We'll have to look for them." Fran was already scanning the room.

"Let's start with pie boy's rucksack," Marcus said.

"He could have hidden them outside," Harry said.

Eleanor flopped back into the corner of the sofa. They'd searched Archie's rucksack, then the room, then the rest of the bothy and there was no sign of the batteries anywhere.

"Gee, that narrows it down," Marcus sneered.

"I was only saying."

"Sit down, Harry," Hazel said. Harry obeyed.

Cal warmed himself in front of the fire.

Marcus loomed from nowhere and stood over Eleanor.

"We found these on the cliffs." He dropped two daypacks in front of her. One Rob's. The other the one she'd bought for the trip.

Marcus's body blocked the heat from the fire. Eleanor shuddered. Marcus stayed where he was.

"No sign of your boyfriend in case you're interested."

Her instinct was to stand up, get on equal footing with him, but he was standing too close. Crowding her. Giving her no room to move.

She glared up at him. "What do you mean *if I'm interested?*"

"Well I haven't heard you mention his name since we got back."

"What are you getting at?" Knots tightening inside her. Did Marcus know about the row. About her kicking Rob? No, he couldn't possibly know. And what did it matter anyway. It had been an accident. She'd tried to help Rob. Had reached out to him.

Her thoughts came to a dead stop. She stared up at Marcus. His face was in shadow, but she could feel him staring at her. Sense the sardonic smile snaking across his lips.

"What do you mean *no sign of him*?"

"Okay, okay - time to calm down." Cal took Marcus by the elbow and steered him across the room.

Marcus did not resist. He sat down at the table, a smirk on his face. He'd been toying with her. He was a sick jerk who got off on winding people up. Creep.

She looked away from him, disgusted.

Cal sat beside her.

"He could have expressed himself differently, but I'm afraid Marcus is right. We didn't see any sign of Rob. We found your daypacks, and we could see where the cliff had given way, but there wasn't any sign of Rob. We scoured the coast, but..."

Cal shrugged. "I'm sorry," he said.

No-one said a word then. Not even Marcus.

Silence pressed in on Eleanor as Cal's words whirled through her mind. *No sign of him.* His body was gone. Swept off the rock. She realised that she'd been hoping for a miracle. Hoping that somehow everything was going to be okay after all. That somehow she hadn't actually kicked her boyfriend to his death.

Swept into the sea. It seemed so harsh. So final. She closed her eyes. Poor Rob.

An arm across her shoulder. Cal. He pulled her towards him at first she tensed, but then she let herself sink into his side. Let him comfort her. She kept her eyes closed. Felt like she never wanted to open them again. That this was only the start of the nightmare.

Marcus's voice sliced through the silence. "I hate to break up a moment, but what exactly happened up there?"

38

Light glowed from the small window at the front of the bothy. A warm invitation on this desolate day. Jonathan battled his way towards it. Gusts of wind battered him from the side. Rain came down in sheets. It had penetrated his jacket at the shoulder seam. Was slowly soaking him from the inside out.

One of his boots was letting in water through the lace-holes. Not much. Just enough to squelch down between his toes. Just enough to make him think of flesh rotting in water.

He pushed the thought aside. Almost there now. Time to look forward, not back. Never back. He ran through his story one more time. There wasn't much to it. He had deliberately kept it simple. The most believable lies were the ones closest to the truth.

They would all be back by now. Preparing food. Pouring drinks. Enjoying a relaxing dram by the fire. Laughing and happy. Exchanging stories from the day.

He reached the door, turned the handle, stepped inside, quickly closing it behind him. Locking out the scream of the squall. He turned to face the room, the bright expression he'd fixed on his face fading as he registered the solemn eyes staring at him.

He stared at them staring at him. Why were they looking at him like that? Why weren't they being loud and irritating. Making noise with their idle chit-chat?

Did they know what he'd done?

But how could they?

Fran took a step towards him. She was clenching her fists. Her knuckles white. She was wired up. Grinding her teeth again.

The tendons in her neck clearly visible.

"Where's Gemma?" she asked.

Jonathan almost laughed. Of course they didn't know. Whatever the hell was going on in the bothy had nothing to do with him. The fact that they were distracted by something else only made it all the better for him. All he had to do was stick to his plan.

He smothered the laugh, replacing it with a concerned frown. It was surprising how easily it came to him. He should have been on the stage.

"Isn't she here?"

No-one bothered to answer. They all just kept on with the staring thing.

"She slipped into a bog," he said. "Got her feet wet. We were almost done anyway, so she came back here, and I finished going around the bait stations."

It was a straightforward story. Plausible, and not so far from the truth. After all, Gemma had got her feet wet. Along with the rest of her.

He looked around. "Where is she? Look, if this is a joke, it's not a very funny one."

Oh yes. Nice touch. Especially that note of pissed-offness he'd managed to inject. He was a born actor.

"It's not a joke," Fran said. "In fact, there's nothing funny about what's going on here."

"What do you mean?"

No need to act now. He was genuinely curious.

He stood where he was, rain dripping from his face and clothes, listening as Fran explained about Rob and Archie and the missing batteries.

Whatever he'd been expecting, it wasn't this. He'd mentally prepared himself for some scrutiny over the Gemma situation, but with a three-ring circus already going on, he wasn't going to be under anyone's magnifying glass anytime soon.

Too bad about Rob and Archie. Especially Rob. He hadn't thought much of the guy, but bloody hell, what a way to go. At least Gemma's demise had been quick. She'd gone from live to dead in the blink of an eye. Poor Rob had to endure two hundred feet of Torridonian sandstone cliffs flashing by him. Plenty of time to contemplate the world of pain coming his way when he landed on the rocks below.

Looking on the bright side, the fact that the entire weekend had gone belly up really worked in Jonathan's favour.

No wonder Fran was all drawn out. She looked like something inside her was about to go *ping*. She didn't deserve this. Any of it. He wanted to comfort her. Get her out of here, away from this lot. Just the two of them. They could go to her room. Light the stove. Get cosy.

He started undoing his jacket.

"What are you doing?" Cal asked.

"Taking my jacket off." Wondering what did it have to do with Cal anyway?

"I don't think there's much point."

Jonathan looked at him blankly.

"We're going to have to go out and look for Gemma."

39

They organised themselves into two search parties. Jonathan, Fran and Harry would walk out to the last place Jonathan had seen Gemma, whilst Cal, Marcus and Eleanor headed for the jetty.

If Gemma had lost her bearings, she would most likely have headed for the coast, following it round to the jetty and making her way back to the bothy from there. Hazel stayed behind in case Gemma made it back under her own steam and so that she could keep an eye on Archie.

Archie whimpered. His sleeping bag rustled as he shifted in it. Hazel stared at him. Despite Fran's assertions that he wasn't getting any worse, it looked to Hazel as though he was deteriorating. She didn't know what to do. Archie twitched and started to moan. It was a pathetic sound. The very weakness of it filling Hazel with guilt and fear.

How much pain must the wretched man be in to make a sound like that? It didn't bear thinking about. Except that she couldn't think of anything else.

So much pain. And she was responsible for it. She couldn't stand the thought that she was to blame. She couldn't harm a spider, let alone another human being.

It struck her that actually she had intended this pain and suffering for another human being - Harry. But that was different. Her husband was the exception who proved the rule. Harry was the only living being on the planet she had any desire to hurt. She rated a spider in the bath above Harry.

Hazel winced as Archie moaned again. Either he'd gained in strength or the pain was getting worse.

She stretched her hand out to stroke his cheek. It would be a reassuring touch. One which would let him know that he was not alone. That she was there for him. Kind and caring. Feeling his pain. Sharing it with him.

Her fingers hovered hesitantly above his face. She couldn't quite bring herself to caress him. His skin had such an unnatural pallor. It looked taut, as though the feel of it under her fingers would be unpleasant. As if it would split wide open at the lightest touch, revealing a red raw mass underneath.

The thought made her feel squeamish.

A sudden noise erupted from Archie. He sounded like a cow in pain. Hazel snatched her hand away. The mournful cry went on and on. Low, persistent, full of anguish. She didn't want to touch him. It didn't seem right. Too intimate a gesture. She hardly knew the man. But she had to do something to help him. She couldn't let him continue to suffer in agony like this. If he was a dog he would be put out of his misery.

Hazel grabbed hold of the thought. She eyed Archie, weighing up the facts. The man was in agony. His condition was getting worse. Fran's hopeful words amounted to no more than wishful thinking. The truth was, not only was Archie dying, he was doing so in a slow, undignified and excruciating manner.

They had no communications. No way of getting help. The storm would no doubt continue through the night, unsettling the sea for days to come. There was little chance of Zander making it to the island tomorrow. They were looking at Tuesday at the earliest before help arrived.

Everything was getting worse. Nothing was getting better. Why prolong Archie's agony? Why delay the inevitable?

Why not put him out of his misery?

Hazel stood up and took the pillow from Marcus's bunk. Her fingers curled into it, squeezing it tight. The pillows belonged to the bothy. Volunteers brought their own pillowcases. Marcus's was plain white. It felt smooth, clean and crisp. High thread-count. Egyptian cotton, perhaps. She'd long had a quiet yearning for Egyptian cotton sheets.

Hazel had a sudden vision of Marcus's home. Everything organised. No mess. No clutter. Not a greasy smudge in sight. A minimalist, stain-free life.

Life with Harry was a life filled with stains, splodges, and crumbs. The man could not make a simple sandwich without leaving a trail of devastation in the kitchen. Buttery fingerprints on the fridge. Dollops of small chunk pickle on the work top. Cheese-smeared knife left lying on the bread board. The cheese not wrapped properly afterwards so that it dried at the edges.

She had been cleaning up after Harry for decades. Washing his stains, wiping his smears, sweeping his crumbs.

She plumped the pillow. The movement released familiar odours. Top notes of fabric softener dancing over a base of bothy mustiness. That musty smell permeated every soft fabric in the building. The pillows and mattresses soaked it up like sponges. Even in the height of summer they seemed damp and fusty. Hazel never looked too closely as she fitted clean sheets and shrugged on pillowcases when they arrived. It was best not to dwell on the stains.

She wondered if Marcus minded using his good Egyptian cotton on soiled pillows. Perhaps he had so much good linen it didn't matter. She could easily imagine him disposing of a used pillowcase after a stay on the island. There was something quite pernickety about the man. She flexed the pillow, musing whether it would be easier to live with a pernickety man than someone like Harry.

Grasping the pillow firmly, she looked down at Archie. He didn't seem like the pernickety type, though you never could tell. The admirably spick-and-span front Harry presented to the world belied his crumb-laden private life.

Whatever Archie's preferences, she sincerely hoped that the pillow would not be an affront to his sensibilities. She could take comfort from the fact that the last thing his skin would be in contact with was quality fabric.

Hazel brought the pillow down on Archie's face.

40

The entire exercise was pointless. They weren't going to find Gemma. Not unless they dredged the bog-hole. A fact Jonathan could hardly point out, and so he went along with the charade.

The rain had eased off a little. Not that it made any difference now. The water which had seeped through his clothing earlier had crept across his shoulders and down his back, leaving a cold damp trail. He was wet and wet was how he was going to stay until he could get stripped off.

"GEMMA!"

Jonathan flinched as Harry bellowed in his ear. Again.

He'd tried to move away from the man, to keep some distance between them. It wasn't as if they didn't have the space. But Harry kept on filling the gap, apologising every time he bumped against Jonathan. Harry wasn't exactly light on his feet. In between the yelling, there were a lot of apologies.

Jonathan couldn't believe how he'd lost his focus back in the bothy. It was seeing Fran all strung-out like that. All he could think about was getting her away from them. He'd forgotten all about looking concerned about Gemma. Had taken a side trip to la-la land. He thought he'd got away with it, but if anyone said anything, he'd put it down to shock. That was feasible. There had been a lot to take in - Rob falling off the cliff, Archie ill, Gemma missing - but if he was going to come through this thing he'd have to watch himself.

He had to act normal.

Easier said than done. After an hour of pointless tramping in the near dark, Harry's yelling stirred up murderous thoughts. Jonathan's foot was wet, his back was damp. Every gust of wind drove the cold deeper into his bones.

"GEMMA!"

Jonathan was tempted to tell him the truth just to shut him up. It would almost have been worth it to see the look on Harry's torch-lit face. Almost. Instead, he picked up his pace and moved ahead a little, but Harry stuck with him. Maybe he was scared of the dark. Maybe that's why he was making so much noise. Covering up his fear.

Ahead of them, Fran swept the beam of her torch around, looking for any sign of a lost or injured Gemma.

"GEMMA!"

Jonathan gritted his teeth. Sounded like Harry was getting hoarse. With any luck his voice would give out on him and they could all get a bit of peace.

Fran stopped and waited for them to catch up. Jonathan stepped it up, taking mild pleasure from the sound of Harry breathing hard. Harry was more of a rambler than a hiker.

"This is it," Fran said. She swept her torch around.

"Yeah," Jonathan replied. "This is where we were when she left to go back to the bothy."

"Well, there's no sign of her. She could be anywhere - she could be less than ten metres away and we wouldn't see her."

"GEMMA!"

Jonathan jumped. "For fuck's sake, Harry."

"Sorry, I-"

Harry flashed his torch in Jonathan's face, dazzling him.

"Harry!" Jonathan shielded his eyes.

"Sorry," Harry lowered his torch.

"Get a grip, man," Jonathan said.

"Okay, let's calm down," Fran said. "We've made enough noise out here to wake the dead. If Gemma was around, she'd have heard us."

I hope not, Jonathan thought.

"Stumbling around in the dark isn't going to achieve

anything," she continued. "I suggest we get back to the bothy before we catch pneumonia and start searching again at daybreak."

"You've got my vote," Jonathan said.

"Harry?"

"Yes, I think that's a good idea. You never know, she might be back there already."

"Maybe," Fran said. "And Harry?"

"Yes, Fran?"

"Keep your torch down."

"Yes, sorry about that, Jonathan."

"No worries," Jonathan told him. "After you."

No worries at all, he thought as he followed behind Harry, dawdling a little so that a space opened up between them. They would trudge back to the bothy and then it would be a warm fire, a drink, something to eat. Food. Oh, yes. What a thought. He was ravenous. Yeah, food, drink then bed with Fran.

He started as a scream shredded the night. His first thought was Gemma. Back from the dead. Haunting him. And then he realised - it was Fran. Fran was screaming.

"Fran!"

Jonathan scrambled towards the torch beams. She was sitting on the ground, rubbing her calf. Harry bumbling around her. Apologising.

Fran looked up as Jonathan arrived. Jaw clenched, eyes watering.

"What did you do?" Jonathan yelled at Harry.

"I'm so sorry," Harry blustered. "I slipped, lost my footing- I stumbled into her..."

"You're a bloody liability, man," Jonathan spoke through gritted teeth. "Fran, are you okay?"

"I'm fine," she said. "I got more of a fright than anything."

"Oh Fran, oh dear me - I'm sorry. So sorry."

"We've got it, Harry. You're sorry, right?" Jonathan said.

"Simmer down," Fran told him. She got to her feet. "I'm fine, okay?"

She took a step and winced.

"You're not okay, are you?" Jonathan asked.

"It's my calf. It'll be fine, but I'll have to go slow. Harry, you go on ahead, Jonathan can help me."

"Fran, I'm so sorry, really."

"Please, Harry. You don't have to keep apologising. If you want to do something for me, get back to the bothy and get the kettle on."

"If you're sure?"

"I'm sure." She gave him a reassuring smile.

"Okay then."

Fran leaned into Jonathan for support as Harry turned and plodded ahead of them, whistling to himself.

"You were a bit harsh," Fran whispered when Harry was out of earshot.

"The man's a pest," Jonathan replied.

"He was just trying to help."

"Yeah, and you know what they say - the road to hell is paved with good intentions."

41

Eleanor had once told Rob that if she was ever in a horror film it would the shortest movie ever. No way would she go down to the cellar on her own. Or up to the attic. Or out to the woods. She'd stick with the group. Everyone together, all keeping an eye on each other's backs. Yet here she was, in the dark, by herself. It was okay though because there weren't any monsters or axe murderers on the island. There was a battery-removing idiot, but he was confined to quarters. That is if it was Archie who'd taken them. But surely if it had been anyone else, they would have owned up by now.

Unless it was Rob who had taken them? No, couldn't have been Rob. He didn't go in for practical jokes. It must have been Archie.

There were no wild animals on the island. Not big scary ones anyway. No bears or wolves and she didn't believe in any of that supernatural twaddle. There were no ghouls or vampires. No such thing as ghosts. And yet, she couldn't help but feel a little spooked. A little nervy. A little bloody terrified. Out here. By herself. With nothing but the whine and wail of the wind for company.

Marcus had suggested it. They'd split up so that they could cover more ground. They were sweeping up from the coast towards the bothy. Great idea in theory. In reality, Eleanor's sweep was more of a scuffle over the rough terrain. This was not what she had signed up for. And then she thought of Gemma. Out in the dark, alone. Injured. With perhaps a twisted ankle, or even a broken leg. Easily done. Eleanor's own bruises could attest to that.

Gemma could be anywhere. Maybe she wasn't even on the island. She could have gone over a cliff. Like Rob. They hadn't thought of that, had they? No, and she didn't want to think about it either. But she couldn't help herself. The expression on Rob's face as he realised he was falling was seared into her brain. No matter how hard she tried to push it to the back of her mind, it kept bursting through to the front.

Bad enough to know he was falling to his death. Worse still to die knowing that the woman he loved, the woman he wanted to marry, had rejected him. That she hated him so much she'd kicked him over the edge.

"No!"

Eleanor jumped at the sound of her own voice.

"No," she repeated, softly this time.

She hadn't kicked Rob over the edge. She had kicked him in self-defence. Rob had gone crazy up there. She had no choice - she'd had to defend herself. Rob going over the cliff - it had been an accident. She'd reached out to him. Tried to help him.

Tears flowed down Eleanor's cheeks. They'd been threatening, on and off, all day since it had happened. Now she gave in to them.

When she was done crying, she started walking again. She shone her torch around and realised that she had no idea where she was. The thin beam of the torch did not reveal much. Rocks, scraggy plants, uneven ground. She swept it around. Boulders. Gorse. Heather. Moss. How the hell was she supposed to find Gemma when she was lost herself?

The torch flickered. Was it her imagination, or did the beam seem weaker?

Eleanor swore under her breath. To be stumbling about in the dark was all she needed. She'd end up breaking her neck, then they'd all be looking for her as well as Gemma. In fact, maybe that's exactly what had happened to Gemma. Maybe she was lying somewhere with a broken neck.

The torch flickered again. Eleanor smacked it against her leg. The beam steadied.

It was definitely weaker.

42

Hazel pressed down on the pillow with her upper body. Archie thrashed around like a big fish landed in a small boat. It was surprising how much energy he had. He'd seemed so weak she'd thought he would give up without a struggle. That it would be a peaceful end. Not like this. Writhing and jerking like he was on fire. Perhaps his movements were involuntary. An instinctive reaction to air deprivation.

She talked to him through the pillow. Though it required some effort, for Archie's sake she kept her voice as gentle and soothing as possible. She told him that what she was doing was for his own good. That it was best not to struggle. He would have peace soon. The pain would stop. There would be no more bleeding. No more indignity. What she was doing was an act of mercy. She was bringing the pain to an end. That was all.

Archie's movements lessened. Not so much writhing as twitching. He was listening to her, she was sure of it. Listening and understanding. There was no malice in her heart. All she wanted to do was help him.

It was easy now. All he had to do was relax and let nature take its course. No more pain.

The door clattered open behind her. Hazel stiffened at the sudden draught of cold air but stayed where she was. Half-lying on top of Archie, her head resting on the pillow over his face, looking towards the wall, away from the room. He was almost gone.

"What are you doing?"

A voice demanding an answer. The tone strident. Tearing into the gentle peace she had created. She ignored it. Archie had stopped struggling. He would soon be at peace. She closed her eyes, feeling peaceful herself.

Hands on her. Fingers digging into her shoulders. Gripping her roughly. Trying to pull her away from Archie. From the peace they'd created together.

"No!" she screamed.

She let go of the pillow. Batted the hands away from her. Archie moved. His peace disturbed.

Hands, grabbing, pulling, mauling. The voice shouting. Telling her to stop. But she did not stop. Could not stop. Couldn't they see? She was helping Archie. It was all for Archie. She was an Angel of Mercy. On a mission to put him out of his misery. She would not be stopped. She thrust down on the pillow, pressing it into Archie's face. The hands moved from her shoulders to her neck. Still trying to pull her away. The voice still yelling at her to stop. The sound filling her head. She struggled fiercely. Energised by righteous indignation. The voice begged her to stop, but she wouldn't. The fingers squeezed.

Pressure built up under Hazel's jaw. The voice pleaded with her to stop, but she struggled on. Tighter. The fingers squeezed tighter. Still she resisted. Her tongue bulged. Became too fat for her mouth. It burst between her lips. Protruding, wet and swollen. Black spots swarmed in from the periphery of her vision. Horrible noises emanated from her throat. Gargling. Gasping.

She realised that she was listening to the sound of herself being strangled. And then it all went dark.

43

Eleanor's torch dimmed and went out.

"Shit."

She banged it against her leg, willing it to flicker back into life. Nothing. What the hell was she supposed to do now? She peered into the dark. And dark was all she could see. No stars tonight. She gave her eyes a few moments to adjust, thinking maybe she'd develop some night vision. After several minutes of standing there like a turnip, all she could see were patches of dark that looked maybe a shade darker than the rest of the dark. She couldn't stand there all night. She'd either get pneumonia or die from hypothermia. Pneumonia had a nasty ring, but she was sure she'd read somewhere that hypothermia wasn't such a bad way to go. A relatively painless slump into oblivion. The way she was feeling now, it had its attractions.

Eleanor sighed. She knew fine well that she wasn't going to stand there waiting for hypothermia to sneak up on her. She took a couple of tentative steps into the dark. Not being able to see where she was putting her feet was disconcerting. She wobbled, as though she was on a tightrope. As though any second she could take a step into the void.

She probed the ground in front of her with the toe of her boot. It seemed solid enough. She took another step forward then sighed in exasperation. This was no use. She could spend the entire night going round in one tiny circle. She could even be standing right beside Gemma and not even know it. That was an idea.

"Gemma!" She hollered.

It was worth a try. Anything beat standing in the dark doing nothing.

There was no answer but the low moan of the wind and the distant boom of the sea. This place was depressing.

"Gemma!" She yelled again.

No response. She stared into the dark. Looked all around. She began to wonder if she even had her eyes open.

Frustration finally got the better of her. She lunged a few paces forward. She couldn't see a thing but nothing bad happened and at least she was moving. She took another few steps. It was fine. She was miles from the cliffs. As long as she headed up the slope away from the sea she was bound to come in sight of the bothy. She walked faster. It was scary but exhilarating. Forging her way through the dark with no idea what was ahead of her. It was death-defying madness.

She was sticking two fingers up at this treacherous island. A stream of giggles bubbled up from her throat. So what if she plunged to her death? What did she care?

Her foot snagged, jolting her body. Her laughter turned to a scream as she pitched headlong into the dark.

That was when Eleanor realised that she cared very much.

44

"Did you hear that?"

Jonathan froze, pulling Fran to a halt beside him.

"It sounded like a scream," Fran said. "Maybe it was Gemma."

He stared into the dark. No. It couldn't be. Gemma was dead. There was no way she'd still been alive when he'd dumped her in that bog-hole. Not with that huge fucking hole in the back of her head. But there was always a chance. Anything was possible.

He tried to remember if he had checked her pulse. He had. He was sure he had. There had been nothing. She was dead. But maybe it had been faint. So faint that he'd missed it. *Anything was possible.*

Persistent as a mosquito, doubt pricked at his mind.

"Jonathan?"

Think man, think. Even if she had survived having part of her brains dashed out - even if she had been alive when he'd dropped her into the bog-hole - she'd have drowned within minutes.

He'd stayed by the hole watching her pale hand float beneath the surface of the water. He'd stayed long enough for drowning time. Long enough for her lungs to fill with dark, peaty water. She could not have survived having her skull crushed *and* being drowned.

"Jonathan - are you okay?"

Fran staring at him, her face pale and ghostly in the torchlight. He wanted to pull her close. Take the worry clean out of her. Tell her that everything was going to be alright. He wasn't going to lose her because of that bitch. Not now. Not after everything he'd done to keep her.

"Yeah. Yeah, I'm fine."

Did his voice sound okay?

He had to act normal. He also had to cover himself.

What if by some chance - some tiny inexplicable miraculous chance - Gemma was still alive? What if, even as he was walking away, she'd managed to drag herself out of the bog-hole like some bitch from hell? What if that had happened and one of the others got to her before he did? She'd tell them everything.

Bubbles popped inside him. Pop. Pop. Pop. Panic fizzling in his gut.

"Maybe it was Gemma. I have to go and help her," he said. "Do you think you can manage back from here by yourself?"

He sounded normal. He was sure of it.

"I'll be fine," she said. "It's not far from here - you go on."

Fran's response was normal too. That proved that he was acting normally.

A-1 Normal all round.

"You be careful," he said.

"You too," she replied.

"See you later."

He kissed her on the lips then headed into the dark. He moved quickly, in the direction of the scream. He had to get to her first and kill her again.

45

Eleanor's plunge into the void lasted a second. Two at the most. Her landing cushioned by a tangled mass of scratchy heather. She spat out a twig and got to her feet. She felt a little stupid about the scream she'd let out, though given the circumstances she guessed she was allowed at least one petrified squawk.

She took a couple of exploratory steps. Was she still going uphill? It felt like it. This time she'd take it easy. A nice steady plod and maybe she'd get back in one piece.

Yes, she was definitely going uphill. It couldn't be far now.

Something caught her eye. She stopped and peered into the gloom. Light - there was light. The bothy. She gave a small cheer.

No, not the bothy. It was someone with a torch. The beam sweeping back and forth. She opened her mouth, ready to call out, but before she uttered a sound, a voice came to her, carried on the wind. Her skin goose fleshed as she strained to hear.

"Gemmaaaaaa. Gemmaaaaaa."

The name repeated again and again in a sing-song tone.

Eleanor shivered. There was something wrong here.

"Gemmaaaaaa - I know you're there. I can hear you."

Eleanor took a step backwards.

The light turned and came towards her.

46

The pain in Fran's leg was easing off. When Harry had first stumbled into her, it felt as though he had kicked her calf muscle into her knee. Poor Harry. He'd been so contrite she had ended up feeling sorry for him. There had been no reason for her to lose her temper with him - Jonathan had been angry enough for them both. Angry beyond reason. She suspected that the real target of his anger was not Harry, but himself. He'd been acting rather oddly since Gemma's disappearance. Having spent the day working with her, no doubt he felt some kind of responsibility. It was only natural. She would feel the same way, even though other than abandon their work to accompany her back, Fran didn't see what he could have done.

If it was anyone's fault, it was Fran's. Gemma's flirting had caused a minor dispute the previous year. Fran should have had her removed from the volunteer list then. But she hadn't. That group of volunteers had left. Another arrived. Everything moved on, and until she showed up yesterday, all thoughts of Gemma had evaporated.

She'd been walking for an age. She couldn't be far from the bothy now. It would be wonderful to get there and discover that Jonathan had found Gemma. It would be one less problem to deal with, though they'd still be in a big mess.

Fran limped on, over ground she barely recognised. In the summer, it barely got dark at night, but it was a different place now.

The island she knew so well had become a stranger to her.

47

Jonathan's scalp prickled. Pop. Pop. Pop. Went the bubbles inside. She was out there. He knew it. He could feel her watching him. Her eyes staring. He should have closed them properly when he'd had the chance. Maybe that's where he'd gone wrong. There were a lot of superstitions surrounding the eyes of the dead.

He didn't need to be thinking about that. Being out here in the dark, looking for a woman who was supposed to be dead was freaking him out enough. He didn't need to be winding himself up any further. As far as he was concerned, the dead should stay fucking dead. Another bad thought, making him think about zombies.

He heard something. Pop. Pop. Pop. Wind rustling the undergrowth - or footsteps.

He swung the torch around and sang into the dark.

"Gemmaaaaaa."

His voice low, soothing. No need to alarm her. No need to attract the attention of others. No need to give away the fact that his heart was hammering fit to burst.

"Gemmaaaaaa - I only want to help."

He swept the beam around. He held the torch in his left hand. In his right was his pocket knife. It didn't have much of a blade, only two inches, but it was sharp. It would be enough.

Another sound. He pointed the torch towards it, half expecting a zombiefied Gemma to hurl herself at him out of the dark. He tightened his grip on the knife as adrenalin swamped his system. Right now two inches seemed very fucking inadequate.

"I know you're there. I can hear you."

He peered into the dark, flashing the torch this way and that, trying to catch her out.

There! Something pale flashed in the light. He jerked the torch back to it. It was her. Gemma! Her eyes wide, staring at him. He strode towards her.

He'd get her this time.

48

"Jonathan?"

Eleanor stared at the man striding towards her. He pumped his arms as he strode. The torchlight catching his face. It was definitely Jonathan. But there was a crazy expression on his face. Looked like he'd been chewed up and spat out by a bear.

"Jonathan - are you okay? It's me, Eleanor."

He didn't say anything, just kept coming. Marching relentlessly, determinedly, towards her. She swithered. Thinking she didn't fancy the look on his face. Telling herself, it was only Fran's partner, Jonathan. Vegetarian. Outdoors type. On the wiry side of skinny. A bit moody but running away from him seemed like an odd thing to do. Then the light glinted on something he was holding in his right hand. The something was a shiny, sharp blade. It was a no-brainer. Eleanor ran.

"*Ssstoppp!*" he hissed behind her.

Ignoring the command she tore over heather, the creepy sound of his voice sizzling into the air behind her. What the hell was going on with him? Maybe he was on drugs. No matter. Getting away. That was main thing. Get away now. Ask questions later.

"*Gemmaaaaaa.*"

But the questions kept on coming. Tumbling through her head as she scrambled up the hillside. Gemma? Why was he calling her Gemma? Even in the dark, she didn't look anything like Gemma. Heart pounding, lungs burning and still her mind was churning. Where was Gemma? What happened to her?

She couldn't be far from the bothy now. She hoped not. Jonathan was fitter than her. If it came down to a chase, she had no chance. He'd run her down. Her only hope was to get to the bothy and get help.

She was already short of breath. A stitch stabbing under her rib-cage. Throat on fire. He was gaining on her. She could hear him breathing heavily behind her. But he wasn't going to stop. She couldn't lose him. There was nowhere to hide. She was trapped in the beam of the torch. The light sending her shadow leaping before her. The beam strong and sure. Burning into her back like a laser.

The hill steepened. Using her hands, she scrabbled up the incline. Grabbing at roots and rocks. Propelling herself away from him. But he was gaining. She could hear him behind her. Grunting.

As every second passed, he was gaining on her. Any moment now, he would reach out and grab her. Wrapping his long fingers around her ankle. Or he'd stab her. Slicing the blade into her Achilles tendon. She'd have no chance. She had to change tack, or he was going to get her. Going to kill her.

She was on her final reserves. Whatever she did, she had to do it soon. He was right behind her. His breath hot on her back. Burning into her like acid. She couldn't out-run him, couldn't beat him physically. All she had going for her was the ability to surprise.

Without warning she whirled around and lashed out with her boot hoping to hell that it would connect with more than fresh air.

49

The pain came out of nowhere. Flaring across his face. Blinding him. She'd been within grabbing distance. He'd put the torch in his mouth. Gripping it with his teeth. Freeing his hand. He'd reached out to snatch her. Pull her down. Suddenly she turned. Whirling around. Landing on her back. Kicking out at him. He should have been able to dodge the kick, but his momentum carried him forward.

The sole of her boot smashed into his face, pulverising his nose. The torch clattered against his teeth, knocking two loose. His eyes teared-up, blurring his vision. He saw bright lights. Shooting stars.

Blood and snot spurted from the mash of broken bone and gristle that used to be his nose. The torch ripped the roof of his mouth. Making him gag as it hit the back of his throat. His mouth filled with blood. Thick, metallic.

Jonathan staggered. The torch fell to the ground, strobing crazily as it rolled and bounced down the hill. He lost his balance. Fell over and kept on going. He tumbled backwards, heels over head over heels.

When he came to a stop, he was still gripping onto the knife. He lay in a heap, too stunned to move. Too shocked to make a sound. Feeling like he'd been broken into a hundred pieces.

It felt like his brain was rolling loose in his skull. He was getting pain signals from one end of his body to the other. Whoever had said that the pain from one wound would blot out the pain from another had been a lying bastard. What Jonathan couldn't figure out was why his leg was singing holy fuck over and above the chorus of hurt from the rest of his body.

He winced as he prodded at it. His trousers were torn, the skin beneath was tender and wet. He was bleeding. He had a notion that he'd sliced himself with the knife on the way down.

He gritted his teeth and explored further. His nerve endings screeched like they'd been scalped. Hurt like hell, but he figured it was a superficial wound. He'd skinned himself. Could have been worse. He could have stabbed his femoral artery, in which case he'd have bled to death already.

He was doing plenty of bleeding as it was. Felt kind of light-headed. Rolling down a hill like Humpty fucking Dumpty would have that effect. He was lucky he hadn't dashed his brains out on a rock.

Face it, he knew how easy it was for that to happen.

50

The whitewashed walls of the bothy were just visible beyond the dark silhouette of the copse. Fran let out a sigh of relief. She'd been walking for an age without seeming to get anywhere. Truth was, she'd been getting a little spooked out there on her own. Had begun to wish that Jonathan hadn't gone off and left her. Not that he could have done anything else. Not given the circumstances. At least she hadn't heard any more screams. If screams were a bad sign, the lack of them had to be good, right?

She didn't usually get spooked. Especially not here, on the island. There was nothing to get spooked about. But once you got a case of the jitters, it was hard to shake them. She was tired and she was weary, that was all. Nerves stretched by the events of the day. Maybe she should have used the time alone to figure out a new career for herself.

There she went again, thinking about herself when people had died, gone missing, were ill. Thing was, she didn't want to dwell on those subjects. Nor on the thought that Archie had removed the batteries from the radios, thereby contributing to his own dire situation. Why on earth had he done such a stupid thing? She'd never have thought it of him.

Oh, she was shattered. A hot drink and a warm bed were all she wanted right now. But she wouldn't be able to do that. Until help came from the mainland, she was in charge of this mess.

The bothy was tantalisingly close, but she could barely put one limping foot in front of the other. She stopped for a moment to rest. Goodness knows, as soon as she walked through the door they'd all be looking to her for answers, guidance, reassurance.

She saw someone moving. It was difficult to be sure when everything was in shades of black, but it looked as though they were coming out of the trees. That was odd. Why would anyone be in the copse? The person walked to the bothy and disappeared inside.

She glanced around. A pinprick of light was approaching from the southwest. A torch. Maybe it was Jonathan and Gemma, though she'd have expected them more from the south east. She hoped it was them. They could do with a bit of good news.

If Jonathan had found Gemma they would be down to one missing person, presumed dead, and one seriously ill. Would that make it a disaster rather than a catastrophe? Degrees of darkness, degrees of awfulness. Every which way, it was a mess.

Marcus produced a bottle of malt whisky from his rucksack. He put it on the table, fetched four glasses and sat them beside the bottle. It had been his torch outside. Fran had returned just ahead of him. She drummed her fingers against her leg as Marcus made his preparations.

"I don't think that's going to help," she said.

"*Au contraire*," he replied. "Right now I think it's the only thing that will help."

He pulled the plastic seal from the bottle and uncorked it. It made a small, pleasant pop. He glugged a decent of measure of whisky into one of the glasses, eyed it for a moment then added another couple of glugs.

"Anyone care to join me?"

"I'll have one," Cal said, "and Harry looks like he could use one. Fran?"

She only hesitated for a moment before nodding. If you couldn't beat them and all that.

Marcus poured a generous measure and handed it to her. She sniffed at the whisky. It filled her nose with its rich, peaty perfume. She could taste it before she took her first sip. It lit up her mouth, sending a flare of heat down the back of her throat. It warmed her, perked her up. What's more, it seemed to have a similar effect on her companions.

"You were right," she said to Marcus, "It does help."

He raised his glass in acknowledgement. There was no hint of sarcasm in the gesture. They sat for a moment, sipping the malt.

"Now what?" Marcus asked of no-one in particular.

"We eat," Cal said.

"What about the others?" Fran asked.

"They can eat when they get back."

"*If* they come back." Marcus said.

"I wish people would stop disappearing," Fran said.

They'd managed to lose another three people. Jonathan and Eleanor hadn't returned from looking for Gemma and, Marie Celeste style, Hazel hadn't been at the bothy when the others returned. Her jacket was hanging up, but she wasn't anywhere inside. It was downright weird.

They argued the toss about going out and looking for all three, but they were cold, wet and exhausted as it was. In the end, they decided not to risk losing anyone else. They'd stay at the bothy, for now at least, warm themselves up, dry themselves out and hope that the missing people made it back to them.

Fran sipped at the whisky. It was making her feel delightfully woozy.

"Whatever happens we still need to eat," Cal said. "Look at us - we're all out. I don't know what the hell's going on any more than the rest of you, but I do know this - before we even think about anything else we have to get some food down us. Unless anyone has any better suggestions?"

Nobody did.

Cal went to the kitchen and rummaged about. Marcus poured himself another large dram. Harry stared at the fire, clutching his empty glass.

Fran was sure it had been Harry's silhouette she had seen emerging from the copse, but when she'd asked him about it, he'd denied it, asking why would he go into the trees? He'd made slow progress back, that was all. So slow, Fran had almost caught up with him. He said that when he got back, Hazel was gone and he didn't understand it.

She'd felt all the more sorry for him then. She and Jonathan should never have sent him on ahead on his own like that. It had been cruel and unnecessary. Everyone was tired and hungry. Bad decisions were being made. Like the one Cal, Marcus and Eleanor made to split up.

The only good decision anyone had made lately, was Cal insisting they took time to eat. To give Marcus his due, the whisky wasn't such a bad idea either.

Harry tore his gaze away from the fire and gave Marcus a profoundly grateful look as he poured him a generous refill. Looked like he was ready to drink himself into oblivion. And who could blame him?

"A small one please," Fran said when Marcus proffered the bottle. She didn't usually go near spirits, but there was nothing usual about the situation. She glanced at Archie, lying in his bunk.

Marcus caught the look.

"I don't think it will do him any good, do you?"

Fran looked away. They'd checked on Archie earlier. He didn't look good. Understatement of the year. Didn't look good, didn't smell good, didn't seem as if he was going to last another five minutes, yet there he was still hanging on. There was nothing any of them could do and so they did nothing. As long as he didn't moan or move around too much it was easier to pretend that he wasn't there. Not that it was much of a challenge. He was barely breathing let alone moving, and the small sounds of misery emanating from him were very faint and easily covered by the low rumble of wind sucking at the chimney.

Cal rattled a pan on the stove and within seconds the heavenly scent of garlic and onion wafted through the bothy. Fran's mouth watered. Cal was right. They needed to eat, and if she wasn't doing so soon, she'd be chewing off her own arm.

Fifteen minutes later Cal presented each of them with a large bowl of steaming hot pasta and tomato sauce.

"It's pretty basic, but it'll do the job."

They sat around the fire to eat. Fran thought it was pretty much the best thing she'd ever tasted in her life and said as much. Even Marcus said it wasn't bad. Harry ate his food mechanically and said nothing.

Silence seeped and spread from him like a creeping mould until each of them was shrouded in it, sunk in their own thoughts. Everyone chewing and swallowing and staring at the fire like it held the answer to everything.

Fran had almost finished her meal when the door banged open. She jumped to her feet, dropping her bowl as she did so. It shattered on the stone floor, splattering remnants of pasta and sauce over her boots. Along with the others, she gaped at the apparition standing in the doorway. It was Eleanor. She'd lost her hat. Her was hair tangled and matted. Her clothes wet and muddy. Her face streaked with grime.

Ceramic shards and pasta ground beneath Fran's feet as she went to greet her.

51

"No, I don't believe it," Fran said.

"Why would I lie?" Eleanor asked.

Fran glared at Eleanor. Eleanor glared right back.

Her body ached from running, clambering and falling. She had pushed herself beyond her limits. She'd had no choice - she had been in fear of her life. Her hands were covered in tiny cuts and grazes. Cal had cleaned them up, but they stung like hell. Her remaining acrylic nails were either broken or had torn off altogether. There was a large graze on her cheek. In fact, she had cuts and grazes, bashes and bruises all over. Somewhere along the way she'd lost her hat. Her hair was matted. She picked bits of heather from it. She was filthy from head to toe. She was exhausted. She felt like hell and now she was being called a liar.

Fran was the first to look away.

"It *was* Jonathan, and he thought I was Gemma," Eleanor said.

Fran screwed her face up. "Why would he think that? You don't look anything like her."

"I don't know - maybe because he's crazy. What I do know is that he thought I was her and he was trying to kill me."

"Jonathan wouldn't do that."

"But he did, Fran. He did. He came at me with a knife, for goodness sake. Look at the state of me. I'm not making it up."

Eleanor's words hung heavy in the air, everyone weighing them up. And look at her they did. They stared at her like she was a freak in a sideshow.

Marcus broke the silence. "Well I guess we know what happened to Gemma."

"We don't know anything," Fran said.

"Oh come off it, sweetheart." Marcus said. "Okay, maybe we don't know exactly what happened to her, but it's clear that whatever it was, it wasn't good, and your boyfriend is involved."

Fran shook her head. "Jonathan would never-"

Eleanor sucked in a deep breath. If Fran stuck up for her demented boyfriend one more time, she would slap her. "Fran, wake up - smell the coffee. He's not the great guy you think he is. He came at me with a knife."

"Have a drink, calm yourself down." Marcus thrust a glass of whisky at Eleanor.

"Thanks." She knocked it back in one go.

"You should eat something," Cal said.

Within minutes she was holding a bowl full of pasta shells and tomato sauce. She stirred her fork through the congealing pasta. She should be ravenous, but she didn't feel hungry at all. Her insides were all knotted up. Every time Fran defended Jonathan, the knots pulled a little tighter. Eleanor wanted to grab hold of her and shake the truth into her.

"Go on, eat," Cal urged.

She poked at a piece of pasta. The rich, garlic smell of the sauce made her feel nauseous, but she forced a forkful down. Chew, chew, swallow. Chew, chew, swallow. Repeat ad nauseam.

"Don't suppose there's a glass of red to go with it?" she asked.

The question, directed at no-one in particular, was meant as a joke. Sort of. A mood lightener. A tension-breaker. Something to say for the sake of talking. All the same, the pasta would slide down a little easier with a sloosh of wine. And it might knock the edge off her nerves. Loosen the knots a little.

"I don't know about red, but you could have some champagne. I assume it was intended for you, so you may as well drink it."

Eleanor swallowed a half-chewed pasta shell and stared at

Marcus. "Champagne? What are you talking about?"

"It's in Rob's daypack. Look yourself if you don't believe me."

"Why were you looking through Rob's things?"

Marcus smiled. His eyes hard and reptilian behind his glasses. "Trying to find the batteries. of course. I couldn't help but notice that he had a half-bottle of champers stashed away. He must have been planning something special."

Eleanor slumped. "He was - he did -"

Marcus still staring at her. Unnerving her with that creepy smile of his. Making her squirm. The others watching. Listening.

"I mean," Marcus said, "You don't carry a bottle, or even a half-bottle, of champagne halfway across an island for no reason."

"He proposed to me. Up on the cliffs. Rob proposed to me. I didn't know he was going to do it and I-" Eleanor dropped the fork in her bowl and covered her face with her hands. She let out a long groan. Nightmare. She was strapped in a nightmare.

Someone put a hand on her shoulder. Gave it a squeeze. "Hey, take it easy." Cal's voice. Soft. Understanding.

She didn't want him to be understanding. Didn't want him to be nice to her. It would finish her off. She'd break down. Cry. And if she started, she might never stop.

She removed her hands from her face, looked up at Cal.. "I'm okay."

"Sure?"

She nodded.

"What did you say?" Marcus asked.

"What?" Eleanor frowned at him.

"When Rob asked you to marry him - what was your answer?"

"That's none of your business."

Marcus shrugged. "I don't suppose it is. I was just curious as to whether or not he died a happy man. I mean it would be a terrible thing to go over a cliff just having had your proposal of marriage thrown back in your face - oho, there's a thought. He didn't throw himself over because you turned him down, did he?"

"Who says I turned him down?" Knots tightening inside her.

Marcus raised his eyebrows, started to speak. Eleanor stood up. Banged the bowl on the table. Cut him off.

"What is your problem?" Her voice loud. Verging on a scream. Losing it. Letting Marcus get the better of her. Knowing it, but unable to contain herself.

"Hey, enough already."

Cal's hands on her arms, pulling her away from Marcus. She swivelled her head to see him.

"You are a complete bastard, you know that?"

He tilted his head. "Yes, I know."

There, right there in that moment, Eleanor knew that she was capable of murder. Before she could explore the thought, Cal propelled her away from Marcus. He took her to the sofa. They sat down together. Him right beside her. Close enough so that they were touching. Arms. Legs. Protecting her. She felt that he was protecting her. Maybe from herself.

Marcus started up again. Why wouldn't he just shut up?

"So, I think we can assume that Jonathan is responsible for whatever happened to Gemma. And maybe Hazel too. But not Rob. I mean, whatever happened up on the cliffs, we can't blame Jonathan."

"It was an accident."

Eleanor spoke through clenched teeth, but her words were lost beneath Harry's agitated voice.

"What about Hazel? What are you saying about Hazel?"

He stood up, eyes popping, chin jutting. Looking all worn out and saggy but confronting them all the same.

"I am saying, Harry, that whatever happened to Hazel, it's likely that Fran's psycho boyfriend had something to do with it."

"Oh yeah - let's blame everything on Jonathan," Fran said.

156

She stood up beside Harry. The room was starting to feel crowded.

"How very convenient," she went on, "I suppose he took the batteries out of the radios and made Archie ill while he was at it?"

Harry turned on Fran. "What did he do? What did he do to my Hazel?"

"*Nothing!*" Fran screamed at him.

Harry stepped back, startled. Fran reached out to him. Harry flinched from her touch.

"I'm sorry Harry. I didn't mean to yell at you, but Jonathan didn't hurt Hazel - I know that."

Now it was Eleanor's turn to leap to her feet. Or it would have been if Cal hadn't held her back.

"How do you know?" she barked at Fran. "If he can come at me with a knife, who knows what else he's capable of."

Fran stared at her, quite still and stony-eyed. "If he was out there attacking you like you say, then he couldn't have been here with Hazel, could he?"

She gazed around the room. "No, it seems that not even my *psycho boyfriend* is capable of being in two places at the same time. I've had enough of this," she said. "I'm going out to look for Jonathan. Who's coming with me?"

52

The night air felt cool and clean against Fran's flushed cheeks. The wind had dropped back to a breeze. She leaned against the stone wall, taking a moment to compose herself. She was glad of the darkness, of the cover it gave her. Glad to be out here, by herself.

The atmosphere in the bothy was poisonous. Everything - everyone - was out of control. Herself included. She had no reason to scream at Harry like that. It had been awful. An utterly undignified way for her to behave. But they had no right to heap the blame for everything on Jonathan. It was terrible the things they were accusing him of. It was little wonder she had resorted to screaming. She shook her head. Now she was making excuses for herself. For her own bad behaviour. At least she had come to her senses. They were still at it inside. Arguing.

She could hear the low sneer of Marcus's voice. Eleanor sniping back at him. She had been through a lot. Seeing Rob going over the cliff must have been terrible. Especially after he'd proposed. How on earth had it gone so badly wrong? It was hardly surprising that Eleanor was so upset. And maybe a little hysterical. That's why she'd said the things she had about Jonathan. The tragedy with Rob had skewed her mind. Was playing havoc with her senses.

That's why she'd gotten it so wrong. And she had got it wrong. She must have done. Jonathan just wasn't capable of the things Eleanor had accused him of. He was very sensitive. You might say highly-strung. Certainly not the type of person to attack someone. He was kind and caring. A gentle soul. Though he hadn't been any of those things when Harry had blundered into her. Harry had been clumsy. He was always a bit like that. Heavy on his feet. Jonathan had over-reacted. Had revealed a side of his personality she had barely glimpsed before. A part of himself he kept hidden. Buried deep.

Doubt seeped into Fran's mind. How well could one person really know another. Jonathan's anger may have been well concealed, but it was still there. She herself had caught a glimpse of it. But that didn't mean... no. Surely not. Eleanor had been mistaken.

Something inside Fran curdled. She thought about whisky and pasta and the smell of garlic and onions sweating in a pan. Despite the cool air, sweat broke out on her upper lip. For a moment she thought she might throw up.

Jonathan wouldn't - couldn't... She felt like a traitor for even having the thought.

The sound of Cal's voice came from inside. His steady tone muffled by the door.

"I'm not going anywhere while there's a psycho on the loose."

That had been Marcus's sneering retort when she'd asked for someone to help look for Jonathan. Cal said he would come. She suspected more out of concern for her, than to help Jonathan. But Eleanor said he should stay. That it was dangerous. That they should not split the group again.

Marcus seemed to enjoy the discord. The thought flashed through Fran's mind that it had been him who had removed the batteries. That he'd somehow orchestrated the entire fiasco for his own amusement.

Harry said nothing. He just sat there, morose. Contributing nothing. When Fran looked him in the eye, he dropped his gaze. She'd walked out then. Alone.

She toyed with the idea of locking herself in her room for the duration. She could stay there by herself until help arrived from the outside world and sanity was finally restored. But the urge to find Jonathan was stronger. She had to find out the truth. No matter what it was. Just as she started walking, the bothy door opened.

She turned, watching as Cal stepped into the night beside her.

53

"And then there were three," Marcus said.

Eleanor kept a wary eye on him but said nothing. She could not believe that Cal had gone out looking for Jonathan with Fran. Splitting up what was left of the group was crazy. She couldn't see Harry being of much use if the knife-wielding maniac turned up, and Marcus would most definitely look after number one. He was a dead cert for sacrificing others to save himself.

Fran was off her head when it came to Jonathan, but Cal should have stayed.

Harry hadn't said a word since they had gone. He just sat by the fire, whistling to himself. And very irritating it was. With his saggy jowls and baggy eyes he looked like a faithful old bloodhound about to be shot by its master. He stirred now, in response to Marcus.

"That's not funny," he said.

"What's not?" Eleanor asked.

"*And Then There Were None*. It's an Agatha Christie book," Harry said. "Hazel was a great fan of them."

Eleanor looked away as tears welled in Harry's eyes.

"It's a murder mystery," Marcus said. "With the emphasis on *murder*." He flicked a crumb from the table, blithely ignoring Harry's emotional crisis.

"Of course the original title was changed," Marcus continued, "Considered rather offensive for modern mores. Nevertheless, it's a neat little tale. Ten people on an island. One by one they are bumped off. Strong parallels with our plight, wouldn't you say?"

"Harry's right," Eleanor said. "That isn't funny. Besides, there are four of us here."

Marcus glanced at Archie, lying in his bunk. "Well, yes. Technically you are correct, but given our chum's condition, I don't think he really counts, do you?"

"Of course he counts. Don't be ridiculous.

Marcus shrugged and took a sip of whisky.

"And then there were four," he muttered.

Eleanor shifted in her seat. Then she shifted again. It was no use. Some things could not be denied, and this was one of them.

"I need to go to the loo," she said.

Marcus raised an eyebrow. "Well, you're a big girl. I'm sure you can manage. Go on, off you toddle."

The urge to stab Marcus repeatedly in the heart was strong in Eleanor. Never before had she met someone so profoundly annoying. He was quite simply the most irritating, self-satisfied, sarcastic, creepy, pig-of-a-man she had ever met. But right now she needed him.

"I don't want to go through there on my own."

Marcus laughed. It was a cold, mirthless sound. "You want me to come with you - maybe hold your hand while you peepee?"

"No, not particularly. But I don't want to go through there on my own while Jonathan is on the loose. For all we know he could be hiding through there right now. And if he gets me, you'll be left with just Harry and Archie for protection."

Marcus stared at her for a moment.

"Actually, you have a point. Maybe we should stick together. Harry?"

54

Never had the night appeared so shrouded in gloom. Not a glimmer of moon or starlight penetrated the thick blanket of cloud. Their torch-beams penetrated the dark in pathetic slivers, rendering the surrounding shadows deeper than ever.

Dark upon dark upon dark. No replies to their repeated calls. Just the sound of the wind and the sea and of boots squelching over wet ground, and of their own breathing.

An ache had spread across Fran's shoulders. The kind that made it painful to stand up straight, even more uncomfortable to slouch. There was no respite from it. Stress pain. Anxiety pain. The pain of exhaustion and fear and sheer and utter helplessness.

"Fran, wait up."

She turned to face Cal. Not wanting to stop. Thinking the only thing keeping her going was the force of her own movement.

"This is pointless," he said. "We're getting nowhere."

She sagged. "You're right," she said. "Jonathan could be anywhere. So could Hazel."

"Or Gemma."

"Or Gemma," she echoed.

Not wanting to think about Gemma. Not wanting to listen to the insistent nagging inside herself. The persistent voice that said yeah, maybe Jonathan did have something to do with Gemma's disappearance.

The thought was disloyal. More than that, it frightened Fran. If she had been so wrong about Jonathan, then what else had she got wrong? How could she ever trust herself about anything?

She was in the dark on a whole stack of levels.

"There's nothing useful we can do out here," Cal said.

"Let's go back. You never know, maybe some or all of them are already back there waiting for us."

Fran wasn't sure she had it in her to get back. She was empty. But she put one foot in front of the other and kept on going. She didn't think Jonathan, Hazel or Gemma were going to be waiting for them. Especially not Gemma. She doubted if Cal really expected any of them to be there either. It was just something to say.

But then, what did she know?

"Almost there," Cal said. "It'll be okay, you know. We'll get through this."

Fran was suddenly very grateful for his calm and steady presence.

As they approached the bothy, Cal naturally started heading for the door.

"No, wait a minute," Fran said. She had stopped and was staring at the black mass of the copse.

"What is it?"

"I think we should look in the woods."

"Why?"

"I'm not sure. I just want to take a look."

She started towards them, ideas forming in her head. Harry had said that he hadn't been in the woods, that he'd only walked around them. But she'd seen someone *coming out* of the woods. She was sure she had.

The thought that she might be on to something gave her an energy boost. Her heart beat a little faster as she drew close to the dark tangle of trees.

Cal followed behind. "I don't think this is a good idea," he said.

"Just a quick look," she replied.

She was already beyond the first of the gnarled branches.

Plunging through the maze of native species. Birch, ash, willow, hawthorn. Elm, poplar, pine.

Hazel.

55

Eleanor held her breath as Marcus slowly turned the door handle. He glanced at her. She gave the nod. He thrust the door wide open. They filled the bunkroom with torchlight. When nothing jumped out at them, they entered the room, clutching kitchen knives in white knuckled grips.

Marcus checked under the bunks. Clear. Eleanor glanced around the sparsely furnished room. There was no sign of Jonathan and, bar under the bunks, nowhere for him to hide.

Harry shuffled into the room behind her, his lips pursed in a silent whistle. He held a torch in one hand. A wooden rolling pin dangled from the other. He didn't look as if he had it in him to raise it above waist level, let alone use it to defend himself.

They crossed the room to the internal door and repeated the process. Harry was with them in body only. Where his head was at was anyone's guess. If the knife-wielding maniac did pounce, his ass would be mince. Marcus, on the other hand, seemed to be enjoying himself. The guy was just one layer of weird after another.

Eleanor peered over his shoulder. Nobody there, but Norman Bates could be lurking behind any of the doors, or around the corners at the end of the hall.

Marcus opened the doors to the two toilets in quick succession. Both empty. Eleanor glanced at the other doors. She didn't think she could hang on until they'd checked them all out.

She looked at Marcus. "I'm desperate," she said.

"Go on then."

"Will you wait outside?"

Having to ask was mortifying, but Marcus nodded without

looking at her. His attention was fixed on the far end of the hall. She glanced, saw nothing. It was now or never. If she hung about any longer she'd end up wetting herself. She slipped into the toilet and bolted the door.

There was nothing in there but a toilet bowl and sink, but she flashed her torch into every corner before sitting it and the knife on the cistern. The thought of Marcus and Harry standing outside listening to her was excruciating, and so she flushed the toilet to mask her own personal sounds.

She tried to flush again when she'd finished, but the cistern hadn't filled up. She worked the handle a few times and managed to pump a bit of water through. It would have to do.

When she opened the door, Marcus moved along the hall to the store-room door without so much as sneering grin.

"Aren't we going back?" she whispered after him.

He spoke over his shoulder at her. "We may as well check everything out while we're here."

She followed him, while Harry trailed behind in a catatonic state. He wasn't going to be much use if they had to defend themselves.

Marcus paused at the store, listening at the door for a moment before thrusting it open and checking inside. It was empty, as was the shower room.

They crept along the hall to the T-junction. They stopped, listening for any clues that someone was lurking around the corner. Breathing, a creak, a rattle, the sound of light footsteps, of material rasping. There was nothing.

Marcus and Eleanor gave each other the nod and jumped out, torches sweeping, knives raised.

The corridor was empty. They grinned at each other. Comrades in arms. An alliance borne of a common enemy. And there, in front of them, the door leading to the room Eleanor had shared with Rob.

She hadn't been there since this morning. Back when Rob was

still alive. Planning his proposal. Planning his life, his future. And all she was thinking of was how soon she could dump him. An end. Not a beginning.

That morning was a lifetime ago. Now Rob was dead, and his mother didn't even know it. Nobody outside of the island did. Not his sister, not his friends, nor his colleagues.

Marcus approached the door. Something thudded in the room. Marcus jumped like he'd been electrocuted. He turned to Eleanor, ashen faced. Eyes wide behind his glasses, his mouth open, breathing sour whisky fumes on her.

They stared at each other. Locked in ear-straining, gut-clenching, terror.

Another bang. Eleanor clutched on to Marcus. Felt him trembling beneath her grasp. His alcohol-fueled bravado had evaporated, leaving him as exposed and defenceless as a snail without a shell. He was even more scared than she was. A realisation that did not make her feel any better.

Another bang.

Marcus jerked in response. Eleanor let go of his arm.

"The window," she said. "I left it open."

"You sure?"

She nodded and opened the door. They flashed their torches inside. Right on cue, the window swung on its hinges and banged against the wall. Marcus rolled his eyes at Eleanor. She grinned. He broke out in a rash of relieved giggles. She joined in until they were laughing like they were having the time of their lives.

Their merriment was brought to an abrupt halt by an explosive scream.

"What the hell was that?"

"Outside, come on."

Eleanor ran down the hall to the external door, Marcus right behind her. She looked over her shoulder as she yanked it open.

"Where's Harry?"

Marcus looked around. "I don't know."

They flashed their torches around but there was no sign of the man.

From outside, another scream. It whipped through the night, stinging Eleanor's nerves. If anything it was more piercing than the last. She looked at Marcus.

"The woods," he said.

56

The sound of her own scream was still ringing in Fran's ears when Cal tugged at her sleeve.

"Don't look," he said.

"Get off."

She pulled away from him and approached the body. Maybe it was the shock of the find. At first glance, Fran hadn't been entirely sure of what she was looking at. Only that it was bad. Bad enough to be worth screaming at. Or maybe it was the way the corpse's face was so hideously distorted. Whichever, or both, there was no doubt now. Fran had found Hazel.

She was lying on her back. Dumped behind a fallen tree. Her bulging eyes staring at bare branches she could not see. Her tongue, black and swollen, protruded from her mouth. It looked obscene. Around her throat was a cruel necklace of stark bruises. Her death had been brutal.

"Oh, Hazel," Fran whispered. "Who would do such a thing?"

She turned to Cal but when she saw his face the words dried up in her mouth. He looked up from Hazel and stared at her, a strange look on his face. A quiver ran under his skin, as if he was trying to get his expression under control. Trying to cover up.

"Oh no," she said, her words barely audible.

Cal's eyes widened as he understood her meaning. He shook his head. "No - I didn't-"

"It was you," Fran said. "It was you, not Harry, coming out of the woods. You - you killed Hazel."

"No, it wasn't like that - you don't understand."

Cal reached out to her. One hand clutching his torch, the other palm up, imploring her to believe him.

She looked at his open hand, at his long, strong fingers, then back at his face.

"You strangled her with your bare hands and then you cooked us pasta."

Fran's voice rose as she spoke.

"Please Fran, you have to let me explain."

"Hazel's dead, you killed her - what the hell else is there to explain?"

Screaming at him.

Cal moved towards her. She stepped back.

"No. Don't you come near me."

"Please Fran..."

57

Archie heard the grinding scrape of a chair leg on the stone floor. Sometime later, maybe only seconds later, he felt a warm weight on his bare shoulder. He opened his eyes. It was Harry. Harry sitting beside him, his hand on Archie's shoulder. Harry was touching him, but he wasn't looking at Archie. He was looking at something Archie couldn't see. Archie closed his eyes.

He wondered if Harry had come to finish the job his wife had started. If that was the case, he was likely to be more successful than Hazel. There was no fight in him now. He had about as much strength left in him as an over-dunked tea biscuit and was just as likely to disintegrate.

He'd been floating in and out of consciousness all day. He hadn't managed to grasp everything that had gone on, but he'd worked out that Hazel had poisoned him. That had been a mistake, which, for reasons that were beyond him, she had tried to make up for by smothering him. To think, she'd seemed like such a pleasant wee woman. Eat your heart out Lizzie Borden.

Cal had yelled at him about batteries but that too had been beyond him. There had been a lot of yelling. A lot of noise. People coming and going. Voices. Talking. Arguing. A lot of arguing. Words he couldn't follow. It was all too hard. His head hurt. He had brain-ache. But it had been quiet for a while. Until that is, Harry had scraped the chair and laid his hand upon him.

It had felt warm at first, but now it was hot and sweaty. And it was too heavy. He'd have liked Harry to get it off him, to unhand him, but he couldn't summon the energy to speak. If he had the ability to speak, he would have asked why he was still lying in the bothy when he should so fucking clearly be in hospital.

Archie may have lost the power of speech, but Harry had not. "Something bad happened to Hazel," he said.

Archie fluttered an eyelid. Harry was still staring into space. Archie didn't know if he was being addressed, or if the man was talking to himself.

"It's all my fault," Harry said. He droned on about some woman he'd been having an affair with. Harry having an affair. Who'd have thought? Archie listened as Harry mumped on. It wasn't as if he had any choice in the matter. He wasn't going anywhere. He didn't have the energy to tell Harry to shut up or get a life or ask him where the bloody helicopter was.

Archie's body was going nowhere, but his mind drifted off a couple of times. Even so, he got the gist of Harry's tale. It was a confessional. Hazel was angry with Harry. So angry, she had tried to poison him, but Archie had ended up with the bad curry. Harry blamed himself for the state Archie was in and for what had happened to Hazel. And so, thought Archie, he fucking-well should.

As Harry unburdened himself, Archie thought that this is what it must be like to be a priest. If he'd had the strength he would have laughed at that. Father Archie. Aye, right. Ten Hail Marys and a kick up the arse for you, Harry boy.

"I'm sorry. I'm so sorry," Harry snivelled.

He squeezed Archie's shoulder as if to impress on him just how really fucking sorry he was. It hurt like a bastard.

I'll give you sorry, Archie thought. He cranked an eyelid open. Harry was crying now. What the actual fuck did he have to cry about? Archie was the one with his insides melting like an Orange fucking Mivvi on a hot day. Archie was the one being punished for Harry getting his end away. Fucking cheek. Sitting there with snot dripping off the end of his nose.

Crying like a big fucking squonk.

58

Fran crashed through the undergrowth. She had to get back to the bothy. Warn the others. Cal was a killer.

Something came at her. It loomed out of the trees. She let out a scalding scream and skidded to a halt in front of it. It reached out to her. Fran gasped. Screaming beyond her now. Whatever it was, it wasn't Cal. He was thrashing about in the woods behind her. Calling her name. Trying to get her. She tensed as the creature in front of her trailed a bloodied finger down her cheek.

"Fran, it's me."

She peered at the thing, looking beyond its splattered nose, beyond the blood and muck it was smeared in.

"Jonathan?"

"Yes, Fran baby, it's me."

"Oh, thank God."

He slid his hand around to the back of her head and tilted her face towards his so that their foreheads were touching. They stood like that for a moment. She closed her eyes and let out a small groan. Just for a second she could relax. Jonathan was with her. Somehow everything would be sorted out now. The mess, the accusations, the mix-up. All would be resolved.

"Easy now," he said.

His voice was thick. As if he had a cold. The result of his splattered nose. Eleanor had kicked him. She'd panicked in the dark, that was all. Easy thing to do. Panic.

Fran opened her eyes. She was looking down. Her torch illuminating moss, twigs, old leaves... the small, blood-encrusted blade dangling from Jonathan's hand. She pulled away from him.

"Jonathan, why-"

Her question was cut off by Cal calling her name again. He was nearby. Almost upon them. She turned. Saw his torch glinting through the trees.

"Who is it?" Jonathan demanded. "Who's after you?"

"It's Cal."

He emerged from the trees behind them, stopping when he saw Jonathan.

"Fran are you okay?" he asked.

"Don't you speak to her," Jonathan snarled.

"He killed Hazel," Fran said.

"Fran, you've got to listen to me. It's not the way you think -"

"I told you not to speak to her," Jonathan said.

He pushed Fran aside and went to the other man.

Jonathan was limping. His leg bound in material Fran recognised as his t-shirt. Questions, so many questions hurtling through her mind. He'd been so tender. Was trying to protect her. But the knife - his face -

The two men eyeballed each other.

"Put the knife down," Cal said.

"I'll put you down first."

Cal threw his torch at Jonathan's face. Jonathan flinched. Cal grabbed hold of his wrist and tried to prise the knife out of his hand. Jonathan punched Cal on the side of the head. Fran screamed at them to stop. Cal bit Jonathan's hand.

"Bastard vampire!" Jonathan yelled.

He battered a series of short punches into Cal's head.

Cal leaned into him. They toppled. Crashing into a bush. Fran watched in horror as they rolled to the ground, grunting and grappling. Snarling like dogs in a slum. Each trying to knock lumps out of the other.

"What the hell?"

Fran whirled around at the sudden voice in her ear. It was Marcus. Eleanor by his side.

"What's going on - are you okay?" Eleanor asked.

"Does it look as though I'm okay? No, I am not okay. Nothing is okay. Cal killed Hazel. Nice guy Cal killed Hazel. And Jonathan is carrying a knife just like you said, so no I am not okay."

The words spilled out of her in a torrent, one on top of the other.

"Cal?" Eleanor said. "I don't-"

"Don't dare tell me you don't believe it," Fran screamed at her. "Don't you dare."

"Come on, let's get out of here," Marcus said.

"What about them?" Eleanor asked.

"The hell with them, let's go."

Jonathan let out a screeching howl. Eleanor and Marcus flicked the beams of their torches on him. Illuminating the scene in time to see him plunge a knife into Cal's neck. Cal's mouth gaped open. His hands went to his neck. A fountain of blood spurted from the wound. Too much to hold back.

Jonathan let out a holler of victory.

Marcus grabbed Fran by the arm.

"Jesus fuck, let's go."

59

Harry stood up, managing to knock over his chair in the process. Archie took a peek at him and wished he hadn't. Harry's face was bright pink and awash with tears and snot. It was no way for a grown man to behave. Especially not with an audience. Then again, as far as Harry knew, Archie was out of the game. For all intents and purposes he was on his own.

It was still no way to behave.

Harry stormed out of the bothy. Who knew what that was about.

Archie was on his own again. Maybe just as well. There was some weird business going on in these here parts and he was better off out of it.

They all thought he was dying. Maybe he was. Maybe he wasn't. And if he wasn't, maybe it was better if they all thought he was. The way things were going, the only safe place to be was in his stinky bunk. He was beginning to think that if he wanted to get what was left of his sorry arse off this island, then his best chance was to play dead. Or at least unconscious. Shouldn't be too hard. He didn't exactly have a lot of energy for doing anything else.

He was still mulling over these thoughts when the door slammed open and Fran and that fucker Marcus tumbled into the room. Archie squinted through half-closed eyes as Marcus bolted the door behind them. Time to settle down for the next instalment of who-knew-what-the-fuck.

60

"What about Eleanor?" Fran asked.

"If she shows up we'll let her in - until that happens, this door stays locked."

Locked in a room with Marcus. Fran turned away from him before her feelings showed on her face.

The room was a mess. It was a mess and she was locked in it alone with Marcus. Being outside was beginning to feel like a better option. No, it was crazy out there. The world had gone mad. Besides they weren't entirely alone. There was Archie.

She righted the upturned chair by his bunk and took a peek at him. He was sleeping. Peacefully, it seemed. For a moment she almost envied him. For now at least, he was out of the nightmare.

She looked at Marcus. Caught him watching her. She shivered. Couldn't help herself.

"Where's Harry?" she asked.

"I don't know. He disappeared before we went to the woods. Are you cold? You look cold." he stepped towards her.

"The fire's almost out," she said.

He glanced at it, then back at Fran.

"I'll soon get it going, then we'll be as snug as two bugs in a rug."

His smile made the hairs on her arms stand up. She moved out of his way as he went to the fire. Stepping back as he came forward. They were locked in a dance. Predator and prey, waltzing.

He busied himself, stoking and poking. Good idea, keeping busy. Fran fetched the dustpan and brush. She'd scooped up most of the mess from earlier, but some small shards of crockery remained. Tiny sharp slivers, mixed with traces of sauce, pieces of congealed pasta, muck and mire trailed in from outside. All the good housekeeping rules gone to hell.

As she swept, she broke the skin which had formed on the spilled sauce. Smeared by the nylon hairs of the brush, the sweet pungent aroma of tomatoes and garlic was released. It had been a simple sauce, but very good. Cooked by a killer.

How could Cal have stood there, slicing onions, simmering pasta, knowing what he'd done to Hazel? How could he just carry on like that? But that's what murderers did, wasn't it? They killed and then they carried on as normal. And the neighbours always said, *but he seemed like such a pleasant man.*

When she was done clearing the floor, Fran started on the splattered mess Eleanor had left on the table. One by one, she peeled off pieces of rubbery cold pasta and flicked them into the bowl. *Peel, flick. Peel, flick.* Where was Eleanor anyway? Fran had thought she was with them. Following them back to the bothy. She hoped Eleanor was okay. *Peel, flick.*

"Leave that," Marcus said. "Come and sit by the fire. Come on, you look exhausted."

"I feel exhausted."

She felt like an empty shell. She looked at the fire Marcus had built up. It would be good to just sit down for a while and enjoy the warmth.

"Up to you," he said.

He settled in the armchair. Fran shrugged and sat on the sofa. Him over there. Her here. Almost immediately, she began to doze. Twice her head jerked forward. Twice she snapped awake, but the urge to sleep was irresistible. She pulled one of the limp cushions towards her and did her best to plump it up. She laid her head on it and pulled up her feet. She closed her eyes and fell asleep listening to the comforting crackle and spark of the fire.

61

Eleanor hesitated when Fran scarpered with Marcus. It seemed plain wrong to abandon Cal when he was injured, no matter what he'd done. If he'd done anything. She didn't believe he'd killed Hazel. He wasn't the type. Then again, last night Jonathan, hadn't seemed the type either.

Cal slumped forward. His head thudded onto the ground, face twisted towards her. Not injured. Dead. Jonathan stood over him. He nudged Cal's head with the toe of his boot.

"Murdering bastard," he muttered.

Eleanor stepped back. Time to leave.

Jonathan slowly turned his head and stared at her. There was a craze in his eyes.

Eleanor realised she had made a big mistake. She should have run when she'd had the chance.

Jonathan narrowed his eyes. "You," he growled.

He looked at her like he was ready to rip out her throat with his teeth. She tightened her grip on the kitchen knife. He turned towards her. Decision time. Fight or flight. He was wounded, the bandage on his leg dripping blood, but he was pumped up and ready for action. If she turned, he'd be on her back. The knife would be in her neck.

She let out a glass-shattering holler and sprang at him. His eyes widened. Surprise, surprise, killer boy. She was on him before he'd drawn breath. She clenched her teeth and jabbed the knife into the wound on his thigh.

She'd meant to stab him. Stab him hard. But she couldn't let herself go. Didn't have the stomach for driving the knife right into his leg. Jonathan screamed, even though she'd pulled up short. He screamed like a banshee, his mouth a twisted black hole.

Eleanor jabbed his leg again. This time stabbing the knife into him. Jonathan roared. She pulled out the knife and punched him in the chest with her torch. He staggered back. Tripped. Landed in a heap.

This time she wasn't about to hang around.

"Stabbing bitch!"

Jonathan's words screamed through the air behind her. He was down for now, but not for long, she feared. He had the energy of a madman. Fury spurting through his veins, invigorating him. It was Eleanor's hard luck that all that vitriol was now focused on her.

Whip thin branches lashed at her face. In the daylight it had seemed like a small wood. In the dark, it had magnified to a forest. She stumbled this way and that, with no idea of direction. Jonathan's screaming sent the chills through her, but as long as he kept it up, she knew she was getting away from him.

Her foot caught on a root. She stumbled. Got caught in a coil of bramble, thick with thorns. It snagged at her trousers, ripping the material, scratching her skin. She tried to keep on running but became more ensnared. The thorns digging deep into her flesh. She had to stop. Gingerly peel the bramble from her legs. All the while looking around nervously. Terrified that Jonathan would find her while she was trapped.

Thorns caught in her hands. Pierced her skin. Pricked into the tender skin under her nails. Jonathan's howls spurred her on. Ignoring the pain, she freed herself and ran on. Seconds later she was clear of the trees.

She stopped running. Caught her breath. Tried to orientate herself. She flashed her torch around and figured that she was on the opposite side of the trees from the bothy. If she skirted around the copse she would find her way back.

Jonathan howled from within the woods.

"*Bitch*!"

The same word Rob had used against her. he sounded angry, but at least wasn't close. She half-trotted, half-limped in what she hoped was the right direction.

She had to get to the bothy. Get inside. Bolt the door. Then what? Wait for help to come? What help? Stop asking questions. keep moving. Got to be better off n there than out here with the howling madman.

A strange sound. She slowed down, tilted her head, listening hard. Stopped, listened harder. There it was again. A kind of snuffling. The kind of sound a small mammal might make. Definitely not Jonathan. It was a strange noise but not alarming. She whizzed the torch around, expecting to catch the gleam of two small eyes. Maybe a hedgehog. The light shot by something pale. She jerked the torch back.

"Owww!" A wail of protest. Not a small furry creature, a person.

"Get that light out of my eyes."

"Sorry." She dropped the beam.

Harry dropped his arms from his face. "You shouldn't go around blinding people like that. It's not right." He looked past her, into the woods. The lines in his face were etched dark and deep. His eyes were red and swollen from crying. Snot ran from his nose.

Despite all the evidence to the contrary, she asked him if he was okay.

"I have to find Hazel."

It hit Eleanor like a brick. He didn't know. The poor sod didn't know that his wife was dead.

"Harry - don't go in there. Come to the bothy with me."

"I have to find Hazel."

"Please Harry - it's not safe - we have to go to the bothy."

"*Bitch!*"

Jonathan. Closer now. Sounding like a wild animal. Harry cocked his head, listening to the disturbance.

"Please Harry - we have to move. Now."

Harry walked by her like she didn't exist. Jonathan was getting closer. Harry wasn't listening. Eleanor gave him up as a bad job.

It was every woman for herself.

62

There was nothing Archie liked better than an open fire. Marcus had stoked up a blaze Auld Nick would be proud of. The heat was luxurious, bringing comfort to Archie in his dank bunk. He turned his face towards the warmth, as a flower turns towards the sun. He closed his eyes, taking pleasure from the crackle, spit and hiss of the logs.

It wasn't long before unconsciousness once again enveloped him in a black, velvet embrace.

63

Eleanor reached the gable end of the building, Jonathan howling behind her. He sounded close. Too close. She had to get inside. Get a locked door between them. She ran on, hoping it was her imagination at work and that she could not actually feel his hot breath blistering the skin on the back of her neck.

The door was lying wide open, the way she and Marcus had left it. She went inside, ready to swing it shut, when she paused. Marcus and Fran - they'd be in the kitchen at the other end of the building. She didn't want to be locked in here by herself. Safety in numbers. She should be in the bothy.

She was going to check if the way was clear when she heard the pounding of feet on flagstones. The gait uneven. As if the runner had a wounded leg. She closed the door. Threw down the knife. Fumbled at the key. Her fingers were stiff with cold. She could not get them to work properly. Jonathan slammed into the other side of door. She yelped. The handle moving. Him, trying to get in. If he got inside, she was dead.

She grasped the key with numb fingers. Turned it. The tumblers fell into place. The sound of safety in a small click. She leaned against the door, fingers still grasping the small piece of metal that was keeping the lunatic at bay.

Realising the door was locked against him, Jonathan hollered. He yanked at the handle, pressing it up and down making it squeak and creak. The end of the handle on the inside banged against her knuckles. She let go of the key, put her fist to her mouth. All went quiet. The assault had ceased. Eleanor pressed her ear against the door, listening. Nothing. Maybe he'd given up.

She let out a long breath. Just as she thought she was safe for now, there was a huge thud on the other side of the door. She squealed and dropped the torch. It bounced and cut out, leaving her in the dark.

The door was solid wood. He'd dislocate his shoulder before breaking through, but he wasn't going to give in easily. He screeched through it at her.

"Bitch. I know you're in there!"

He pounded and kicked the door. Told her what he was going to do when he got his hands on her. Screamed that it was all her fault. His voice scraped and scratched at the inside of her head. His voice, the words he used, scared her. He'd dehumanised her. Made her a thing he was going to hunt down and destroy.

She covered her ears with her hands and slid down the door until she was sitting on the floor. He kept on banging. Beating a madman's tattoo. Every thump, every bang, smack and bash reverberated through her body. She sat in a tight ball, cold, damp and shivering. He went on and on banging and hollering, but as long as he did, she knew where he was. She knew she was safe.

64

Someone was raising a din outside. Archie opened his eyes. What the hell was going on now? It was a high-pitched racket. Screaming and squealing. But it sounded like a bloke. Not Harry. A younger man. Jonathan or Cal then.

Not Cal. Surely not. It had to be that Jonathan one. Yeah, that made sense. Archie had marked his card as being a queer bastard. Not queer in the sense of being homosexual. Queer in the old-school style. Weird. Odd. Peculiar as fuck. He'd been after that one - what's-her-face? The one with the make-up and nails. She liked the red wine. Eleanor, that was it. Eleanor - he'd been after her.

She said that Jonathan thought she was Gemma. But Gemma was gone. Gone baby gone. Gone where? Maybe the bogey man had got her.

All that banging and hollering - it wasn't a good sign. Someone should do something about it. Archie peeked at Marcus. He was sitting in the armchair, calm as you like. As if he couldn't hear a thing. Archie began to think he was suffering from auditory hallucinations. Everything else in his body was buggered. Why not his hearing?

He covered his ears with his hands. No noise. He uncovered his ears. Noise. Archie repeated the experiment. The results were the same. His hearing was not buggered. Someone really was kicking up a stooshie out there. So why was Marcus sitting there doing nothing?

Archie watched Marcus for a while longer. After a short time he realised that Marcus was not doing nothing. Marcus was in fact staring at Fran. Watching her as she slept. Drinking her in with his eyes.

The din outside stopped. Marcus gave no indication that he noticed the sudden lack of commotion. All of his attention was on Fran.

He was looking at her the way a hungry dog might eye up a butcher's counter. The man was practically drooling. And there was Fran, all curled up. Unawares and completely vulnerable. It gave Archie the heebie-jeebies watching him watching her. He wanted to do something. But what? It was taking every ounce of energy he had just to keep on breathing.

65

Eleanor uncovered her ears and listened. The noise had stopped. She pressed her ear against the door. Still nothing. Maybe he'd given up.

She groped around for the torch. Knocked her hand against it. Sent it rolling further away. She followed the sound, shuffling forward on her knees, fingers reaching into the dark until she found it again. She grasped it tightly and felt for the switch, whispering *please, please*, as she pressed it. She did not want to be alone in the dark.

The light came on. *Thank you.* She saw the knife. Picked it up, staring at the blood smeared on the blade. Jonathan's blood. Thick, sticky, dark. She could hardly believe she'd stabbed him. Not once, but *twice*. She'd pulled up short the first time. Didn't have the stomach for it. But when it came down to it, she did it again. The second time she'd felt it go in. Felt it cutting him.

Her hand shook at the thought. She dropped the knife. She screwed up her face, looking at the blade with disgust. Then she thought about Jonathan. About what he'd done to Cal. And about what he'd do to her if he got the chance.

No. She was not going to let that happen. She would do whatever it took to survive. She would not die on this miserable island.

Eleanor picked up the knife. She studied the congealing blood for a moment before wiping the blade on her trousers. By the time it was clean her hands had stopped shaking.

She had not liked being shrouded in darkness, but there was precious little comfort to be had from the torch's small pool of light. Shadows pressed in from all sides, threatening to overwhelm the weak beam.

Lack of light was not the only thing preying on her nerves. The silence ensuing after Jonathan's onslaught turned out to be not much of a silence after all. Small sounds seeped out of the dark. Each one of them icing her spine, increasing her unease. A creak that was hardly there. An odd little click. A soft groan. The building settling, that was all. Yes. No. Footsteps in the hall? Couldn't be.

Slowly, trying not to make a sound herself, she stood up. The darkness could click and groan at her all it wanted, but she was not going to bite. No sirree. She would simply slip outside, nice and easy. Then, quiet as you like, she'd nip along to the other end of the building where there were people and light and safety.

She wrapped her fingers around the key. Ready to turn it. To unlock the door. But what if Jonathan was trying to trick her? What if he was out there all this time, patiently waiting? She steps outside thinking he's gone and bam! He's on her like a fox on a hen. She pulled back, not knowing what to do. There was no way of telling if he was there or not, not without sticking her head outside for a look-see.

Not without risking her life.

66

Fran groaned and shifted on the sofa. She was in the midway zone between being asleep and being awake. The state of sleep had been so delicious, she wanted to sink back into it. Let it fold her into itself. Jonathan, she had been dreaming about Jonathan. He was beside her, touching her, caressing her. The world had been righted. The dream was real. Everything else was false.

If only she could go with it. Let herself believe this was true. If you believed something strongly enough, could you make it so? No, she couldn't kid herself like that. Even in this delirious half-state between the sleeping and waking worlds, she couldn't kid herself. The world had not been righted.

Images of Jonathan's snarling face flashed through her mind. And of Cal's, twisted in agonised surprise. Clutching at the wound in his throat. Powerless to stop his blood spurting into the cold, dark air.

Those images were the reality. And this: someone really was touching her. And if it wasn't Jonathan, then who?

She opened her eyes. Caught her breath. Marcus's face was only a few inches from her own. One side in shadow, the other illuminated by firelight. He was close. So close she could see his scalp through his receding hair and the open pores on the side of his nose. His forehead had a greasy sheen. He was kneeling in front of the sofa, staring at her intently as he used one hand to stroke her hair and face, the other to grope its way around her body.

"It's okay," he said.

She winced at the sour smell of alcohol on his breath. He pushed his hand in between her thighs and rubbed it hard up against her.

Fran jerked out of the horrified trance she'd been in.

"What are you-?"

He clamped his hand over her mouth, suffocating her words. Panic flared and exploded inside her. She pulled at his arm and twisted her head, trying to get his hand off her face. He pressed down harder. He pulled his other hand from between her thighs and worked at the button on her trousers. She tried to fight him off. Punching and kicking.

"Don't be difficult now," he said, his voice low, controlled.

He swung himself onto the sofa. Used the weight of his body to pin her down. She felt his hand working at her trousers again. A moment later the button popped free. The skin of her belly was exposed as he pulled down the zip. She bucked under him, trying to push him off, twist herself free, but her efforts had little effect. All he had to do to control her was bear down on her with his body weight. He had about twelve kilos plus gravity on his side and she couldn't do a thing about it.

There was no chance of her kneeing him in the groin or gouging at his eyes. She bit at the hand he had clamped on her mouth. The salty taste of his sweaty skin made her want to vomit, but she kept on gnawing at him until he shifted his hand roughly up her face so that the V between his thumb and forefinger was jammed against her nostrils. Her eyes rolled as she tried to get a breath.

"Now you listen to me you little prick-tease." He spoke with his mouth pressed against her ear, his breath hot. His dry lips scraping her skin. "I don't want to hurt you, but I will if I have to. Do you understand?"

She gave a short nod.

"Good girl."

He eased his hand from her nose so that she could breathe.

She took in small snatches of air, breathing in his stale breath. She concentrated on controlling her breathing. Steadying herself. Panicking was no use. Hyperventilating was no use.

Keeping one hand over her mouth, he pushed the other inside her pants. Her face flushed, burning hot with shame and embarrassment.

She breathed in sharply as his fingers probed roughly between her legs. She tried to pull away from him, but she was pinned down tight. There was nowhere for her to go. Tears of anger and humiliation welled in her eyes. Marcus pressed his mouth against her ear, grunting as he pushed his fingers inside her.

"Easy now." He licked the side of her face. "You know you want it so just relax and enjoy it."

He pulled his hand from between her legs and trailed his fingers under her nose. She squirmed. "You smell that?" he asked. "Do you smell that? Cunt, Fran. Wet, juicy, cunt. Nothing else in the world smells like that."

He made a show of sniffing his fingers, closing his eyes and breathing in deeply. When he opened them again, they were cold and hard. He looked at her like he hated her.

"That's foreplay over, Fran, let's get down to business."

She tried to scream as he yanked down her trousers, but her cries were suffocated by his hand. Even if she could call out, there was no-one to hear her. No-one but Marcus, and he was going to rape her.

67

Eleanor heard a sound from the other side of the door. A soft scrape. It wasn't much but it was enough to convince her that she'd been right to be cautious. Jonathan was lying in wait for her. He was sneaky alright, but that was okay. She could do sneaky too.

There was a reason he was staying put. A reason he knew she was there. Eleanor sat the torch on the floor beside the door. As long as there was a chink of light getting through, he would stay put. Waiting for her.

Moving as silently as possible, Eleanor moved away from the door. She would slink along the corridor to the bunk room and from there she would flee to the safety of the bothy. Sure, she'd have to go outside to get there, but it was only a few short feet from one door to the other, and Jonathan couldn't be everywhere. Psychopath he may be, but he was still a man, and a man could only be in one place at a time.

Once she turned the corner, she'd be feeling her way in the dark. She glanced back at the torch. At the comforting light it gave. But better to give up the light than alert him to the fact that she was on the move.

Her teeth chittered. Partly nerves, but mostly because she was so cold. Her clothes were damp. Chafing her skin. The room she'd shared with Rob was right in front of her. She could nip in there before heading down the dark hall. It wouldn't take a minute. She was only a few feet away from warm, dry clothes. No point in surviving the maniac to die of pneumonia. Even if she just changed her top half she'd feel warmer. So much warmer.

She peeked around the corner. The hall was still and dark. She was loathe to leave the security of the wall, but clinging to it wouldn't do her any good. Deep breath. Two quick steps and she had crossed the void to the opposite corner. No stopping now. Straight into the bedroom.

It did not take her long to find a rucksack by touch. She took it to the open door. The light from the torch barely penetrated this far, but there was enough illumination for her to see that she had picked up Rob's bag. No matter. She felt inside and pulled out a few of items of clothing. Among them was some kind of thermal t-shirt and a fleece top. Perfect.

She quickly stripped down to her bra and put on the dry clothes. The effects were immediate. She no longer felt like a shivering wreck. She thought about changing her trousers too, but no, time to get moving. She picked up the knife. All she had to do now was get to the bothy.

She crept back to the T-junction, wondering if she should have taken the time to look for a spare torch in Rob's bag. Too late now. No going back. Just move, move, move.

A loud, rumbling, noise stopped her dead. She froze, eyes wide, back of her neck prickling. The sound was coming along the long, dark hall from the bunkroom. It grew louder. It's source approaching. Eleanor stepped back. A rolling pin trundled into view. She jumped as it clattered against the wall. Stared at it as it rolled to a halt. Harry had been carrying it. Now someone had spun it along the hall, and she did not think that someone was Harry.

She backed into the bedroom.

Footsteps in the hall.

Hide. She had to hide. There was no place for her to go but under the bunks. He'd know she was there. But no choice. Either that or face him. She'd got the better of him twice already. Had no stomach for it now. She was scared. No fight. it was all about flight. She got down on her belly. Squirmed under the bunk until she was tight up against the wall, side of her face flat on the floor. Choking on mildew. Breathing in dead spiders and dust. Straining to hear.

Silence. Nothing but the sound of her own breathing. Too heavy, too loud. Booming out. She'd be as well yelling, *I'm in here. Come and get me psycho boy.*

A sudden noise. She tensed. Scraped her shoulders on the bedsprings above. Trundle, trundle. The rolling pin again. Echoing. Then silence. She listened so hard she thought her ears would burst. Footsteps. Yes, footsteps. Retreating. Moving further away. Yes. Relief. Maybe. He. Would. Just. Go. Away.

Yeah, right. In your dreams.

Eleanor's fingers tightened around the knife handle as the footsteps came closer. A beam of light splayed into the room. Her torch. He'd picked it up. That had been the footsteps retreating. But not now. Now they were up close and personal. She tried to press further back into the wall. Tried to sink into it. Become part of it. But it was made of stone and she was flesh and blood. Eleanor had gone as far as she could.

He flashed the light around the room. She should never have backed herself into a corner like this. But what else could she have done? Where could she have gone? It wasn't like in the movies. There were no handy air ducts she could wriggle into. No trapdoors leading to tunnels. It was just a small, smelly room. Unless she could fold herself up small enough to fit in one of the drawers, she was hiding in the only hiding place there was. Which meant it wasn't anyplace to hide at all.

The boots walked alongside the bunk. She clutched the knife so tight it felt as though her knuckles were going to split her skin.

Maybe she could stab him in the foot. But she had no room to manoeuvre. No space to work up enough force to penetrate the thick leather.

The boots stopped level with her face. So close she could

smell the mud trapped in the deep treads of the soles. The smell gave her a flashback of lying sprawled on the clifftop. She held her breath, waiting for him to duck down and see her trapped there, like a rabbit in a snare. Waiting for his lean, grinning face to appear.

Seconds stretched like spun sugar, becoming elongated strands of time. The tension was killing her. He knew she was there. Had to know. He was toying with her. Screwing with her mind. But she'd get him. She had a plan. When he bent down, she'd stab him in the eye. Even if she had to dislocate her shoulder to do it. Push the blade right into his brain. Kill him stone dead. But if she had to do it, she wanted to do it right here. Right now. Wanted it over and done with.

Tension. Impossible tension. Knotting her tendons. Frying her brain. She wanted to cry out. To scream *I know you know I'm here you bastard!* But she kept quiet. And the boots turned and went away.

68

Fran was trapped. Immobilised by the weight of Marcus's body bearing down on her. She could barely breathe. Had no room to struggle, to fight back, to inflict damage of any kind. Marcus was going to rape her and there was nothing she could do about it.

Perhaps if she relaxed, gave into him, it would hurt less. She could not save her body, but if she withdrew from the situation, perhaps she could save her mind.

She closed her eyes. Her chest was constricted by his weight, but she inhaled as deeply as she could. Better if she could breathe out through her mouth, but his hand was still covering it. No matter. Do what you can. Air in. Air out.

Fran sank into herself. She could no longer smell the sweat curdling on his skin. The product dripping from his hair. His rancid breath. She could not hear him grunting. His muttered obscenities were a distant drone. Could not feel him mauling her. Trying to get inside her. She was far away. In a place, dark and blank. A place of nothingness.

Fran was suddenly jerked back to the here and now. She opened her eyes as Marcus screamed. His body jolted. Went into a spasm. He stiffened before slumping on her. Unconscious. His dead weight suffocating her.

Seizure. He'd had a seizure. A stroke. Or maybe a heart attack. She pushed at him. Wriggling, shoving and kicking until he rolled and thudded to the floor.

She scrabbled at her pants and trousers, pulling them up, fastening them, thinking that whatever had befallen him was better than he deserved. She was on her feet before she noticed Archie standing with the poker in his hand.

"You're naked," she said.

Archie looked down at himself. "So I am." He swayed, looked like he was about to keel over.

Fran stepped over Marcus and took the poker from Archie. She put her arm around him and helped him to the armchair.

"Sit there," she said. "Don't move."

She pulled the sleeping bag from Marcus's bunk, unzipped it and wrapped it around Archie. He gave her a crumpled grin. It wasn't up to his usual standards, but it was a big improvement.

"I thought you..."

"Were going to die?" he finished. "It's okay," he said. "So did I." His voice was raspy.

"Would you like some water?"

Archie nodded. She fetched him a glass. Told him to sip it slowly. When he'd had all he could take, she took it from him and knelt in front of him. She felt his forehead. It was clammy, but not feverish.

"How are you feeling?"

"I'm still alive and right now, that will do."

"Archie?"

"Yeah?"

"Thank you."

"It's okay," he said. "I knew I'd get the bastard."

Fran went over to Marcus's prone body. She stood over him, staring down for a moment before giving him a sharp kick in the ribs. He groaned but did not move.

69

Eleanor slumped as the footsteps retreated. It had been a close call. She couldn't believe her luck. She lay for a moment, giving her heart time to slow to a regular rhythm, for the tension in her body to ease, then wriggled across the floor to the edge of the bunk and peered out. There was no light. No sound. He had gone.

She dragged herself from beneath the bed and stood up. Her left arm had been crushed up against the wall, the weight of her body on top of it. Pins and needles tingled and jabbed through it now. She waggled her fingers, trying to shake off the unpleasant sensation, then rolled her shoulders. She was all kinked up.

Loosened off, she stretched out her hand till it touched the wall and felt her way along it to the door and looked out. Total darkness.

It was a different kind of darkness to what she had experienced outside. Nerve-wracking though that had been, being in the fresh air had made a difference. There had been a sense of freedom, of excitement. This was different. Thick and claustrophobic, it felt menacing. As though it would swallow her if she stepped into it and never release her.

She'd never been scared of the dark before, now she leaned against the doorframe, feeling sick and light-headed. She had to fight the childish urge to climb into one of the bunks and hide her head under a pillow. But what if he came back? What then? She had to go on. Had to get to the safe place at the other end of the building. People and light. That was the plan. She did not want to be on her own in the dark anymore.

Feeling her way along the wall, she stepped into the hall.

It was okay. Just one foot in front of the other.

One step.

Two steps.

Three steps.

Her foot hit something. Eleanor caught her breath. A familiar trundling sound thundered through the dark. A rash of sweat broke out over her body. A trap. He'd set a trap. Turn. Turn now. Lock yourself in the bedroom.

A click killed the dark. Before she could turn, she was blinded by a dazzling light.

A voice - Jonathan's voice - came from behind the light.

"Hello, Eleanor."

70

"Where's Cal?" Archie asked.

He was sitting by the fire, huddled in the folds of the sleeping bag. He ached from his insides out and felt like he had the mother of all hangovers, but he'd taken one step away from death, one closer to life. Was beginning to think he might yet live to see another day.

The water had eased his throat. Fran told him to take it easy, but he wanted to know what was going on. Wanted to know what he'd actually heard and what he'd hallucinated.

"Cal's dead," Fran said. She looked away from Archie. Stared at the fire. "Jonathan killed him. It was horrible. Everything spiraled out of control." She looked back at Archie. "Cal killed Hazel. He strangled her. I don't know why. He strangled her and hid her body in the trees and when I found her he came after me."

Archie frowned. Shook his head. "No, that's not right. Cal didn't kill Hazel. Harry did. Hazel was suffocating me with the pillow and Harry tried to pull her off, but she put up a fight. The woman wanted me dead."

"What?"

"Hazel - she was trying to kill me."

"But why?"

"That, Fran, is something I do not know. The poisoned curry was meant for Harry because of the affair, but I ended up with it."

"Affair?"

"Yeah, Harry was having an affair. Hazel found out, poisoned me instead of him and then she tried to suffocate me. Harry tried to stop her and ended up strangling her in the process. It would be funny if it wasn't so fucking tragic. He went to pieces when he realised what he'd done. Slobbering and wailing. Snot dripping everywhere. He blamed himself for the whole thing - me getting poisoned, Hazel getting strangled. If you want my opinion, he did have a fuck of a lot to answer for."

"But Cal-"

Archie shook his head. "Cal had nothing to do with it. By the time he came back, Harry was dribbling and howling all over Hazel. He was hysterical, pulling and mauling at her, trying to make her wake up. It was a bit much to stomach to be honest. The only way Cal could calm him down was by saying that he'd look after Hazel, that everything would be all right. So he hefted her up and took her off. So you see, it wasn't Cal who killed Hazel, it was Harry."

"Oh my God." Fran said.

"What?"

"It's all my fault Cal is dead."

"How do you figure that one?"

"He knew where the body was, so I thought he'd killed Hazel. He kept trying to explain, but I wouldn't let him. I thought he'd murdered her you see, so I ran away from him and then when I found Jonathan and Cal came after me…"

"Jonathan killed Cal, thinking Cal was going to kill you. What a fucking mess," Archie said.

"Mess doesn't begin to cover it."

"So why haven't you called the coastguard?"

"I couldn't - there's no batteries in the radios. I thought you knew?"

Archie shook his head. "I was drifting in and out. I thought I must have been hallucinating a lot of this crazy shit, but apparently not."

Fran fetched the radios and showed Archie the empty battery chambers.

"He said you'd taken them." She nodded towards Marcus.

"Why would I want to do a stupid thing like that?"

"I don't know - why would anyone? We looked everywhere for them, but, as you can see, no batteries."

Archie leaned back and closed his eyes.

"Are you okay?" Fran asked.

"Gimme a minute. I'm thinking."

After a few seconds, he leaned forward and opened his eyes. "It was that bastard. He took them. Did anyone look in his bag?"

Fran looked at Marcus then went to his rucksack. It was fastened up tight. She started going through the compartments, pulling apart Velcro fastenings, undoing zips, emptying the contents onto the floor.

"There's a bit I can't get into."

She took the bag to Archie. Showed him the tiny, but very sturdy, padlock locking the compartment. She felt through the material.

"This could be them. It is! The batteries are in here. But why, why would he do something like this?"

"Because he's a bastard. He likes to play games. Like winding up Eleanor about Rob. He does it for kicks."

"Eleanor - oh what's happened to Eleanor?"

71

"Nice to see you again."

Eleanor could hear the grin in his voice. He was enjoying his moment. Savouring his own cleverness, her stupidity. He had known all along that she was under the bunk. Now he was getting his kicks, playing games with her.

He was standing only a few feet in front of her, shining the torch right into her eyes. He'd been standing there the whole time. Waiting, silently laughing to himself in the dark, while she fumbled her way towards him. But she wasn't going to give in that easily. She hurled the knife at him.

She took no time to aim. Threw it without warning. He screamed at her. The light jerked as he dodged the blade. It missed him, but he was thrown off balance for a second. A second was all she needed.

Eleanor darted into the bedroom and slammed the door. She felt for the chair, dragged it to her and wedged it under the handle. It was a spindly thing. She hoped it would be strong enough to hold him off for a few minutes.

She groped her way to the window. Opened it. It would be a tight squeeze, but she had no choice. Jonathan pounded on the door. Rattling the handle. Shaking the door in its frame.

Eleanor clambered on top of the drawers. Behind her the chair creaked ominously. She lunged at the window. Creaks gave way to splintering. She pushed herself through the small gap. The frame scraped at her shoulders. Too late she realised she should have gone through the window feet first and dreeped down. No matter. Better to break her neck than have Jonathan catch her.

She wriggled, her fleece catching on the wooden frame. Her head dangling over an abyss. She pushed on. There was nothing else she could do. No other course of action. A huge splintering sound behind her. He must be in the room by now. About to grab her legs, drag her back. *No.* No matter what, she was getting off this island.

The fleece snagged. She felt the fabric tear. Warmth as a sliver of wood sliced her arm. Blood. It felt like lots of blood. No pain. Not yet. That would come.

She put her arms out to protect her head as she fell. Stopped short. Was left dangling. Her hips had wedged in the window. She pressed her hands against the wall, trying to pull herself free, twisting, legs kicking frantically, feet banging against the top of the drawers. And then she was out.

Falling.

It was a short fall. She landed with a splash before her feet were through the window. Water splattered on her face and into her mouth. Tasted earthy.

She rolled onto her hands and knees, spat it out. Felt thick mud oozing up between her fingers. Cold and gritty. She was coated in it. Soaked to the skin again. At least she was free and that was all that mattered.

From the room the sound of wood cracking and snapping as the chair imploded. The door slamming against the wall. Torchlight flashing. Jonathan's wild laughter turning to a screech as he realised she had gone.

She hadn't gone far enough though. No generous hips to wedge him in. He'd be through that window like a whippet any second.

Hugging into the side of the building, Eleanor paddled through the mud on her hands and knees. Stones dug into her, bruising and scraping. Pieces of rock and debris swept down from the hill gouged into her knees and shins. Tiny particles of grit embedded themselves in her hands, cutting in deeper with every move forward.

She ignored the pain, the discomfort, the cold, the wet. All she could think about was getting to the end of the building. Turning the corner before he pinned her down with the beam of the torch.

A cold draught on the side of her face. She felt for the wall. It was gone. She was at the corner. She scrabbled around it. Got to her feet. She was battered, bruised and bleeding. She was on the opposite side of the building from where she wanted to be. But she was out of sight. And she was alive.

She breathed in the cold night air. Not a hint of mildew.

She was very much alive.

72

Fran screwed up her face. She hated being so close to Marcus. Couldn't stand being in the same room as him. Breathing the same air as him. But this was the quickest solution to their problem.

Being Marcus, his gear was top-notch. The material of his hi-tech rucksack too tough to hack through with what was left of the kitchen knives. They'd be as well trying to chew their way into it. Unlocking the padlock was the answer. Which was why Fran was kneeling on the floor beside him, easing her fingers into his trouser pocket.

She leaned forward for easier access, putting her face close to his. Flecks of dried saliva flaked in the corners of his mouth. He groaned, sending a plume of sour whisky breath into her face. She'd never hated anyone the way she hated Marcus. Had never before experienced this overwhelming sense of loathing.

She turned her face aside, pushed her fingers deeper into the pocket. They jarred against metal. She wormed her fingers in, started working the keys out.

The way he was lying made it awkward, but finally she managed to get some and eased them out a little. Up they came. Soon the padlock would be open, the batteries replaced, the coastguard called. Almost there. Then nothing. No movement. The keys had caught fast. She pulled. They would not budge.

Frustration made Fran less cautious. She pulled out her hand and pushed at his hip, shifting his weigh, then tried for the keys again. They were catching on something. Maybe a thread from the seam of his pockets. She tugged. Suddenly they came free.

"Got them."

Marcus opened his eyes as she dangled them from her finger. He grabbed her by the wrist, squeezing tight, a sick grin on his face. He took the keys from her.

"Naughty girl."

"Let her go."

Archie jabbed Marcus in the chest with the poker. Marcus winced. He glared at Archie, narrowing his eyes at the poker. Looked back at Fran. Weighing up his chances. A sneer furled his lips as he slowly uncurled his fingers.

She pulled back from him. He'd gripped her tightly enough to leave marks. She rubbed at her wrist. Wanting to scrub his touch away. Would have used steel wool to do it. He trailed his fingers lightly under his nose, sniffed and winked at her.

"Bruise like a peach, don't you?"

Fran blushed. Marcus smirked.

"Shut up." Archie jabbed him hard with the poker.

Marcus shut up.

"Give me the keys." Fran put her hand out.

She held his gaze, hating him. Hating the fact that she'd been right about him and wrong about Jonathan. Thinking she'd never be able to trust her own judgement again. Wondering what she'd done wrong, why he'd picked on her.

He'd called her a prick teaser, but she had never led him on. Never flirted with him. Never given him any indication that she was attracted to him. In fact, she had tried to avoid him.

With a flick of his wrist, he casually tossed the keys at her.

She went to the rucksack and put the smallest key in the padlock. It sprang open. She undid the zip and took out the batteries, holding them up for Archie to see. He nodded.

He was sitting guard over Marcus, holding on to the poker as if it was taking all his strength and concentration to do so.

She should have felt triumphant that she'd found the batteries. Or relieved that they could call for help. Instead, she felt furious. She screamed at Marcus.

209

"*Why? Why did you do it?*"

He seemed amused by her outburst.

"Fran." Archie croaked.

She looked at him. He nodded at the batteries. "The radio," he said. "We can deal with him later."

He slumped on the sofa, eyes closed. The poker fell from his hand, clattering on the stone floor beside Marcus.

"Oh no, Archie," Fran said.

She ran to him, checked that he was still breathing.

"How touching," Marcus sneered.

She grabbed a radio from the table. Movement in the corner of her eye. Marcus sitting up. She opened the battery compartment. Slotted in a battery. Glanced at Marcus. He was probing at the back of his head where Archie had whacked him with the poker. Fran snapped the battery compartment shut, eyed the poker. Leaning on the edge of the sofa for support, Marcus got to his feet. The poker. She should have grabbed the poker. Hands shaking, she switched on the radio.

Marcus bent down. When he straightened up, he was weighing the poker in his hands.

73

Jonathan flopped on the bed he had shared with Fran. He couldn't see that happening again. He lay on his back staring at the ceiling. Every now and again he switched the torch on and then off again. *Click. Click.*

Everything was screwed up. He was caught in a maze and he could not see a way out. Could not get his thoughts in order. Felt like someone had taken a big wooden spoon and stirred up his brain.

His leg hurt too. *Throb. Throb. Throb.* Pulsing pain.

He'd liked being with Fran. It had felt good. Had made him feel the way he imagined other people felt all the time. Being with her was so easy when it was just the two of them. He didn't have to try. Didn't have to pretend. That's when it was best. When it was just the two of them. That's when he'd felt-

Whatever.

It didn't matter now. It was over. Even though he'd taken care of the Gemma problem, everything was still screwed up.

He had been freaked, out on the hill. When he thought she was still alive. That she was going to tell Fran what had happened. Ruin things. He'd lost it then. Flipped out. Then he realised that it wasn't Gemma. That he had been right in the first place. He had taken care of her. But now he had a new situation to deal with. The Eleanor problem.

It was just one thing after another. *Click. Click.*

The truth was, Gemma had pretty much taken care of herself. Once she'd bashed her own brains out, all he'd had to do was tidy up. But the Eleanor problem. That was something different.

211

He'd clocked her right from the start. Hard-faced, snotty bitch. Looking down at everyone. He'd heard Fran yelling at her in the woods *you were right about my boyfriend*. He could just imagine the kind of hatchet job she'd done on him. Had no doubt made everything sound a lot worse than it really was.

It wasn't fair. Everything he'd done, he'd done it for Fran. Including killing Cal. He'd been chasing her. Was after her. It was a big deal sticking a knife into someone's neck like that. It didn't just happen. Took a lot of guts. A lot of energy. It was the kind of thing that if you did it at all, you had to do it with feeling. But the way she'd looked at him afterwards - like he was some kind of a monster. Her expression, caught in a strobe of torchlight, was etched on his mind.

There had been others who had looked at him that way, but he never thought Fran would be one of them. He had thought she was different. But no, she had given him that look and then she had run away.

He knew then that the connection between them had been cut. That there was no going back. No way to fix it. He'd killed for her and she hated him for it.

Fran was lost to him forever, and it was all the fault of that stabbing bitch Eleanor. He'd let her go, for now. But she would pay. Oh yes she would.

Click. Click.

74

Fran switched the dial to channel 16, the international distress frequency. Marcus took a step towards her. Fran adjusted the dial to lose the static.

"It's over Marcus," she said. "Whatever sick game you've been playing, it's over."

A slight shake in her voice. Could he sense her fear?

"You think so?" He threw the poker aside.

She cringed at the violent action. Shrank back as Marcus crossed the room towards her. The ugly sound of metal hitting stone was still ringing out as the gap between them closed.

He grabbed her by the throat. Threw her against the wall. She dropped the radio. Heard it clatter as it hit the floor. He came at her. His eyes dark. A sneer on his face. She tried to dodge him, but he was too quick. He pinned her against the wall. Pressed against her, forcing her to breathe in his hot, rancid breath again. Making her want to vomit. She twisted her face away from him.

"You know what?" he said. "Up close, you're quite an ugly bitch."

75

Eleanor bit down hard on her lip. Her shin had banged against something hard. Metal. The pain rang like a bell, but she kept it in. Kept it silent.

Jonathan had been ominously quiet. She had no idea if he'd followed her outside or if he was skulking around inside. There was no hint of light behind her, but that meant nothing. The torch battery could have died or maybe he was keeping the light hidden from her, sneaking up on her in the dark. She pushed the thought aside. She'd come this far. She had to keep it together for a little while longer. Not let paranoia get a grip of her.

Following the wall around the building was proving to be more difficult than she thought. All manner of junk was piled up against the gable end. She'd already negotiated her way around the log pile and something covered in tarpaulin before banging into whatever the hell this thing was. She felt her way round it with her hands, hoping she didn't slice a finger off in the process.

Finally, she reached the corner. She looked around it. Saw light emanating from the window at the far end. Light, people, safety.

She was on hard ground now. Walking on the flagstones that ran along the front of the building. She tread as lightly as she could, but still the heavy boots sent out a hollow tap as she went. Like bloody tom-toms. She hated those boots. If Jonathan was anywhere nearby, he couldn't fail to hear her.

She paused and listened, but there was no hint of his presence. She wondered where he'd gone but decided that, as long as he wasn't anywhere near her, she didn't care.

She passed Fran's bedroom window. Gasped when a light flashed on.

Screamed when Jonathan smashed the torch against the window, cracking the glass.

76

Outside - a scream. Eleanor, it had to be Eleanor.

Marcus grinned. "Sounds like your boyfriend is still-" He stopped mid-sentence. He stared at Fran before staggering back, eyes wide, a look of bewilderment on his face.

He put two hands on the table. Leant on it, steadying himself. He didn't seem to notice the pounding on the door.

"Let me in, let me in."

Fran ran to the door and opened it up. Eleanor rushed in and immediately slammed and bolted it. She double-checked the bolt then leaned against the door, breathing heavily. She was wild-eyed, coated in mud, streaked with blood. Her clothes were torn and sodden. There were scratches all over her hands and face.

Marcus had left the table and was fumbling his way to the armchair. He sat down and held himself very still, paying no mind to anyone.

Fran picked the radio up from the floor. It was still in one piece. She reset the dial and spoke into it.

"Mayday - mayday - mayday."

She watched Marcus as he gingerly felt his head, a stunned expression on his face.

"Stornoway coastguard, this is Fran Hutchens."

The tremble in her voice lessened as she spoke. She didn't know what had happened to Marcus, but it didn't look as though he would be giving them any more trouble.

"My location is fifty-eight degrees, twenty minutes, forty-seven point five one seconds north."

But she wouldn't be turning her back on him.

"Zero five degrees, nine minutes, forty-six point one six seconds west."

Eleanor was still leaning against the bolted door, but her breathing had steadied.

"There are ten people on the island. Three injured, two dead, four missing. Emergency treatment required."

Eleanor's eyes were closed. She was whispering *thank God*, over and over.

"There are two dangerous men. Repeat, two dangerous men. One loose on the island, one injured and contained."

Marcus stopped picking at his head and glowered at her.

"Assistance urgently required."

"*Cunt*," he spat at her.

Eleanor opened her eyes. Fran put the radio down. "Ignore him," she said.

Eleanor stared at him. Looked like she was deciding whether to punch him or not. Instead she took Fran's advice and went to the sink. She filled it with water and washed her hands and face.

"There are some old tea-towels in there."

Fran pointed to a cupboard under the sink. Eleanor took a handful out and dried herself. When she'd finished, they were streaked with blood and mud.

"Let me bandage that arm for you," Fran said.

She fetched the first aid box. Then they sat at the table together. Fran cleaned the wound on Eleanor's arm with antiseptic, apologising when she flinched from the sting.

"Don't worry," Eleanor said. "That's the least of it."

"What happened?" Fran asked.

Eleanor told her about Jonathan coming after her. Fran bound her arm with a bandage, telling Eleanor about Marcus trying to rape her, that Archie had saved her by hitting him with the poker. The blush rising to her face as she spoke about the assault angered her.

217

Eleanor glared at Marcus like she wanted to tear his head off.

"I gave you what you wanted," he said.

His face was pale, and he was holding himself very still. Like he was scared to move in case his head cracked wide open and his brain fell out. Maybe Archie had done some real damage.

"You were playing at it," he said. "I gave it to you for real."

Using a pair of tweezers, Fran picked pieces of grit from the palm of Eleanor's hand. Her nails were broken and grubby. Her skin grimy with ingrained dirt. It would take more than a splash at the sink to get her properly cleaned up.

"You all wanted to be cut off from the rest of the world. I cut you off." Marcus spoke in a monotone. "You should be grateful."

This was the worst bit. Waiting.

"Yes, grateful."

Picking grit. Waiting.

And listening to Marcus.

"Ungrateful bitches."

77

Eleanor stared at the dying embers of the fire. Help was coming. The nightmare was almost over. All they had to do now was sit tight. Once she and Fran had shared with each other what they knew, the conversation dried up. The void was too big to fill with small talk. Even Marcus, no doubt depressed by the lack of reaction to his goading, had shut up.

When the rock crashed through the window Eleanor jerked like a fish on a line. Fran yelped and grabbed the radio with one hand, the poker with the other. The women leapt back from the table as the rock skidded across it. Jonathan's face appeared at the window, framed by jagged glass.

It was a sash window. Wooden frame, four panes. Eleanor didn't think he could get through it. Not without knocking the whole thing out and that would take some work. The window recess was deep. Maybe a foot and a half. Maybe more. They'd be able to beat him back before he got far.

Not that they were having to do any beating. Not yet. He was too busy staring at Fran. Having some kind of creepy moment with her. No talking involved. It was all in the eyes. Some kind of telepathic exchange.

Fran was gripping onto the poker and radio like her life depended on them. She was probably right. Tendons roped her hands and arms. Her face was ashen as she stared right back at him.

Without taking her eyes from him, Eleanor stepped towards the kitchen intent on arming herself with something. Anything. The movement drew his attention to her. Their eyes locked. She clenched her fists. Pain needled through her hands as tiny cuts were forced open. Grit forced further into her flesh. She held his gaze. If he was trying any telepathy crap on her, it wasn't working. There was only one message she was receiving, and she was getting it loud and clear. The guy was nuts.

He started to speak, then stopped. He cocked his head, looked up.

Eleanor strained her ears. Couldn't hear anything. No, there it was. The steady *whoomp whoomp whoomp* of an approaching helicopter.

Jonathan looked back at her. He stared at her intently for a moment, then he was gone and all she could see was a broken window.

The sound of the helicopter grew louder. Search lights flashed outside. Marcus rolled his eyes and gazed at the ceiling.

"Saigon. Shit, I'm still only in Saigon."

78
MONDAY

Jonathan felt as though his mind had fragmented. Pieces had come together when he was staring into the bothy at them. Fran and Eleanor. But it was too late by then. He couldn't undo what had been done. Could not wipe out the last twelve hours. Could not recreate himself. Not in their eyes.

He'd started down this road the minute he'd decided to hide Gemma's body. He should have come clean then. Explained what had happened. It wasn't as though he had put the rock there, but now he'd gone too far. There was no way back for him.

The funny thing was, he hadn't meant any of it. All he'd wanted was for Gemma to shut up. The rest was just... well it was just shit that happened. Out of his control.

There wasn't anything he could do about the helicopter churning the air overhead either. He glanced up at the lights. The noise thrummed through him. Maybe they would listen. Would understand that it was all an accident. That he hadn't meant any of it. Not Gemma. Not Cal. Not Eleanor. Emotions had been running high. A sense of perspective had been lost.

Then he thought about the way they had looked at him. Fran and Eleanor. They had already made up their minds. Wasn't anyone going to believe that it wasn't his fault. The way they'd stared at him. Like he was some kind of a monster. Maybe he was. He didn't feel like a monster. He felt the way he always did. Except maybe a bit more screwed up. No wonder. Anyone would feel the same after what he'd been through. He needed time to think. Time to sort his head out. If he gave himself up now there would be questions. Endless questions. He'd have no headspace. They would crucify him.

The spotlight was coming his way. Before it caught him, Jonathan slipped into the bunk room and closed the door. His thoughts were settling down now that he had something practical to deal with. He had a decent chunk of time to play with before the helicopter landed and the crew made their way to the bothy, so he took his time. Stayed cool.

His torch had broken when he used it to smash the window in Fran's room, but there was enough light now from the helicopter for him to find his way about. There were four rucksacks in the room. He went through the first one, looking for anything that might be useful. In the pockets he found a Mini Maglite, a couple of bars of chocolate and a purse. He flicked on the torch, opened up the purse. Credit, debit and store cards in Gemma's name and sixty quid in paper money. He left the cards, stuffed the money into his pocket.

The helicopter developed a high-pitched whine as it prepared to land. He went through the remaining rucksacks quickly and found a few cereal bars, more chocolate, a packet of mints and enough paper money to bring his haul up to near two hundred pounds. Time well spent.

There was a carrier bag neatly folded in Hazel's rucksack. He shook it out and threw his loot, into it, then added a pair of socks and a fleece from Cal's rucksack and a pair of trackie bottoms and a t-shirt he spotted lying on a bunk. He grabbed a sleeping bag and went through the internal door into the hall, a plan forming in his mind.

During his previous visits to see Fran, he'd helped out with maintenance tasks. Knew all the nooks and crannies. The toilets and shower had been installed only a few years before. Seemed to be, that even those wanting to get away from it all, didn't want to get from it so much that they had to use a primitive outdoor toilet. The new facilities were basically boxes created within the building, complete with their own, white-painted ceilings. Between the boxes and the original roof, there was an angled space used for storage.

Jonathan dropped his loot and, using one of the toilet door handles to stand on, he hoisted himself up for a look. There were a couple of cardboard boxes filled with junk at the front of the space, but nothing at the back, where the roof angled down to meet the toilet ceiling. It wasn't much of a space, but he would be able to lie flat and stretch out.

He pushed the boxes to one side then jumped down to the floor, wincing as he landed. He tied the carrier bag shut then tossed it and the sleeping bag up on the ledge. He climbed back up and squirmed into the space until his head scraped against the roof and he could go no further, then pulled the boxes back into place.

His leg throbbed. He untied the makeshift bandage he'd tied around it and inspected the damage Eleanor had inflicted on him. Her first stab hadn't been much more than a nick. The second was much nastier. It was deeper and looked as though it could do with a couple of stitches. He hoped to hell it didn't get infected. Couldn't do much about that now.

After taking off his boots, he lay down and gingerly peeled off his trousers then used the t-shirt he'd taken from Cal's bunk to make a fresh bandage for his leg. Once it was bound up nice and tight he changed into Cal's dry clothes. He stacked his own wet gear in a pile behind one box, his boots behind another.

He wasn't able to sit upright. Every action carried out in a hunched or twisted or semi-prone position. His shoulders and back ached from the effort. It was a relief to be able to lie down properly and worm his way into the sleeping bag. All zipped up, he wriggled as far into the eaves as possible.

The hall was narrow. If anyone bothered to look up, all they would see was a few old cardboard boxes. If they decided to explore further, well, there wasn't anything he could do about that. He was physically and mentally exhausted. He was weary. He had done everything he could. If they found him then so be it.

Jonathan switched off the torch and pulled the sleeping bag up around his head.

79

From outside: shouting and yelling. Banging. Voices raised high. Bordering on hysteria. You'd think they would have calmed down now that their rescuers had arrived. Their heroes.

It sounded like a mob out there. Explanations, instructions, orders. Authoritarian bark. Taking charge. Getting this situation under control. The thrum-whine of the helicopter underscoring it all. Finally, the hall door opened. Strong flashlight beams bounced across the ceiling.

Jonathan had the hood of the sleeping bag tight around his head. Only his eyes and nose uncovered. He lay on his back listening to the commotion. Watching the torch beams dance. His heart keeping time with the pound of heavy boots on the floor. Waiting for the moment when the boxes would be pushed aside. When he'd be spotted and pulled from his roost, a big, meaty, coastguard hand wrapped around his throat.

Shudders going through him as the doors below were opened and banged shut. They moved noisily along the hall, checking every room, finding nothing. They checked the rest of the building then went back outside. More shouting. More confusion. He closed his eyes, picturing torch beams in the dark.

The noise went on and on. He began to think that they would never leave. That they would come back and search again. Looking above their heads this time. But no. The helicopter's whine suddenly grew in intensity. Screaming frantically, until it sounded as though the rotors would shear off, and then, magically, it lifted. The roar increased for a moment, vibrating through his body, shaking his molecules, before moving off, becoming distant, until it faded away. He was safe for now. But they would be back.

He woke with a jolt. Wondered what had awakened him. Had he heard a noise? Were they back already? What time was it anyway? The dayglo dial on his watch told him that it was almost six. It would be light soon.

He lay quietly and listened. There were no human sounds apart from his own.

He switched the torch on and wriggled out of the eaves until he had room to sit up. There was a pain on the back of his head like a headache on the outside. He shuffled out of the sleeping bag and pulled his damp boots on. He made a space between the boxes, swung his legs over the side and dropped to the floor.

Feeling creaky, he limped along the hall to Fran's room and looked out of the broken window. There was a hint of steely cold light creeping across the sky from the east. He figured they'd wait until it was properly light before coming back, so he had a little time.

After using the toilet, he washed his hands and inspected his face in the mirror. Covered in cuts and scrapes, bruised, swollen and lumpy, it looked like a kilo of raw mince. His nose was broken, and a crust of dried blood had formed around his nostrils. No wonder Fran hadn't recognised him in the woods. He'd have walked by himself on the street.

He grinned. As disguises went, it was cheaper than plastic surgery. Maybe Eleanor had done him a favour.

His stomach growled and gurgled. He hadn't eaten anything since yesterday morning. Was feeling light-headed. Not good. He'd intended to scoff the cereal bars the night before but had fallen asleep.

He wandered through to the bunk room and peered out of the window. Getting lighter all the time, but still no sign of anyone. If he made a more thorough search of the rucksacks he might scrape up another cereal bar or two, but the only place he was going to get enough food together to have a chance of seeing this thing through was in the kitchen. There was no choice but to venture outside.

Heart thudding, he opened the door a smidgeon. Peeked out through the crack. Couldn't see anything but empty island, empty sea. Wondered if there were police snipers lying in the heather. Waiting, just waiting.

Scalp prickling, Jonathan stepped into the cold light of pre-dawn.

80

There was no rifle crack. No pain. No shouting. No-one there.

In the kitchen he slapped a slice of bread onto the counter, smeared a thick layer of peanut butter over it, used a fork to mash a banana on top, slapped another slice of bread on top of that, squished the lot together and bit a mouthful off. He gave it a few chews before swallowing it down in big, soft, claggy chunks.

Tasted good.

He checked the food stores while he ate. Mostly pasta, pulses and flour. Stuff that had to be cooked. But there were oatcakes, digestive biscuits, fresh fruit and some snacks. Trail mix, nuts and chickpea noodles. He'd have to eke it out, but he reckoned there was enough.

When he'd finished eating he had a rummage through the first aid kit. Satisfied with its contents, he took off his trackie bottoms, undid the t-shirt bandage and inspected the damage. His hill-tumbling wound looked the worst. Like wet corned beef with added grit. He'd taken a slice clean off himself. Couldn't have done it better with a ham machine.

Of the two stab wounds Eleanor had given him, the first was as superficial as he'd initially thought but the second wound was much worse. The skin around the puncture was white and tender. The wound itself gaped red like a mouth full of raw meat. It was begging for an infection.

He'd had a tetanus jab a couple of years before. Wondered if that would be enough. It would have to be. Couldn't exactly mosey on down to his nearest health centre.

He washed out the wounds with clean water and removed all

the foreign material he could see. When everything looked as good as it was going to get, he sloshed them with Dettol. Burn baby, burn. Should have diluted it first. Stung so bad he felt it had to be doing him some good.

He dabbed the wounds dry with the corner of a clean-looking tea towel and took a plastic tub from a shelf. It was filled with the kind of crap people didn't throw away in case it came in handy one day. This was that day.

He sat down and rummaged through the contents. Biros, chalk, a miniature screwdriver, a roll of tape, a few screws, a couple of grimy sachets of English mustard and, at the bottom, in amongst the rusty thumb tacks and bent paperclips, a tube of superglue. It was twisted. Had been used. Was most likely dried up. But it was worth a go. He unscrewed the cap, grinning when a globule of clear glue formed on the tip of the nozzle.

He pinched the sides of the deep stab wound together and applied a thin line of glue along the seam. He held it closed for a few seconds then let go. The wound stayed closed. He didn't know if it would heal. Suspected it needed packing but given the circumstances it was the best he could do.

A plaster covered the other stab wound just fine. He applied a gauze pad to the skinning he'd given himself, bound it with a crepe bandage and fastened it with a couple of small safety pins.

The wounds still nipped but it was a good kind of nippy. Like everything had been scoured clean and was on the mend.

He considered taking the entire first aid box back to his ledge, but it was an essential piece of kit and maybe someone would notice it was missing. Maybe they'd look for it in all the unlikely places. Maybe he was being paranoid. Maybe he was. But he wasn't going to take any chances, so he satisfied himself with a couple of packs of Paracetamol and a few plasters.

He filled a glass with water and swallowed a couple of the painkillers before putting the rest of the pack in his pocket along with the plasters. He was fed. He was watered. He was all patched up and good to go. He'd just put the glass down when he heard a low humming noise. He looked out of the broken window. Zander's boat, crossing the water to the island. Growing bigger, coming closer, every second.

Shitfuck.

Panic fuzzed his thoughts. He hesitated for a moment, then grabbed the first thing that came to hand and ran.

He was only outside for a second. A dark figure against a white wall. But the light was grey. He could only hope it was grey enough and they were still too far away to see him. He dodged through the bunkroom, into the hall, threw the packet of biscuits he'd grabbed up on the ledge, then clambered up after it.

The bandage. He'd tied it too tight. Couldn't flex his muscles. His foot slipped from the door handle. He slithered clumsily to the floor, scraping his face on the door on the way down. There was a one second pause before his nose began pulsing like it was being beat with a hammer.

He got up. Tried again, taking it slower this time. He sat on the ledge for a moment until his breathing steadied. When he turned to move, his hand brushed against the biscuits. The packet rustled as it rolled to the edge of the ledge. He snatched for it. Missed. Heard it hit the floor.

He shone the torch down. The packet was beautifully highlighted in the circle of light. Shiny red wrapper. White print. Photograph of a digestive biscuit. It looked very bloody incongruous lying on the floor outside the toilet. Anyone seeing it would wonder where it had come from. Sometime soon, they'd look up. Wonder what was up on that ledge. Maybe take a closer look.

Voices outside. They were here.

They'd go into the bothy first. He had some time. Couldn't leave the biscuits there. Might as well have a big neon arrow pointing up at him. He slung himself over the edge. Dropped to the floor. Heard the door opening into the bunkroom. Heard someone saying, *this is where the missing girl slept.*

His throat tightened. He was one closed door away from being caught.

He picked up the biscuits. Couldn't risk throwing them up on the ledge. Couldn't risk the noise. No pockets deep enough to hold them. He shoved them down the neck of his fleece into the upper sleeve. The wrapper crackling like thin ice. One eye on the door, waiting for it to burst open.

Then it did.

81

He was on the ledge. But only just. Hunched up behind the boxes. No time to wedge himself into the eaves at the back. He had to stay right where he was. Couldn't move, not at all. Couldn't risk crackling the biscuits.

"Toilets, store-room, shower along here. The other bedroom and the ranger's room are at the end of the hall."

Three of them. One guiding the other two.

"Christ it stinks." Different voice. The others laughed.

Jonathan blinked. Sweat trickled down his back. He wondered if it was him they could smell.

They stayed on the island all day. Others came too. He heard them outside. A helicopter flew overhead. Later, he heard dogs. Lots of activity. Lots of movement. They were looking for Gemma. They were looking for him. Maybe they were looking for some of the others too. He was hazy on who was missing. Who wasn't. The important thing was, they stayed outside. Searching the island.

He shifted. The sleeping bag whispering around him. His feet were cold. Felt numb. But the rest of him was warm. He was stiff though. Wished he had a pillow. And he was thirsty. He should have brought a pillow. And water. Shouldn't complain. At least he was lying down in relative comfort, not all hunched up scared to move.

Every now and then someone came and used the toilets beneath him. He lay very still then, hardly breathing at all. Listening to them piss and fart. They didn't always wash their hands either. Dirty bastards.

He passed the time trying to figure out who they were looking for. Who they might have found. Who they hadn't. They'd have found Cal by now. Wouldn't have to be Sherlock for that. He wouldn't look too pretty. Not with his throat cut. All that blood, dried to a dark maroon, or maybe almost black by now, would make it look really bad. Worse than it was. As if he'd been killed by some kind of maniac instead of a guy who was trying to do the right thing.

Doing the right thing could be very hard. It wasn't always easy to make the right choice, and then, whatever you chose, you were stuck with it. People made up their minds about you on that one thing. It wasn't fair.

Once they found Cal, they'd look all the harder for him. He wondered if they'd ever find Gemma in her bog-hole.

It went on like this for days. They came over at first light. Left before dusk. He came down from his perch then. Like a bat leaving his roost.

He got himself a pillow. And a flask of water he replenished every night. The rucksacks and the other personal stuff had been removed, but the food had been left through in the bothy. There wasn't a lot, but it was enough to keep him going.

He couldn't eat the fresh fruit in case they'd notice it was gone but he cooked some pasta and tossed it in a mixture of brown sauce and ketchup. Tasted pretty good too. He ate baked beans and brown rice flavoured with soy sauce. He cooked porridge once, but the pot was a bastard to clean so he didn't make it again.

He was scrupulous about cleaning up after himself. Only took a little of anything at a time. Put everything back where he'd found it. He came and went without being seen. It was as though he wasn't there at all. He was the invisible man.

One day they didn't come back. They came the next, but not so many of them. They were scaling down. Then they scaled down so much, they didn't come back at all.

He could never be quite sure though. There was always the chance they'd turn up one day, so he couldn't let his defences down, though it was hard not to. Hard not to feel that the place was his. That he'd won.

He couldn't go out during daylight hours. Too much risk of being seen from a passing fishing boat. Maybe Zander's. But at night the island belonged to him. He'd become weak and flaccid lying on his ledge. He built his muscle strength up by exercising and going for walks under starry skies.

He'd long since eaten all the Paracetamol but he didn't ache so much now. Maybe he'd gotten used to sleeping on a hard surface or maybe he ached so much all over that he didn't notice it anymore.

One night, he took his old clothes down to the shore and tossed them in the sea. Maybe they'd be found and identified. They'd assume he'd drowned.

Mostly what he did was think. Lying on his ledge, in the dark. Walking around, in the dark. Always thinking. Thinking about what had happened. What he had done. Replaying it over and over like a movie in his head.

He conjured up different versions of the story. In one, he gave in to Gemma's charms. Had sex with her. But she taunted him afterwards. Her beautiful face twisted into an ugly sneer. She couldn't help herself. It was in the script. Fated. He picked up a rock shaped like a shark's fin and stove in her head. She ended up dead. No matter what, she was always going to end up dead. Cal too. Wrong place, wrong time. Just one of those things. Destined to die. And what of him, what of Jonathan?

He wasn't sure. He didn't blame himself, not for any of it. How could he, when none of it was his fault? If anything, he was as much a victim as any of them. The only thing clear in his mind was that somehow, someway, his fate was bound up with the other one. Eleanor.

He thought about her a lot.

82

The days grew longer. The temperature rose. Spring had sprung. He didn't know how much time had passed since the police had left. Hours and days and weeks merged into each other. It was easy to lose track. He should have kept a tally. He could have scratched it into the roof where he slept.

He collected things. Took them back to his ledge. A small kitchen knife. A couple of books, but mostly he gathered food. Now that they had gone, he could help himself. Not that there was a lot to help himself to. He was hungry most of the time. Could feel that he'd lost weight. He held off opening the digestive biscuits for as long as he could. The packet was intact, the biscuits inside broken. Down one side of the packet they were mostly crumbs. When he opened them his mouth watered. He told himself he would only have two or three. But three turned into four and pretty soon he'd eaten the whole packet. Didn't stop to savour them. Just crammed them into his mouth one after the other, scooping up the crumbs and broken bits. His mouth filled with their crumbly, sandy texture. The sweetness of them like a drug.

He felt sick afterwards. His mouth parched. The long chug of water he took made the biscuits swell in his stomach till he thought he would burst.

He took more care after that. When he found a packet of fig rolls behind the pots and pans, he eked them out, allowing himself one each morning, another in the evening. They were two years out of date. No matter. He nibbled at the stale pastry then sucked on the fig filling, drawing out the pleasure. Making it last as long as he could.

He was desperate to feel the sun on the skin. Wondered how long it would be before vitamin D deficiency kicked in, but he daren't venture out during the day. Someone might see him moving around or spot the door opening.

Finally, the thing he had been waiting for happened.

He'd been counting on them coming back, but walking the island night after night, he'd been worried that they wouldn't. That maybe they'd close the island down for the year, as a mark of respect. How would he survive then?

Even if he ate every pulse, every grain of rice, there wasn't enough food in the bothy to do him till the following year. He'd have to catch rabbits. Set the snares at night. He wasn't sure he knew how to do that. Even if he did catch one, he could not live on rabbit meat alone. Not enough nutrients. He'd die of rabbit starvation. He could probably find something to eat with it. Dandelions. They were edible. It had been a while since he'd eaten it, but a bit of fresh meat would be tasty.

He hadn't meant to lie to Fran. She'd said she was a vegetarian and before he knew it, he'd said that he was too. She'd been delighted and so he went along with it. He hadn't lied. Not really. He'd made it true from that moment on. But the truth changed. It changed all the time.

Funny thing - he could barely conjure up Fran's face now. He would think he had it, but when he tried to focus on her features they hazed over, as if he was looking at her through a gauze. Getting hazier all the time. It was as if she'd never been real.

Eleanor was different. He had her in sharp focus.

He didn't think they would close the island down. Not when there was good money to be made from visitors. Maybe they'd even have a bumper year. The visitor numbers boosted by ghouls and rubber-neckers among the nature lovers. People pretending to be puffin watchers but who were secretly seeking out the spot where Rob had fallen to his death or where Cal had met his grisly death.

There would be visitors aplenty.

They swarmed over the bothy when they came. Cleaning and scrubbing. Trying to eradicate every last trace of that weekend. This was a risky time for him, when he was most in danger of being discovered. All it would take was one nosey sod to take a snoop at his ledge and the game would be up.

He grew tense waiting for it. His hand curling around the knife handle whenever anyone was in the corridor below him. Whatever else happened, he wasn't going to give up without a fight.

He needn't have concerned himself. Turned out they had too much going on at eye-level to concern themselves with what was going on over their heads. He picked up snatches of conversation, but not much because of where he was situated. Mostly he heard them in the toilets. The human sounds of bladders being emptied, bowels evacuated.

He ventured down at night to fill up his flask with water, use the toilet and try to knock some of the kinks out of his body. He waited until the wee small hours, when there was best chance of them being in deep sleep. It was risky, but he didn't have any choice. He figured that anyone hearing him would assume he was someone else in the group.

This was the worst time for him, stuck up on his ledge for over twenty-three hours a day, but it was a necessary privation. One that would lead to his salvation. He couldn't risk going through to the bothy, so he lived on the food he'd hoarded. Lying in the dark chewing and swallowing and thinking about what he would do when he got off the island.

Within days of them arriving, most of them left again. As far as he could tell, only three stayed behind. Fran's replacement - a guy with a nasal whine who liked the sound of his own voice - and two other guys. One of these had a habit of saying, *cool man*, to everything. The other didn't say much. They went out in the morning, didn't come back for hours. The ferry was running again, bringing across the day trippers.

He paid attention to the rhythm of their days. On the fourth day, after they left in the morning he climbed down from his ledge and went through to the bothy. he paused for a moment to enjoy the sensation of sunlight on his face. It was a stunning day. Full of promise. The kind of day that made you feel glad to be alive.

He watched the small dot of the boat as it crossed the sound towards the island. there was no panic in his breast. Anyone spying him now would assume he was meant to be there. The boat was fully loaded. Looked like it was going to be a busy day. Jonathan smiled to himself and went inside.

The kitchen now contained an embarrassment of food. He took an apple from a bowl and crunched into it. His teeth piercing through the smooth skin, biting into the flesh of the fruit. A trickle of juice ran down his chin. He wiped it on his sleeve and took another bite. It tasted like the best thing he'd ever eaten. So healthy. So fresh. So full of vitamins. He could feel the good it was doing him even as he ate it. For the next few minutes, he devoted himself entirely to the pleasure of eating the apple.

When he'd chewed it down to the nub of the core, he tossed the remains in the bin and had a poke around. Someone had made a big pot of soup. He scooped out a mug-full and ate it cold, standing by the repaired window, watching as Zander's empty boat returned to the mainland for another load. The sea was flat calm. The only disturbance on the water the wake left by the ferry.

He put the kettle on the hob and made himself a cup of coffee then rinsed the kettle under the cold tap to cool it down. He didn't want anyone coming back and finding a warm kettle. Mustn't raise suspicions. Not now when he'd come so far. There was a plastic tub on the counter filled with home-baking. He helped himself to a couple of Anzac biscuits and took them over to the window along with his coffee.

He watched for the ferry coming back as he sipped and munched. The coffee was the first hot thing he'd had in days and it invigorated him. He had already decided that if there was another full boatload of passengers then this would be the day.

He'd just swallowed the last mouthful of coffee when the boat appeared. It was full.

Today was the day.

Jonathan rinsed and cleared away the mugs he'd used for the soup and coffee, nabbed himself a couple of apples, checked that no-one was around outside then went back through to the bunkroom without pausing to bask in the sun. There would be plenty of time for that later.

Cool Man and Quiet Guy's stuff was scattered over the room. Jonathan sifted through it and selected a few choice items, then he went through to Whiny's room and did the same, mixing and matching until he had a completely new and non-descript outfit. Grey, zip-off trousers, dark green t-shirt, dark blue fleece, grey walking socks and a navy, waterproof jacket.

The trousers were big on the waist, but Mr Whiny provided a belt to sort that problem. Jonathan completed the outfit with a black beanie and a pair of sunglasses. He pulled the hat down low and checked himself in the mirror in Whiny's room.

Between the hat, the sunglasses and his beard, the only part of his face on display was his nose which, thanks to Eleanor's efforts had been completely reshaped. It was perfect. He looked exactly like dozens of other guys who came to the island and nothing like himself.

Another rummage through Whiny's gear produced an army surplus bag. The kind with the long strap he could wear diagonally across his chest. Perfect. Everyone who came to the island was carrying something. He didn't want to stand out as the guy with no baggage. He didn't want to stand out at all. Mr Invisible.

He collected the money from the ledge, stashing it in various pockets. He filled his flask and put it in the bag along with the apples and a pair of binoculars belonging to someone or other.

He left the bothy and cut south west across the island until he came to the path. He walked along it until he came to a big, flat boulder. He sat on it and waited.

Soon he heard the murmur of conversation followed by a peal of laughter. Heads bobbed into sight. Four people came up the incline towards him. Looked like two couples. Walking at a jaunty pace. Heading back to the ferry. Jonathan lay back on the boulder, using the jacket as a pillow, basking like a lizard, making out odd words as they drew closer. He sat up on his elbows as they approached, casual as you like. They were in their fifties, maybe sixties. On holiday. Having a ball.

"Beautiful day," one of the men said. Not stopping. Just one human being acknowledging another. He had on a red baseball cap, tufts of silver hair sticking out at the sides. The other man gave Jonathan a nod. The women smiled at him without breaking their chatter.

"Sure is," Jonathan replied with a smile of his own. Acting for all the world like one of them. A day tripper.

Another cluster appeared within minutes. A young couple, with a small child strapped into some kind of carrier on the man's back. They were talking in angry whispers. French. They shut up when they caught sight of Jonathan. Kept up a smart pace as they passed him, the atmosphere of a row clinging to them. The woman gave him a sidelong glance, the man a curt nod. He gave a lazy wave in return. The kid waved a soft toy at him. A blue bear.

A single man came hurrying along next. A tripod in his hand, camera on a strap around his neck, massive rucksack on his back. Said, "Morning," on his way past, though it was already afternoon.

Jonathan gave him a head start before following on behind.

His timing was good. Zander had just arrived at the jetty with another load of visitors. One of the bothy residents was collecting tickets as the passengers disembarked. Jonathan wondered who it was. He didn't have to wonder for long.

"Good trip across? Cool, man... I'll just take your tickets here... That's cool, man... Beautiful day, man... Yeah, take of your life jackets and head up the pier... Yeah, just leave them at the side there for these folks... Just head on up the pier folks. Follow the path to the information hut where my colleague, Brian, will tell you what's what."

The people who had passed Jonathan on the path were clustering at the end of the jetty along with another couple he didn't recognise. Sweat tingled in Jonathan's armpits. He hoped Cool Man wouldn't recognise any of the clothes he was wearing. He joined the cluster, positioning himself behind the bulk of Tripod Man's massive rucksack.

Once the new arrivals were out of the way, Cool Man called them along the pier and handed out lifejackets. The first few people boarded but the couple with the kid struggled to get him out of the carrier. The kid started bawling. Cool Man stepped in to help. Told them it was cool, and no problem. Tripod Man came to a sudden halt. Jonathan bumped into him.

"Sorry," Jonathan said.

"My fault," Tripod Man replied, "Got to get this off before I get onboard." He jerked his head back towards his massive rucksack and made to put the tripod down.

"Here, let me help," Jonathan said. He took hold of the tripod.

"Thanks."

Once they had their lifejacket son, Tripod Man turned to take the tripod back from Jonathan.

"It's ok, I've got it," Jonathan said.

"Cheers, mate." Tripod Man turned climbed aboard the ferry with his rucksack. Using the tripod to shield his face, Jonathan boarded behind him. Zander glanced at him. Jonathan's chest tightened. Zander turned back to fiddling with one of the boat controls. Jonathan moved past him and sat upfront beside Tripod Man, hoping it looked as though they were travelling together.

The family with the kid got on and sat behind them, the mother making soothing noises at the child. The father silent. Once everyone was aboard, the boat moved swiftly over the water, back to the mainland. No clanging from the shackles this time, only the steady hum of the engine.

Jonathan imagined Zander's gaze sweeping over his passengers. Then stopping. Thinking there was something familiar about the guy sitting up front. Not being able to pin it down.

He felt an itch in his back, between his shoulder blades. Zander's eyes boring into him. Had he been rumbled? He had a strong urge to turn around, check if Zander really was looking at him. But what if he turned and something in the shape of his cheekbone, or the way he moved, triggered recognition in Zander? Gave him away. No, he couldn't risk it.

The itch intensified. Felt like something was burrowing into his skin. He resisted the urge to scratch it. He stared straight ahead. No squirming. No turning around. No drawing attention to himself.

The boat pulled in smoothly and came to a stop. Everyone stood up to disembark. All they had to do was step off the port side onto the pier. There was hilarity at the back of the boat where the two couples had sat. Something to do with one of the women losing her balance.

When Tripod Man got off, Jonathan was right behind him. They took off their lifejackets. The man pulled on his rucksack.

Jonathan handed him the tripod then followed him up the pier to the car park. The tight feeling in his chest eased. He'd made it. He was back on the mainland and no-one knew a thing about it.

He was at the top of the pier when Zander's voice hollered out.

"Hey, you! Wait there."

Jonathan's face flushed. His chest tightened again. He took another step.

"Wait!"

He stopped and turned. Saw Zander leaping out of the boat. He moved quickly up the pier. Past the two couples. Towards Jonathan. The only obstacle between them was the couple with the kid.

Zander was bigger than Jonathan but if he gave him a quick punch to the nose it might be enough to knock him off balance. He could push him into the water. It was shallow, but the shock would slow him down. Give Jonathan a chance to get away.

Zander came up behind the couple with the kid. Put his hand on the dad's shoulder. Jonathan waited for him to push the man out of the way.

"Wait," he said. Looking at the dad. "You forgot this."

He handed him a blue bear. The kid put its hand out for the toy. Big smiles from the woman.

Jonathan let out the breath he'd been holding. He turned and walked up the pier.

Now he could go and find Eleanor.

MAINLAND

83

"Fear thou not; for I am with thee."

Rob's mother leaned into Eleanor. She was slight. A wisp of a woman, weighted down by the black clothes she wore. Amazing that she had produced a big chunk of a son like Rob, never mind his Amazonian sister.

She grasped onto Eleanor's arm. Her hand was un-gloved, the skin translucent, blue veins prominent. Looked like the bones would fracture into dust with one decent handshake, but her grasp was firm. Almost painfully so.

"Be not dismayed; for I am thy God: I will strengthen thee; yea I will help thee; yea, I will uphold thee with the right hand of my righteousness."

Her grip tightened as the minister's voice boomed. Eleanor winced but resisted the urge to shake herself free. The pain wasn't so bad. At least she was feeling something.

It was Zander who had found Rob's body. He'd been shooting lobster creels close to the rocky shoreline of the mainland. There hadn't been much doubt that it was Rob, but there had to be a formal identification. The duty fell to Rob's mother and sister. They asked Eleanor to come with them. After all, Rob had proposed. She was practically family.

"Behold, all they that were incensed against thee shall be ashamed and confounded."

She hadn't wanted to go but could hardly refuse the two grief-stricken women.

"They shall be as nothing; and they that strive with thee shall perish."

They'd been warned about what to expect, but when the sheet was turned back, it was still a shock.

Rob's body had been in the water for several weeks by the

time Zander found it. By then the skin had blistered and turned dark green. Almost black. They'd done their best to clean him up for the identification, but it was obvious that pieces of his face were missing. Nobody said so, but it didn't take a genius to figure that he'd been nibbled and picked over by fish, crabs and other marine scavengers.

They saw him for only a few second. It was enough to take in the damage. And, despite the damage, it was enough to know it was Rob they were looking at. His mother and sister collapsed into each other's arms, sobbing. Eleanor stood apart from them, before being pulled in to share the grief.

"Thou shalt seek them, and shalt not find them, even them that contend with thee."

She'd felt like a fraud then and she felt like a fraud now. The police were satisfied that it had been an accident, and so it had been. She hadn't told anyone about the fight. About Rob attacking her. About her kicking him.

His mother and sister had their memories. Memories were all they had. Who was she to sully them? What would it achieve? They wouldn't believe her anyway. They would never believe anything bad about Rob. The only result would be them hating her for saying it. Maybe she deserved to be hated. But it had still been an accident. Rob was still dead. Neither of those things would ever change.

"They that war against thee shall be as nothing, and as a thing of nought."

Eleanor shifted in the hard pew. The minister had been thundering on forever. It was all about God Almighty. All very am-dram. Very little about Rob.

"For I the Lord thy God will hold thy right hand, saying unto thee, Fear not; I will help thee."

Still, his mother seemed to take some comfort from it. Her grip eased as she nodded her head in time with the verse from Isaiah.

The photographers kept a respectable distance from the graveside, but with their telephoto lenses they didn't have to be near to get their close-ups. The grieving family. The bereft fiancée. Eleanor wondered what the following day's headlines would be.

The whole sorry mess had been a gift for the tabloids, the 24-hour news channels, social media. There had been several variations along the same theme: *Island of Horror, Death Island, Terror Island* but the one that finally stuck was *Castaway Hell.*

Rob's mother and sister each dropped a single white rose into the grave. Then it was Eleanor's turn. She stepped forward. Aware of every camera and phone in the cemetery focused on her, she dropped a single red rose onto the coffin. The whirr of lenses focusing. The snap of the shutters. Her image captured. *Click, click.*

Fran told her not to do it, but Eleanor had read everything she could about their ordeal. Compulsively poring over endless sensationalised Sunday pages. Scanning Facebook and Twitter. Couldn't help herself. The tabloids had neatly defined everyone involved for easy-to-digest fodder. She'd got off pretty lightly, cast, as she was, in her tragic role. *Castaway Hell Fiancée Grieves for Lost Love.* Even so, they'd managed to scrape up a couple of old boyfriends, one of whom had kept his mouth shut, while the other had sold his story to a Sunday rag.

The interview with him was part of an eight-page *Castaway Hell* exclusive. It had been fascinating to read about the nights of passion they'd shared and how she'd been insatiable in bed when all Eleanor could remember were a few clumsy teenage fumbles. The sex hadn't been good, let alone steamy. The piece was illustrated with an out-of-focus shot of her and the erstwhile boyfriend. Each sporting a seriously bad haircut. Both fully clad. That must have been a disappointment for the dirt diggers.

Elsewhere, over and over again they'd used the same picture of her and Rob together. God knows where they'd dug it up. It hadn't come from her. They were good-looking, young and carefree with smart hair. Seemingly, the perfect couple.

Formalities over, the mourners began to drift away from the graveside. They formed small clumps in the cemetery, offering sympathy, sharing grief, catching up.

Eleanor felt jealous of herself in that picture. Wished she could step back into that reality and change the future. She would have split up with Rob way back when. Then he'd still be alive and she wouldn't be locked into this eternal show of grieving for a man who'd attacked her. A man she'd wanted to leave.

"Hi. How are you doing?"

Fran's face, angular, pale. Framed by loose auburn hair. The heroine of the piece. They hugged briefly.

Click, click.

Eleanor tried not to stiffen.

A function room had been hired in a nearby hotel for post-funeral refreshments. Fran, Eleanor and Archie sat in a quiet corner, at a table away from the bar.

"Why did he change his mind?" Archie asked.

There were occasional nudges and curious glances from the rest of the mourners. Eleanor could hardly blame them. She supposed they were a strange little group. The Castaway Hell survivors gathered together. All three of them.

Fran shrugged. "I don't know, I'm just glad he finally did the decent thing."

"That'll have been a first for that scumbag." Archie, victim-turned-hero, sat his glass on the table.

He'd lost a serious amount of weight. He wasn't the only one who'd been on the Castaway Hell Extreme Diet. Fran looked thin rather than slim and Eleanor's clothes were hanging loose on her. She could have bought new, but these days she had as little appetite for shopping as she did for eating. So much for the material girl.

"I wonder if it had anything to do with those women coming forward - the ones he'd worked with," she said.

Although Jonathan had ultimately triumphed as the villain of the piece, Marcus had become a national hate figure. A history had emerged of him sexually harassing female colleagues.

"He was a rapist in training" Archie said.

"And I got to be the one he was training for," Fran said, "Lucky me."

"Sorry, I wasn't thinking."

Raucous laughter fueled by alcohol belted out from the bar. Rob's rugby mates. Old stories retold, good times remembered.

"It's okay, really. I don't want you treating me like I'm made of fine crystal. I'm not going to shatter into a million pieces. Seriously."

She smiled at Archie. He smiled back. It looked to Eleanor that the friendship between her fellow survivors was developing into something more serious.

"To be honest," Fran continued, "It's his wife and kids I feel sorry for. Imagine being married to a man like that or having him as a father."

In Eleanor's mind, the frozen tabloid image of Marcus's ex-wife. She'd been caught in an unguarded moment. The slightly blurred image gave the impression of a well-groomed woman, eyes hidden behind over-sized sunglasses, mouth set in an unyielding line. She looked impressive, like an old-style movie-star whose face you recognise but can't pin down. Hard to imagine that once-upon-a-time Marcus had charmed her into marrying him.

She'd kept a low profile, had refused to speak to anyone from the media. The broadsheets reported her as maintaining a dignified silence. The tabloids said she was brittle. Hinted at pills and alcohol.

"At least you don't have to go to court now," Eleanor said.

"Thank God," Fran said. "I was dreading the whole court thing."

"He should have pled guilty in the first place," Archie said.

"I think he was playing with me." Fran replied, "Letting me know that he was still in charge. They say that's what rape's about, don't they? It's not about sex. It's about power."

"Well he's not so bloody powerful now, is he?" Archie said.

He gave Fran's arm a squeeze.

Watching Fran and Archie together, seeing the bond that had developed between them, made Eleanor feel emptier than ever. Crazy though it sounded, the last time she'd felt alive was back on the island when Jonathan was hunting her.

A couple of his ex-girlfriends had taken their bite at fame, telling tabloid tales of his weird moods and how much he'd scared them. That they always knew there was something about him that wasn't quite right.

Everyone an expert after the fact.

84

Eleanor's colleagues made furtive little movements as she walked into the office. Eyebrows raised. Sidelong glances. Hastily clicking away from the images of Rob's funeral. Eleanor pretended she hadn't noticed. She couldn't blame them for being curious. She was the same.

She woke early these days. Spent the unsleeping hours between the night before and the start of the next day browsing Castaway Hell stories on the internet.

She'd already pored over the images from the funeral. Rob's mother leaning on Eleanor's arm. Eleanor and Fran embracing. Eleanor throwing the rose into Rob's grave. Eleanor, Eleanor, Eleanor.

She didn't know who she was any more. If it wasn't for all the images of her on the laptop screen, she felt she might not exist at all. Even in the images she hardly seemed to exist. She looked hollowed out.

Fran was ethereally thin. Looked as though she was spun from spider's webs. As if one decent gust of wind would blow her away like cherry blossom. It seemed that the only thing anchoring her to the earth was Archie. Despite his drastic weight loss, he looked solid, like nothing could shift him if he didn't want to be moved.

The pictures lied. It looked as though she and Fran were clutching onto each other when they'd embraced for the briefest of moments. Fran was made of steel, not cherry blossom. It was Fran giving strength to Archie, not the other way around. And Eleanor didn't look hollow because she'd lost Rob. It was because she'd lost herself. She felt as though someone had taken a big metal spoon and scraped out everything that had been her.

Below the images of the three of them was one of Marcus being escorted into court. He looked puffy and pudgiefied. As if he'd been injected with the fat the three of them had lost. He stared straight out of the screen at her, eyes peering from behind broken spectacles. They'd been taped together on one side and sat slightly squint on his face. Maybe, like Archie said, he wasn't so powerful now, but the hint of arrogance in the curl of his lip still made her feel as though she had maggots crawling under her skin.

Scrolling down, there was a picture of Gemma. Laughing. Blonde curls shining. Blue eyes sparkling. A vision of loveliness. They'd found her body. Dumped in a bog-hole. And they'd found the rock that had gone through the back of her head. It stuck out of the ground like a shark's fin. Attempts had been made to wipe it clean, but they'd found tiny pieces of *matter* caught in the fine crevices. Eleanor didn't want to know or think about that. She didn't want to think about anything.

She functioned well enough to get through the day, but people didn't know how to behave around her. Ask her about the ordeal? Pretend it hadn't happened? That they didn't know anything about it? She suspected that many of them were dying to hear about it in explicit, gory detail but she didn't feel much like sharing. It was a had-to-be-there kind of thing.

She declined all offers of counselling and paid leave from her employers. Thought that if she wasn't obliged to turn up at work she might sit in her flat until what was left of her turned to dust and disintegrated. As for counselling, she'd turned that poisoned chalice down flat. Didn't want anyone messing with what was left of her.

Fran and Archie were going on a trip. New Zealand. Or maybe it was Australia. Six months. Something like that. Now that the funerals were over and Marcus had decided to plead guilty, they wanted to get the hell out of Dodge. Eleanor couldn't blame them.

She thought about it herself. Going away. But where would she go and what would she do when she got there? More to the point, who would she go with?

Everyone she knew had commitments. Careers, children, partners, mortgages. All the usual constraints. Even if she could find someone who'd be willing to pack it all in for a few months, she couldn't bear the thought of the inevitable questions. Either asked or hanging between them unasked. She felt like a freak. What had happened on the island had turned her into an object of morbid fascination.

She could go away by herself, but the idea held little allure. She craved company. Someone she didn't have to explain herself to. Fran and Archie were lucky. They had each other. Queer kind of luck though it was.

She didn't think they'd make it as a couple. Not in the long run. Not with this always hovering in the background like a toxic mist. But for now at least they had each other. Good luck to them. What did she know anyway? Could be something good would come out of this mess. Maybe they'd make it to their Silver Wedding and beyond.

She had seen Silver Wedding pictures of Harry and Hazel. She had seen all sorts of photographs of them, all over the papers - weddings, birthdays, Christmas, holidays. Looked like someone had flung the family album wide open and invited the world in.

They'd found Harry in the woods, clasping Hazel's body to his chest, sobbing into her hair. It had all come out - his affair, her poisoning Archie by mistake, Harry strangling Hazel because she was trying to suffocate Archie. He'd been arrested. Family loyalties had been divided. He'd wanted to go to her funeral, but some of the family didn't want him there. It didn't matter in the end. He was too ill to attend. He was in hospital. Suffering from hypothermia after being out in the cold and wet all night.

Eleanor had gone though. Fran and Archie too. The family had thanked them for coming - Archie in particular. Even though she'd poisoned and tried to suffocate him, Archie didn't hold any ill will against Hazel. Funny that, how one person could do so much to another and yet be forgiven.

Maybe Archie could forgive Hazel because he had Marcus to hate. They all had Marcus to hate.

Harry died of pneumonia ten days later. His funeral was a low-key affair but the three of them had gone. Eleanor supposed that it was sometime during all this funeral attending that Archie and Fran had grown close.

So what brought you and your wife together Archie?

Well, you see it was the multiple funerals.

Multiple funerals?

Yes, they were acquaintances of ours. Their deaths brought about by a peculiar pick and mix of brutal murder, tragic accident and staying out all night in the cold and wet.

She supposed going to the funerals was a way of bringing it all to an end. Of gaining closure. *Closure.* Eleanor hated that glib word. It was the kind of thing a counsellor would come out with.

Cal and Gemma were cast as *tragic victims*.

Cal's family arranged a humanist funeral. It was personal, moving and dignified. And it brought Eleanor to the brink of madness. She swayed on the edge of the void, her mind splintering like a cracked eggshell as she finally realised what everyone else had known all along. Cal was gay.

She was screamingly, hideously, embarrassed by her own stupidity. As she realised the truth, a blush erupted on her throat, exploding on her face. Her skin radiated heat. One tiny revelation had cracked the world wide open and she could see it all in excruciatingly detailed high definition. That night in the bothy. She'd fancied Cal rotten, thought he'd felt the same, but he'd never fancied her. She'd read him all wrong. Way wrong. Way, way wrong. God, it was funny. Hysterical.

Laughter gurgled in her throat. She leaned forward trying to swallow it.

Of course! That's why Rob thought she fancied Marcus.

Hysteria rippled through her body. She tried to stifle it, choked, began to tremble.

Rob knew something was up. But he also knew Cal was gay, so he'd already dismissed him as a threat. He'd seen Marcus winking at her and put two and two together and made a holy bloody mess.

No wonder Marcus had been winking and smirking. She couldn't blame him. It really was hysterically funny. He'd seen it all. Lapped it up. Marcus knew she fancied Cal. Marcus knew Cal was gay. Marcus realised that she didn't know.

No wonder Rob had gone off his head when she'd laughed at him. Laughing then and laughing now. Laughing like she'd never stop. Shaking with laughter. Trembling.

Fran's hand on her back. Gently stroking her, trying to soothe her. They thought she was crying. But she wasn't crying she was laughing. Except that now she wasn't so sure. Laughing? Crying?

She had to take the decision now. Let herself go? Or pull back? It would have been so easy to let go. To cry and cry and laugh and laugh. She felt she could let go of her mind as easily as a child letting go of a helium balloon.

But she didn't.

She stepped back from the edge. Gave Fran a grateful smile for the comfort she had offered, even though her touch had been an irritant.

When the laughter stopped, there was nothing else.

Gemma's funeral was a gossip rag event. My Big Fat Tacky Funeral. The coffin was pink. Her mother hired a public relations manager and had been whoring herself all over the media. Squeezing out tears on demand, wringing her hands.

"She was beautiful. She was my angel. She could have been a star…"

Eleanor wouldn't have been surprised if she'd made a deal

with *Hello* for the funeral photographs. On second thoughts, make that *Take A Break*. She could see it now. A picture of the weeping mother, clutching a photograph of a bikini-clad Gemma in her perfectly manicured hands. *My Personal Castaway Hell.*

The trio declined the offer of a seat up front and sat at the back of the packed church. They slipped out early, to the strains of *You Are the Air Beneath My Wings*.

So that was that. One on remand at Her Majesty's Pleasure. Three survivors. Five dead and buried. One loose end.

Jonathan.

85

They searched the island. They found Cal. They found Harry and Hazel. They found Gemma in the bog hole. But they didn't find Jonathan. There were no boats. He could not fly. They ascertained that he could swim and assumed he'd swam for it.

He was physically fit. He was desperate. The distance wasn't great. Not if you could swim in a straight line from the island to the mainland. But that would be difficult. The currents were strong and there was a riptide not far offshore. There were big tides and a swell on the water. The shore was bad. And the water was deadly cold. Death was almost inevitable.

They expected his body would turn up, just the way Rob's had. But the only place Jonathan turned up was in Eleanor's dreams.

She dreamt she was running. Running and running and running. Funny thing was, she wasn't sure if she was running away from something. Or running towards it.

She dreamt about Rob. Over and over she watched him falling from the cliff with that look of surprise on his face.

And she dreamt about Jonathan. His face looming out of the night. All dark eyes and jutting cheekbones. In her dreams he had metamorphosed into a beautiful, demented angel. He opened his mouth to speak to her, but she woke before the words left his lips.

She lay in bed until she was sure she wasn't going to get back to sleep then got up and browsed the internet until it was time to get ready for work. Sometimes she sat staring at the screen for a long time, looking at pictures of him.

The Jonathan dreams were strange and intense but Eleanor

rationalised them away. A few weird dreams were hardly surprising after what she'd been through.

Then they spilled into her waking hours.

She'd see his face in the crowd but when she looked again, he'd gone. Vanished. Or never been there in the first place. She'd look out of the bus window and catch a glimpse of him on the street, looking at her. Once she thought she'd seen him near where she worked. She did a double take, but he had dissolved like a shadow in the dark. On yet another occasion, she saw him as she emerged from her block of flats. By the time the security door clicked behind her, he was gone. Disappeared in the blink of an eye.

He was everywhere and nowhere.

Finally, driven to distraction, she called the police liaison officer who had been assigned to her and asked if they'd found him yet.

"There's been nothing," the female officer assured her. "Not since his clothes were washed ashore. Don't worry Eleanor. As soon as we hear anything, you'll be the first to know."

She started looking out for him. She'd turn her head quickly or do a sudden U-turn in the street, swiveling on her heels. Trying to catch him out. She did not get so much as a fleeting glance. Either he was too smart for her or he wasn't there at all. Most likely never had been.

The city was her natural environment. Concrete beneath her feet, fumes in the air. Everyone in a hurry to get someplace. Cars and bars and traffic lights. Fast food, fancy food, cinemas and street buskers. People in suits. Smart suits, sharp suits, crumpled suits. Suits with a sheen of grease. Stiletto heels, kitten heels, Crocs and Docs. Big Issue sellers with Eastern European accents. Winos lounging on the grass in front of the multi-storey car park. You could get your hair done, face done, nails done. Tattoo studios out of the backstreets and on the high streets. Department stores and pound shops. Comedy clubs, night clubs, the deli on the corner that sold fancy cheese and artisan bread.

She should have been relieved when he wasn't there. Stalking her turf. He was a psycho, a nut job, a loon. Not the kind of boy you'd take home to mother. Not seeing him also meant that if she had been hallucinating, she wasn't any more. She should have been relieved. But she wasn't.

Seeing his face, experiencing the sensation of him circling her like a shark, coming closer with every pass until he gave her an exploratory nudge, gave her a secret thrill. The thrill reinforcing how dead her life had been since her time on the island. Even the city had lost its edge, its promise that anything could and would happen. Like herself, it was doing no more than going through the motions.

She missed the excitement of the chase. The adrenalin rush. The feeling of freedom and exhilaration she had felt when her life was threatened.

The last time she had felt truly alive was on the island.

86

Marcus was sentenced to eighteen months in prison and placed on the sex offenders register for life. Fran and Archie went on their travels. Good luck to them. Cal, Harry, Hazel, Gemma and Rob were all dead and buried. The only ones left were Eleanor and Jonathan. And Jonathan wasn't real. He was a shadow. A dream.

The story died. Replaced on the front pages by political scandals, overseas disasters and celebrity twaddle. Eleanor began to wonder if she really existed.

She went to visit her mother to prove to herself that she was real, but her mother was having one of her bad days and didn't recognise her. There was a post-card from Fran and Archie waiting for her when she got home. The pictures on the front were vivid, the message on the back short. It opened with a jaunty *G'day* that depressed the hell out of her. Eleanor sat it on the kitchen counter along with the rest of her mail, dumped her bag on the table, kicked off her sandals and slung her jacket over the back of a chair.

There was a bottle of red in the cupboard, two thirds of it drunk already. She pulled out the stopper and poured herself a glass before having a root around in the fridge.

There wasn't much to root through. A piece of cooked chicken that looked as though it was ready to get up and walk out of the fridge by itself. A tray of leftover noodles. A bag of sorry-looking salad.

She had a poke at the noodles. Pulled a couple from the tray. She dropped them into her mouth. Chewed. Swallowed. Cold, slightly greasy, salty tang of soy sauce. Not the worst thing she'd ever tasted but past their best. She should probably bin them along with the chicken and salad.

She closed the fridge door, leaving everything where it was.

She took a sip of wine and grimaced. It had turned to vinegar. She couldn't remember when she'd opened the bottle. She poured the remainder down the sink and picked up the postcard.

G'day! Enjoying Oz. Glad we came. Hope you okay? F & A

Was she okay? She went to work, she visited her mother, she functioned. Yes, she supposed that made her okay.

She put the card down, picture side up. Sydney Opera House, blue skies, sunshine, beaches. She thought of sharks in the surf.

She had a choice. She could do a shop online and get it delivered, stock the fridge right up and leave it to rot. She could order a take-away and get it delivered. That would do her tonight and provide a few leftovers she could pick at tomorrow. Or not. Or, she could do something really radical and haul herself all the way to the deli on the corner of the street and treat herself to some nice food that she might actually eat.

She decided to live dangerously and go to the deli.

The shop was an old-fashioned family affair. Small, densely packed, and suffused with the rich smell of freshly roasted coffee beans. Apart from the coffee counter there were deli and bread counters, and a small ice cream cabinet. The walls were lined ceiling to floor with shelves heaving under the weight of jars, bottles and cans containing everything from smoked octopus to maraschino cherries.

Eleanor had been a late-night customer long enough to earn a cheery good evening from the proprietor along with a surly nod from his wife. She had a face more suited to selling pickles than freshly ground coffee. Eleanor browsed for a while, picking bits and pieces that took her fancy. Rustic bread, pate, tinned soup. A slab of extortionately expensive dark chocolate, a bottle of red wine, a tub of olives and a bag of fancy crisps in a plastic bag designed to look like brown paper.

The proprietor kept up a stream of professional small talk and quick smiles as he packed her goods. Eleanor nodded and agreed in the appropriate places, aware of the wife scrutinising her from behind the coffee counter.

Walking back to her flat, she had the squiggles-down-her-spine feeling of being watched. She glanced around. Saw a family getting into a car. Bickering kids clambering into the back. On the other side of the road, a woman clacking along the pavement in high heels, all dressed up for a night out. She checked out doorways, windows, cars. Watched a man trudging alongside an old, fat dog. Nothing of interest. Nothing in particular to see.

Nothing, nothing, nothing. Still, she stepped up her pace. Kept on snatching those glances. A smug couple walking arm-in-arm. A group of grungy teenage boys messing around.

A gentle breeze blew the skirt of her dress against her legs. She shivered. The dress felt too light, too insubstantial. She should have changed out of it when she'd come home from visiting her mother.

Despite spying nothing untoward, all the way back she could not shake the feeling she was being watched. Sharks came to mind again. Circling in the water, unseen. The hairs on the back of her neck stood up. She walked faster, almost breaking into a half-run. Sweat prickled in her armpits. Nerves, not exertion. She was starting to panic. Could feel anxiety swelling inside her. She would not let fear grab a hold of her like this. She forced herself to slow her pace. Took several deep breaths. Calmed herself.

Nothing was going to happen to her out here in this wide street. It was still light. There were people around. Cars and buses going by. People walking dogs, for God's sake. Nothing bad was going to happen here.

There was a tremble in her hand as she unlocked the security door. She pushed it open, went inside. Felt reassured by the click of the lock behind her. She turned and stared out of the long, narrow window set in the door. The glass was one-way. She could look out into a slightly darkened world, but the world could not look in. All it would see was a limited reflection of itself.

She half-expected to see him standing on the other side of the road. Jonathan. But he wasn't there. Of course he wasn't. She was being stupid. Paranoid. It had been a long day. She turned away from the door.

She was tired, that was all. Tired and overwrought. She started up the stairs. Maybe she'd have a bath instead of her usual shower. Have a soak. With lots of bubbles and smelly stuff. Nibble at the goodies she'd bought. Eat chocolate. Drink wine. Watch something undemanding on the television.

She was on the half-landing between the ground and first floor when she heard the security door opening below. She tensed. Her body seizing up. Footsteps echoed on the tiled floor. Adrenalin flushed through her. She dashed up the stairs to the first floor. Stopped at her door. Keys ready in her hand. Fear quivering through her. Footsteps coming up behind her. Beating a brisk tattoo on the stone stairs. She fumbled the keys. They slipped through her fingers. Silently disappeared. She looked on the floor. They weren't there. Where? Frantic. Sweat beading on her hairline. Change of rhythm behind her as the footsteps reached the half-landing. No clatter. The keys had not fallen on the floor. The bag. They were in her bag of groceries.

She rummaged through it. Too many packages wrapped in grocer's paper. Too many folds. Too many nooks and crannies. Footsteps brisk. Climbing the stairs. Reaching the top. Her fingers brushed against the keys, curled around them. Footsteps on the landing behind her.

Too late. She'd found the keys too late. She made a fist around them, pushing the Yale between her clenched fingers. She'd stab him in the eye. Punch it in again and again. That's what you did with sharks wasn't it? You punched them again and again. Sometimes it worked. Sometimes they went away. Footsteps right behind her. Sometimes they didn't.

She turned to face him.

87

He smiled. The smile as brisk as his pace. An acknowledgement. The kind of smile reserved for faces barely recognised, people half-known. He picked up on the distress radiating from her. His step faltered.

"Are you okay?" Average height. Sandy hair, blue eyes. Dark suit, tie loosened at the neck. Top button of his white shirt undone. Faint scent of aftershave.

Where did adrenalin go when it drained away? Did it turn into something else? Was there a substance called relief? She returned his smile, perhaps too brightly.

"Dropped my keys, that's all."

"Well, if you're sure?" Hesitation in his eyes. Not the kind of man to walk on by, but not really wanting to get involved. Tough day at the office.

"Absolutely. But thanks for asking."

"See you then." His smile warmer now. Couldn't wait to shed the suit. Flick the cap off a chilled bottle of lager.

"See you," Eleanor replied to his retreating back.

She turned back to her door. Shaking her head. Laughing at herself. His footsteps tapping up the next flight of steps as she put the key in the lock. Calling herself an idiot for jumping at shadows. She opened the door. They'd occasionally passed each other on the way in and out of the building. Nodding acknowledgements. Now they would be obliged to exchange small talk.

She didn't have time to scream.

He came at her unseen. Unheard. A shark rocketing out of the depths. He kicked the door shut as he propelled her into the flat. The bag flew into the air. Groceries spilled, splaying across the floor. He clamped a hand on her mouth. His other arm wrapped around her body. The thin material of her dress the only barrier between them.

Her foot hit against the bottle of wine, sent it spinning into the skirting board. She stood on something soft. Felt it burst beneath her foot. The smell of brine and olives. He pushed her along the hall. The front of his body tight into the back of hers. Moving as one they went through the open door into the kitchen and stopped. They stood for a moment, both breathing heavily, locked tight as a pair of lovers. His mouth brushing against her ear.

"Not a sound."

She gave a tight nod. It was all she could manage. He moved his hand down slowly. Away from her mouth. The skin of his palm rough against her chin, then her throat. He let it rest there for a moment. He didn't say anything. He didn't have to. The threat was implicit. She didn't scream. It was just the two of them breathing.

By the time he released her, she was calm. What next, she wondered. She did not turn to face him. Not at first. She just stood there, with him standing behind her. Listening to him breathing. Acutely aware of how close he was to her. Wondering if this was what she had wanted all along. Wondering how it was going to end. Knowing it was never going to be happily ever after. It had been a long time since she'd believed in happy endings.

She turned slowly. No sudden movements. Nice and easy does it. Her eyes cast down. Scuffed black boots. Faded black jeans. Background clothes. Her eyes travelled up. Easy now. No threat. Dark grey t-shirt. Then his face.

They looked at each other for a long time. Deciding whether they could each trust the other.

He looked different. His hair was longer, curling at his neck.

He needed a shave. His nose had been broken. The maniacal gleam had gone from his eyes, replaced by something altogether more knowing. His face now defined in harsher lines.

"They think you drowned," she said.

"I know."

He wasn't the Jonathan she remembered from the island.

"They said Gemma's death was maybe an accident."

"It was."

But neither was he the demented angel who had been haunting her dreams.

"You hid her body."

"I panicked."

This was a different man altogether.

"You killed Cal. I saw you do it."

"It was a mistake."

"You were trying to protect Fran. She told me."

He nodded.

"You could have explained. She would have backed you up."

"Maybe, I don't know. I can't change what happened. None of us can."

She thought about her struggle on the cliffs with Rob. Thought about Jonathan chasing her in the dark.

"I killed Rob." The words were out now. She couldn't take them back. He didn't say anything. Just looked at her. "It was an accident," she continued, the urge to confess too strong to resist. "But I made it happen. He wanted to marry me, and I wanted to finish with him. I could barely stand the sight of him by the time we had the fight on the cliffs. He asked me to marry him and I hated him. He died knowing I hated him and then I sat beside his mother at his funeral. A fraud in mourning."

It was crazy. The one person in the world she could talk to, the only one who could understand, was the man who had tried to kill her.

"What happened on the island changed everything."

Eleanor stared at him. He understood. More than Fran. More than Archie. More than anyone. It was different for them. They hadn't killed anyone.

She ran her fingers through her hair. Had the urge to run them through his. She looked at his unkempt locks, then his face. Those dark eyes. He looked right back at her. Then his mouth was on hers. Hot, hungry kisses. She kissed him back. His mouth moved down to her throat. She threw her head back.

He pulled her jacket off. She let it fall. His hands were all over her. Touching her. Feeling her. Wanting her. They sank to the floor. Bodies writhing, limbs wrapped around each other. She yielded to him as he manoeuvred her onto her back. Watching him as he rode her dress up to her waist and pulled down her knickers. He pushed her legs wide apart, staring at her vulva as he undid his jeans. She flushed as he looked at her but being so exposed aroused her. She felt liberated. Excited by his desire. She was wet and ready for him. Desperate for him to fuck her. He pulled his jeans down, releasing his huge, hard cock and thrust it into her.

She gasped.

It was over in seconds. Wham, bam. Thank you, ma'am.

They lay side-by-side on the floor, not touching. Her heartbeat slowed. Gradually steadying into its usual rhythm. She pulled the skirt of her dress down. Shock tremors beginning deep inside her. He did up his jeans.

"I'm going for a shower."

She stood up. Could feel his semen dribbling onto her thighs.

He looked at her. "Okay," saying it like he was giving her permission.

She snatched up her discarded knickers on the way out. Shock waves growing. In her bedroom she paused, looking at the phone.

"Not thinking about calling anyone, are you?"

She jumped at the sound of his voice behind her. Creeping

up on her again. She turned, clutching her torn knickers in her hand. He was standing in the doorway. Blocking it.

"No," she replied. "I told you - I'm going for a shower."

Her voice was steady, wasn't it? No hint of the shock waves pounding inside her. He smiled. Not moving.

"It's in there," she pointed to the door of the en-suite.

"On you go then," he said.

Her watched as she went into the shower room. She closed the door behind her, wondering if he'd try to stop her. Make her keep it open. He didn't. She locked the door. It wouldn't stop him for long if he really wanted to get in, but it was something. A barrier between them.

She pushed the knickers into the bin. Looked around the small room. They'd been here before. Her locked in a small room. Him outside. Except that last time, his semen hadn't been globbing on her thighs. And there had been a window in the other room. The en-suite was an internal room. There was no window. No phone. No ceiling recess, no trapdoor.

She wondered if he was standing outside, listening. She'd told him she was going to have a shower, so she'd better have a shower. Be compliant. Maybe he'd relax. Let down his guard. Then she could take her chance. She turned the water on, let it run hot. She looked in the mirror. Watched herself disappear in a cloud of steam. She felt soiled. She really did want a shower.

She threw her dress in a crumpled heap by the bin. It was her mother's favourite, but she would never wear it again. She stood under the shower for a long time, the water as hot as she could stand it, and scrubbed herself. Scrubbed herself hard, especially in all the places he had touched. Washing him away. His smell. His touch. Trying to wash herself away.

She'd let him do it. She'd wanted him to. But why? What had she been thinking? What was happening to her? No. No. No. She could beat herself up when it was over. Not now. She lowered the temperature for the last few seconds before getting out, sucking in sharply as the cold water blasted her body.

A brisk rub-down with the towel before wrapping it around her body, securing it under her arms. She combed back her hair then turned to face the door. What if he was there, waiting for her. Wanting sex. Her skin goose bumped. She couldn't stay in there forever. She had to get out. Get dressed. Be ready for her chance. She'd fought back before. Gotten away from him. But what if she'd used up all her chances already? Don't be stupid. It didn't work like that. She had to keep on making new chances. She unlocked the door. Slowly opened it.

The bedroom blind had been closed. The phone was gone. The door ajar. No Jonathan. She crept over to the door and closed it over. Moving quickly now. Wanting to get dressed before he returned. Knickers, bra, jeans, t-shirt, sweater, socks, trainers. By the time she was done, only her head and hands were uncovered.

How to get out of this? Maybe she could climb out of the window. Edge her way along the building like Jason Bourne. Or, as she lacked his CIA training, maybe she could just open it wide and call for help. It wasn't so late. There would still be people around.

She got as far as touching the cord to open the blind when the door swept open behind her. She dropped to a crouch as if tying her laces. Innocently looking round at him as he entered the room.

"Are you ready?" he asked.

She nodded.

"C'mon then."

He directed her through to the kitchen. Orders disguised as requests. The first thing she saw there was her bag sitting on the counter. Its rifled-through contents hanging out like displaced guts. Beside the bag was her mobile phone. It had been opened. The battery removed. The island scenario all over again, except this time it was happening here, in her home.

The wall-mounted landline was also gone. She wondered if it was in the same place as the one from the bedroom and, presumably, the one from the living room. Somewhere in her flat, a graveyard of phones. Communication dead.

The blinds had been closed in here too. He was shutting out the world. It was just the two of them. Locked together in a flat that had once seemed spacious but now felt claustrophobic.

He indicated that she should sit on a chair at the table.

"Do I have to tie you up?"

She shook her head. All meek. Good little girl. No nonsense going on here.

"Okay, but I don't want any trouble. You know what I mean, don't you?"

His voice the personification of reason. She nodded. Gave him a shy kind of smile. "How did you get off the island?" she asked.

Trying to engage. Make him relax.

He looked at her a moment, as if considering the angles.

"Did you swim?" Coaxing him.

He smiled. The idea seemed to amuse him. "No, I didn't swim."

"So how did you do it?" Not hostage and hostage-taker. Just two friends talking.

"Same way I got on. Same way you got on." He laughed, amused by himself.

"The ferry?" she raised her eyebrows. "Tell me about it."

Reeling him in.

88

He knew what she was doing. Trying to get him to talk. Creating a bond between them so that he would let down his guard. She thought she was smart. Maybe she was. But he was smarter. It was tempting all the same.

He'd seen how desperate she had been to unburden herself. Her guilt had been weighing her down. Hardly surprising - it was quite a load she'd been carrying. Killing her big, smug, rugby-playing boyfriend right after he'd proposed to her. What a stinger. No wonder her conscience was nipping.

Nip, nip, nipping. Right from the moment Rob went over the cliff. The knowledge of her deeds preying on her mind. Gnawing away. Making her feel bad. And no-one she could tell her tale to. Not until he came along. She'd had to keep it to herself all this time. Right until he had provided relief. All sorts of relief.

He had been her confessor. Now she was offering to repay the compliment. Buying herself some time into the bargain. Only, he had not done anything wrong. In his own case it was himself who was the victim. He was a victim of circumstance. Ergo, he had nothing to confess. However, he did have a story to tell, and was very much tempted to do so. It was a fair trade. Her confession for his story.

She had an eager expression on her face. Her features open, urging him to talk. Desperate to hear him. So talk he did. He told her the whole story. About how he'd outwitted them all. Cops, coastguard, Zander. How he'd been on the island, right under their noses, the whole time.

He told her about the police using the toilets, not three feet below where he was lying, about how still he'd had to be, hardly breathing at all. He told her the whole thing. It felt good. Finally letting someone know how clever he'd been.

It really was too good a story to keep to himself.

89

She listened. Nodding, encouraging him. Asking what happened next. Underneath, trying to figure a way out of the situation. She didn't know what he had planned. Maybe he had no plan. Was that better or worse for her?

He hadn't hurt her. So far. That had to be a good thing. And he'd let her have a shower and get dressed in private. The fact that he was holding her hostage was a dirty secret between them. Something to avert their eyes from. Each of them complicit in ignoring the underlying threat in his behaviour.

He was being pleasant for now, but she could not see how this would end well. He was not going to finish his story then say, *Okay, time to go. See ya later.* With her replying, *not if I see you first, ha.*

He hadn't tied her up. Not with cords. But she was wedged in at the table. Him blocking the door. She was as good as hog-tied.

He enjoyed telling her how clever he'd been. How he'd fooled everyone - even the police. She smiled. In on the joke, with him. *With him.*

That was her way out. She had to convince him she was in on it. That she was on his side. that she got it. Got him. She'd already had sex with him. Willingly, though the self-confession made her squirm inside. There had been no resistance on her part, in fact, she wasn't sure that she hadn't instigated it. That had to count for something. If she had to, she would do it again.

She focused on what he was saying. Something about how he'd hitched a lift from the man with the tripod.

"Fantastic." She laughed. It sounded real enough in her ears.

276

Hoped it would to his. "Listen, before you go on, you know what I fancy?" Nice light tone there.

"What?" His eyes narrowed.

"A huge glass of wine." She emphasised the word *huge*, dragging out the vowel sound. Pursing her lips. Inviting him in. "I bought a bottle earlier. We could share it, if you like?"

He stared at her. Suddenly silent. His eyes hardened. She'd screwed it up. Pursed her lips too much. Laid on the perky, let's-have-a-party-right-here act, too heavy.

Sinking. She was sinking. Ready to drown.

Then he shrugged.

"Okay," he said, and the tension broke. She could breathe again.

"It's in the hall," she said. "The wine, I mean. I dropped it earlier."

Saying it like it was her fault. Oops-a-daisy-clumsy-old-me. Silly butterfingers. Nothing to do with him forcing his way into her flat. Taking her hostage. Threatening her.

"I'll get it," he said. He shot her a warning look before leaving the kitchen. *Sit. Don't move.* Like she was a dog.

As soon as he was through the door she was looking around for something. Anything. Though she didn't know what. Her gaze hooked onto the knife block. He was back before she'd strung a thought together. Caught her stare. Followed it. Sabatier. Six of them. Handles sticking out from a black wedge. His gaze swung to her face. His eyes cold, like a shark's. Her skin prickled.

"The corkscrew's in that drawer." Voice bright and breezy. *Don't know why you're giving me that odd look. No, really I don't.* She pointed at the drawer below the knives. The tremble in her hand barely noticeable. "In there."

He looked at the drawer. Looked at her.

She clung onto a smile that felt as though it was cracking her face in two. *See,* the smile said, *I wasn't looking at the knives. I wasn't thinking about stabbing you.* Again. *Trust me. I was being helpful. I was thinking about a corkscrew for the wine. That's all...*

"It's a screw cap," he said.

"Even better."

"I found these." He tossed the bag of crisps she'd bought onto the table.

"Yummy."

He shot her a look. She was laying it on too thick. Had better take it down a notch. Or twenty.

"The glasses are in there." She pointed at a cupboard. He opened it, took out two. Sat them on the table beside the bottle.

"A bowl would be nice."

"What?"

"For the crisps. Nicer than eating out of the bag, don't you think?"

"Where?"

"That cupboard."

He fetched a bowl. Put it on the table. Eleanor picked up the crisp bag and pulled it open. The pungent odour of sour cream filled the room. Smelled like baby sick. Thick and milky white. Like his semen snail-trailing down her thighs.

The walls pulsed. Her sweater clung too tight around her neck, constricting her throat. Making it hard to breathe. Images flashing through her mind. Cal couldn't breathe. His mouth had gaped, trying to gulp air into his lungs. But he hadn't breathed. He had gurgled. He had listened to himself dying, his blood splurting through his fingers.

For the first time since Jonathan had burst in on her, Eleanor felt frightened. Truly frightened. This wasn't a game. She could die here. In this flat. How long would it be before anyone even missed her?

After months of moving through life in a fug, everything was in sharp focus. Jonathan had cut into Cal's throat with a tiny little knife. He had murdered him. Cal was dead. Beautiful, handsome Cal would not talk or laugh or love again. She'd been so wrapped up in herself. So self-obsessed. So caught up in her fantasy la-la world that she had lost sight of what was real. Of what Jonathan was capable of.

What had she called him? *A beautiful, demented angel.* My God, she was the one who was demented. She was deluded. What kind of sick fantasy had she woven for herself? He wasn't any kind of angel - he was a murderer. A brutal killer. Someone capable of taking the life of another. Of bringing that life to a sudden and pitiless end. He would do it to her too. He would do it and he would walk away. Her only chance was to kill him before he killed her.

She swallowed the lump in her throat and rattled crisps into the bowl. She pushed the bowl to the middle of the table. For sharing. Then she looked at Jonathan, smiled and told herself she could get through this.

He glanced at her as he twisted the cap open. She couldn't read his expression. He poured the wine. She had no way of knowing what was going on his mind. Maybe he figured the pair of them could hook up. Go on a crazy, sex-fueled, crime spree. Robbing and killing and dodging the cops and shacking up in cheap hotels. Bonnie and Clyde. Mickey and Mallory. Pumpkin and Honey Bunny.

Or…

Could be he was deciding right now, when, where and how he was going to kill her.

He slid one of the glasses towards her, sat down. He slowly drummed his fingers on the table, staring at her all the while. The steady beat unnerved her. Panic fluttered inside her like a caged bird.

"Cheers."

She raised her glass to him. Steady as steady can be. Almost. Barely a ripple on the surface of the wine.

Nothing from him for a second. Then two. She sat, frozen in

tableau, glass raised in the air, feeling frightened and stupid. Dread growing inside her as silence stretched   between them. *Think woman, think.*

She could throw the wine in his face. Then, while he was blinded, she could get up, get past him, out of the kitchen, along the hall, unlock the front door... then she had a choice. She could run upstairs and bang on her newly acquainted neighbour's door (hoping he was still at home and would let her in). Or, she could run downstairs, out onto the street, throw herself on the mercy of strangers and hope for the best. Better still, throw the entire glass at him. Maybe she'd get lucky. Knock his eye out. Knowing, even as her thoughts ran into each other, that he'd be ripping her head off before she'd had the chance to stand up straight, never mind escape.

If she went for it and mucked up, there would be no more pretence, no more chances. For the sake of doing something, maybe she'd throw it over him anyway. Her fingers twitched. He tilted his glass towards her.

"Cheers," he said.

She lowered her arm. They drank, each eyeing the other over the rim of their glass. She took the tiniest of sips imaginable, barely wetting her tongue, before sitting the glass back on the table.

"Nice wine," she said.

"Not bad."

It wasn't much. Just two words - but he was talking. Engaging with her.

"Crisp?" she asked. Working with what she had.

He took one from the bowl. Playing the part of polite guest to her polite host.

He ate the crisp.

"What happened next?" she asked.

"Next?"

"After the man with the tripod gave you a lift."

280

90

She was full of trickery. Most women were. They sucked you in like quicksand. That's what she thought she was doing now. Sucking him in. Thought she had him right where she wanted him. But he knew.

Still, it was nice sitting at the table in the corner of the kitchen, sipping wine, munching crisps. Must be a thousand couples doing the same thing across the city right now. Talking about what had happened during the day. How work had been. Who had said what to whom. He liked this feeling of being normal, even if it was only a game of let's pretend. So he told her what happened next.

He kept himself clean. It was easier to pass by unnoticed if he wasn't repellent to people. Tripod man dropped him off in Ullapool. Jonathan took a stroll around the village. It was the Easter holidays. Plenty of people around. Plenty of strangers in the village. Many of them dressed just like him, in a vaguely outdoorsy kind of way. He wandered into the campsite like he belonged there. Borrowed a towel drying on a line outside an empty campervan. The jolly campers were out for a jolly day. He went to the shower block, checked the cubicles. Found a bottle with a smidgeon of shower gel in it. Had himself a nice warm shower. Feeling good, at one with himself, at one with the world, he even returned the towel.

All freshened up, he went back into the village and treated himself to a fish supper. He ate it on a bench overlooking the harbour. He fitted in with all the other people as they ate ice-cream, drank coffee, watched boats. People just being people.

He was part of the world again.

Meal finished, he walked along the front until he was past the filling station and on the road south, then he stuck out his thumb. A car loaded with kids went by. The driver shrugged a sorry. Jonathan smiled. It was easy to smile on a day like this. A day when the sun was shining. A day when he'd gained his freedom. Two more cars and a van went by without stopping. His smile was beginning to fade. Another car. A lone woman in it. There would be no chance of her picking him up. The car pulled in. He glimpsed blonde hair. The passenger window rolled down. She leaned across to speak to him.

"Where are you going?"

He bent to the window. Looked in at her. She was about Hazel's age, but in every other respect she was the opposite of Hazel.

"South," he said. "Anywhere, south."

He smiled. She gave him a once-over without returning the compliment. He thought she was going to drive off on him, but she told him okay, get in.

She was wearing a dress that looked as though it had been made with her in mind. He buckled up. The skirt stopped at her knees. She had good legs.

"What's your name?" she asked.

He'd told tripod man his name was Ed.

"Phil," he said. The gaze from her sharp blue eyes pinned him to his seat. She was clearly not a woman to be messed with.

"Ruth," she replied. "I'll take you as far as Inverness."

"Thanks."

He spent the rest of the journey staring straight ahead. When Ruth dropped him at Inverness, he felt lucky not to have been ejected en-route. From Inverness, he thumbed his way down the country towards Eleanor. One of the lorry drivers who gave him a lift bought him a meal at a trucker's stop. He was suspicious at first, figuring the burly driver wanted a blow job in return.

Turned out there was nothing to worry about. The driver felt sorry for him, on account of being so skinny, that was all. Made Jonathan feel almost guilty at stealing the guy's secret stash - a roll of twenty-pound notes he kept hidden in the breast pocket of a thick plaid shirt. Shouldn't have left it unattended like that.

People left newspapers lying everywhere. In cafes, on benches, in bus stations. Jonathan picked them up and read them. Read about how they'd found Rob's body. Read about where and when the funeral was going to be. Went to the funeral.

Nobody recognised him. Nobody noticed him. Nobody saw him. He was the invisible man.

"It could have been the big reunion," he said. "You, me, Fran..."

91

He stopped speaking. Stared into his wine.

"It was after Rob's funeral I started seeing you," Eleanor said.

He looked up at her. "The more I saw you, the more I wanted to see you."

"That's how I felt too." Feeling sick inside but taking her chance. Grabbing onto it with both hands. "I kept catching glimpses of you... and I was dreaming about you. I saw you from the bus - do you remember?"

"I remember."

"At first I thought I was going mad, but -"

"Did you tell anyone?" He turned his glass slowly, by the stem.

She shook her head. "I wasn't sure that you were really there. Not at first, and I... I thought I might be going mad."

She mirrored his action with the wine glass, then laid her hand on the table, fingers extending towards him. Wishing she had told someone. Hollered to the world that he was alive. On the loose. Stalking her.

"Then, when I realised that it was you and you really were there, I started looking out for you," she gushed on. "But you disappeared, and I thought that perhaps I had imagined you after all."

"I was still there," he smiled at her. "I was always there."

Though his smile repulsed her, she smiled back. "I knew you were the only one who would understand about the island," she said. "About... everything that happened there."

Truth intermingling with lies. Fact with fiction. She hoped it would be enough. It had to be enough.

"The island changed everything," he said.

He stopped turning his glass. Laid his hand on the table, his fingers stretching towards hers.

"I never thanked you," she said.

"What for?"

"For listening - for letting me tell you about Rob... For not judging me."

"Why would I judge? It was the same as with Cal. An accident." He shrugged. "Accidents happen."

"Good things can come out of accidents though, can't they?" she said.

"Such as?"

She lowered her eyes, looked shyly away.

"Like us," she said, whispering the words.

Hoping she hadn't overplayed it. Hadn't laid it on too thick for him to take the bait. One beat passed. Then two. Then his hand touching hers. *Slam dunk! He swallowed it whole.* She caressed the tips of his fingers. Looked up at him, doe eyed. Gave him the performance of her life.

"I was thinking," she said, stumbling a little over the words, "that you could stay here... If you don't have any plans, that is."

She dropped her gaze. It was Oscar-class material. He entwined his fingers in hers. She looked up at him. He gazed back at her with the same intensity she'd seen him stare at Fran.

"No plans-"

A loud *BUZZZZZZZZ* cut his words short. The intercom. Someone pressing the buzzer downstairs. He jerked back. Knocking his chair over as he stood up. Grabbed her by the arm. Pulled her to her feet. His fingers digging into her. Creating grab-shaped bruises.

"Who are you expecting?" His eyes wild. His face filling her vision.

"No-one," she said.

"Who's there? Who is it?"

He shook her. Her head rattled. She bit her tongue. Tasted blood.

"I told you - no-one. Someone will have pressed the wrong button. It happens all the time."

It came again. The loud *BUZZZZZZZZ* filling the room like a cloud of fat, glistening bluebottles. He grabbed her by the hair. She cried out.

"Liar!" He screamed at her.

Her eyes streamed. Arms flailing as she tried to ease his grasp.

"No... I'm not... I'm not lying."

He pulled harder until she felt as though a screaming great chunk of her scalp would tear off in his hand.

"Do you think you had me fooled with that act?" His spit flecking her face.

"The island..." Her voice a squeak.

"You were lying all along."

Eyeball to eyeball.

"No!"

Her flailing hand brushed against the wine bottle. Almost toppled it. She grabbed hold of it. Wrapping her fingers tight around its neck.

"Sche-ming, cun-ting, li-ar."

Emphasising every syllable with another pull on her hair.

She swung the bottle up. Smashed it into his temple. The crack and crunch of thick glass meeting thin bone. Wetness as wine poured down her sleeve. He released her. Staggered back. Eyes wide. Backed into the worktop. Stood there, slack-jawed, staring at her, as though wondering why she'd hit him.

She'd hurt him. That much was plain. How badly, and for how long he'd be out of the game, she did not know, and wasn't about to hang around to find out. Dropping the bottle, she ran into the hall. Olives squished beneath her feet. She skidded on the pate and thudded against the door. He'd put the chain on.

She fiddled with it, fingers wet with wine. Behind her, Jonathan calling. His voice thick. She glanced back.

He was swaying. Hanging onto the door-handle. Still with that stunned expression on his face. She'd whacked him good and proper. She wiped her fingers dry on her jeans. Undid the chain. Unlocked the door. Ran out. And stopped.

A man in a blue jacket. Coming up the stairs. He halted, one step from the top. Stared at her. Took in the red wine stains. The pate smeared on her trainers. The blood dripping from her mouth. Glanced over her shoulder through the open door. Saw the groceries scattered in the hall. Held out a flat, square box.

"Mexican Sizzler?"

92

Eleanor paid the driver and got out of the taxi. The sky was beginning to lighten. A new dawn. A new day. The world was still turning.

Everything was normal as normal could be. The usual cars parked in the usual places. Grit in the gutter. Dust on the leaves. Everything where it ought to be until she turned the key and opened the door to her flat.

The assault on her nose came first. Olive brine, rancid pate, sour wine. She flicked on the light.

The pate had lost its pink, been greyed by footfall. Ground into the fabric of the carpet. Someone had stood on the rustic loaf, perhaps one of the paramedics. It lay squished against the skirting board, surrounded by large flakes of crispy crust gone soft. Only the tinned soup and the chocolate had survived unscathed. She picked them up and discovered that the chocolate was broken, held together only by the wrapper. The soup tin had a dent in it.

She took them to the kitchen and sat them on a clean spot on the counter.

Jonathan had done a good job on himself. He'd plunged the Sabatier deep. Slicing a trench from his wrist to his elbow. This had been no scratching-at-the-wrist cry for help. He'd almost dug the artery right out of his arm. His blood had arced bright red across the kitchen. The paramedics had never seen anything like it.

Some of the smaller splatters had dried to a crust, but the large pool was still wet and jelly-like in the middle of the tiled floor.

The pizza guy had finally snapped-to and dialled 999. When

asked what service was required he told them to send everything.

Jonathan was still alive when the paramedics arrived, but only just. By the time they carted the gurney downstairs, the sheet was over his head.

Before she left the station, one of the police officers had given her a business card. Said they came highly recommended. She took it out of her pocket.

WE CLEAN
24-hour professional cleaning services
for victims of crime

There were two telephone numbers beneath the words. One landline, one mobile.

She looked around her kitchen. Once it had all been neat and ordered. A place for everything and everything in its place. When bits and pieces belonging to Rob had inevitably arrived, they too had found a home.

She'd been so sure of herself then. Jonathan had been right about one thing. The island had changed everything.

She put the card on the counter beside the broken chocolate and dented soup can. From the cupboard under the sink she took three bottles of cleaning product and one pair of heavy-duty rubber gloves. After one final look around the kitchen she pulled on the gloves and started cleaning.

Erosion is dedicated to
Liz Reid and Phil Jones.
Friends old and new.

If you have enjoyed reading Erosion, please consider leaving a short review on Amazon.

Acknowledgements

For their support, encouragement and feedback, my sincere thanks go to Angela Ford, Marie MacDonald, Aonghais MacDonald, Charlie Thomson, Caroline Thomson, Mary Kate Thomson, Jessica Pyke, Pete Urpeth and Allan Guthrie.

Thanks also to cover models Scott Irvine, Evelyn MacDonald, Phil Jones and Karen Macfarlane. You all look much happier in real life.

A final thank you to Ruth Clark for making a special guest appearance in Erosion.

About the Author

LG Thomson was born in Glasgow and grew up in modernist New Town experiment, Cumbernauld. She now lives in Ullapool on the North West coast of Scotland. She likes coastal rowing and sharks. She does not like custard or mayonnaise and is undecided about people.

By the same author

EACH NEW MORN

Couldn't put it down.
An edge of your seat story right from the start.
A rogue prion disease has wiped out most of the world's
population. Some survivors have been infected by a secondary
disease. Aggressive and erratic, they become known as
Screamers. They are not the only enemy. Society has broken
down. Violent mobs rule the streets. Gangs of raiders swarm
through the countryside and the worst winter in decades is
about to descend. Who will survive *Each New Morn*?

BOYLE'S LAW

A great read with genuinely heart-stopping moments and cool twists.
Cracking good read: hilarious and horrendous at the same time.
BOYLE'S LAW is a twisting crime thriller set in the heart of
the Scottish Highlands. Rippling with dark humour, it's a page-
turning read. But with lust, murder and a diamond heist in the
picture, be prepared for a view of the Scottish Highlands you
won't get on any glossy calendar.

BOILING POINT

Effortless and tight and not a word is wasted.
Full of the gritty, witty action we've come to expect from LG Thomson.
Lenny Friel's hard man reputation is on the line. Petty
criminal Sammy Macallister owed him big-time and was
supposed to clear the debt by way of a diamond heist. Sammy
died before he could pay Friel back and somebody else rode
into the sunset with the stones. Friel wants to know who. And
then he wants to be paid. With interest.
Boiling Point is the second Charlie Boyle Thriller. Boiling
Point can be read as a stand-alone book, but if you want more
of the same be sure to check out Boyle's Law.

291

Writing as Lorraine Thomson

THE NEW DARK
a dystopian trilogy

I couldn't put it down
Great writing and characters!
I can't wait to see how the story concludes.

The world has entered a new Dark Age. There is no internet, no government, and nature is biting back. The Before times have gone; food is scarce, and the world is a hostile place where things are not always as they seem.

Sorrel's home is destroyed by a gang of marauding mutants who snatch her brother, Eli, and her boyfriend, David. She sets out after them, embarking on a journey fraught with danger, spurred on by the thought of them out there somewhere, desperate for help.

In *The New Dark* trilogy we follow Sorrel on her quest in a world where survival depends on the kindness of strangers, and close friends make the bitterest of enemies.

Published by Bastei Entertainment.

www.thrillerswithattitude.co.uk

Praise for LG Thomson

If you like your crime fiction lean and mean, and with a ripple of gallows humour, then check out LG Thomson, one of Scotland's best new writers.
Allan Guthrie, Author of *Two-Way Split*, Theakston's Crime Novel of the Year

Boyle's Law...tough, tightly-packed word-atoms of energy and economy, dangerously building to fury one moment, erupting in humour the next.
John A. A. Logan, Author of *The Survival of Thomas Ford*

Boyle's Law is gripping from start to finish, and what starts out appearing a predictable, easy read flourishes with a twisting climax.
Jack Calvert, Northern Times

If you'd like a gripping, fresh take on the zombie genre, packed with tension and surprises that are equally pleasant and horrible then Each New Morn is for you.
Dr. Austin, Zombie Institute of Theoretical Studies, University of Glasgow

And finally... the Squonk
The Squonk is said to live in the hemlock forests of Pennsylvania. Ashamed of its appearance, it hides from sight and spends much of its time weeping.
According to *A Dictionary of Monsters and Mysterious Beasts* by Carey Miller (First published 1974 by Pan Books Ltd.) "One man thought he had captured the Squonk after he lured it into a sack by mimicking its cry. On his way home he felt his burden get gradually lighter and the sobbing ceased. When he opened the sack all he could find were tears and bubbles."

Printed in Great Britain
by Amazon

65140712R00169